OF FLESH AND FEATHERS

Of Flesh
and
Feathers

L.M. PIERCE

ISBN: 9781735228013
Imprint: Independently published

Cover design by: MoorBooks Design
Edited by: Nikki Rae at Metamorphosis Editing
Library of Congress Control Number: 2020910864
Printed in the United States of America

To all who have ever loved a bird.

And a loving dedication to Richard Adams, whose story about a warren of rabbits and epic adventure inspired in me a love that has burned brightly ever since.

Acknowledgements

So many loving souls helped make this book happen.

Whitney, thank you for raising our first flock of baby dinosaurs with me
and encouraging my big weird ideas.

Thank you to my amazing critique partners,
Dante Medema and Vanessa Palensky, my cheerleaders
and partners in literary crime!

Holy crap, a huge thank you to the astounding Olympia Writers Group,
who saw so many renditions and rewrites of this journey. Some
seriously top-notch writers and readers.

And a long list of everyone who loved me, who loved this book, who
beta read, and contributed to its emergence: Chris Pierce (seriously, the
best partner), Roy Mae, Rebecca, Chris W., Lauren, Jesikah, Johanna,
Diana, Rick, Mica, and so many others!

Thank you.

"All the world will be your enemy, Prince with a Thousand Enemies, and whenever they catch you, they will kill you. But first they must catch you, digger, listener, runner, prince with the swift warning. Be cunning and full of tricks and your people shall never be destroyed."

- *Watership Down* by Richard Adams

"Every morn and every night,
some are born to sweet delight.

Some are born to sweet delight,
some are born to endless night."

- *Auguries of Innocence* by William Blake

1 | The Beginning

"We are brought to the light by Piasa's grace;
All creatures of the world begin as small, naked chicks,
And we all face death the moment life begins."

- *Tales of Piasa*, for Chicks and Hatchlings

The walls of the chicken coop obscured all hint of sunrise, except for the square of light where the ramp led down into the small yard. The caked straw and long accumulated droppings burned Chickory's eyes, and her wind pouch ached with every breath. Outside, the flock squabbled and fought over early worms.

She had watched them rise, watched as they shoved through the small entrance like a squirming mass of grubs. What they hurried for, she didn't know. The tender new season grass was gone. Even the spicy ants with sharp angular mouths were gone. The flock had stalked them back to the nest and once the juicy queen had been dug up, no more had appeared.

Every sunrise they hurried into the yard, even though their caretaker wouldn't be there to greet them with a sprinkle of corn or wheat or knobby vegetables. Their reliable, frizzy-headed Hum, Lady, had gone inside the blue house and never returned. Sometimes that happened—Hums, like all living creatures of Piasa's world, could die, *would* die. And Lady wasn't the only one. Chickory fought against the memory but it dripped through like honey in the sun season. The Hum child from the neighbor's farm was slumped against the back fence, an arm draped over the lowest rail as his body returned to the soil. His flesh squirmed with flies and squishy white bugs, but an unusually terrible smell emanated from every inch of his decomposed body. The smell of his sickness had deterred most creatures from eating his flesh. Even the sky birds avoided the feast of insects that didn't fuss over a diseased home.

No, she really didn't see the point in getting up at all.

"What are you doing in here?" Rosie's brilliant red feathers looked black as she stood in the shadow of the entryway.

"Resting."

"Resting? 'A bird at rest is an easy meal' and you've been resting for many sunrises," Rosie hissed. She had returned to her clutch of perfectly domed brown eggs after a brief journey for water and whatever food she might have found. It was time to nest—and hens nested alone.

"I won't bother you."

"You're bothering me now! Get out, get out, your smell makes me sick." Rosie hopped to where Chickory huddled on the bottom roost and snapped her comb. The wrinkled red flesh nearly tore and Chickory scurried away from her.

"Fine. I'm leaving," Chickory said and stalked out the entrance and into the full light of the day.

She blinked and squinted. Morning mist cloaked the yard. Dark shapes moved across the muted landscape and the pink of the sky, coupled with the haze, made it feel like a dream or a chickhood memory.

However, beneath the dreamlike appearance, the yard had reverted to wilderness. Lady's once careful attention to the plants and creatures she cared for had almost faded. The overgrown and lopsided hedges around the house soaked up slabs of sunshine, and tall flourishing field grass spread across the front like misplaced whiskers. The yard around the coop, once lush with green, was now patchy with dry grass and bald spots of soil. Hills of decayed leaves, left over from the cold season, tangled in the fence surrounding the main yard, and knobby twists of nut trees cast long shadows over the pebbled entrance.

Chickory descended the ramp and entered the mist, already beginning to fade. The mild new season had begun the shift into the heat of the sun season and soon there would be no mist at all—the ponds and puddles would turn into cracked earth and choking dust.

Woodfawn strutted out from behind the coop and shoved Chickory aside. "Go on then, out of the way, you silly sparrow," she said.

Chickory drooped her head and tried to look, well, small. As the biggest of all the birds, Woodfawn commanded the top of the roost, and Chickory was very much at the bottom. Woodfawn puffed out her breast and cackled as she strutted across the yard. The markings of her feathers looked like dappled sunlight, but even she, big and beautiful as she was, eyed the treetops as she went. Wariness of the sky birds ensured a ground bird's long life.

From the farthest field, the dairy cow bellowed, "Owwww. Do you hear me? Owwwww." She had called for many suns, her own calf too big to suckle, but Lady did not answer her call. No one did because no Hums were left and no creature could do anything for her, but the cow bellowed anyway. Chickory's stomach ached at the miserable sound.

A loud chorus of quacks exploded from the meadow pond and a few of the ducks shot into the air and called, "Sharp teeth! Sharp teeth!" The others splashed frantically in the murky water. A sneaky killer bounded away into the dense forest beyond the edge of the farm's outer fence. Maybe a fox, or even a coyote. The ducks preferred the pond and rarely came near the house anymore, even with no dog or Lady to protect them from killers. The foxes, weasels, and raccoons still remembered the big shaggy dog who guarded the yard and though dog was gone too, the smell and memory of him lingered. For now.

The other hens scratched in the yellow grass and Chickory avoided them as she lurked in the shade under the crying tree. She turned over a small stone and a few rotted sticks, but there weren't any worms. A small patch of young grass had sprouted between two tree roots and Chickory hurriedly devoured it. She didn't dare glance at the other hens. They might swoop down on her discovery. Being bigger and older meant you could do what you wanted, and Chickory was neither big nor old. But the others snapped at small flies and hunted for insects, and didn't notice her at all.

"Let go!"

"No, you let go! I found it first," squawked Dolly and Daisy, as they squabbled over the dried corpse of a beetle. They dug their claws into the dry soil and the beetle crumbled between them. They growled at each other, identical double yolks, with the same straw-colored feathers and ruffled red combs.

"I hope you're satisfied, you rotten egg," Dolly said.

Daisy ruffled her feathers. "It was dust anyhow."

By the back edge of the fence, Robert, their rooster, dipped his beak into a mossy trough of water. The body of the little Hum would be just beyond, perhaps Robert would see him. Chickory hadn't mentioned the boy to the others because what could she say? Each sunrise came and went and hunger needled all their innards. Reminders of the dead helped no one.

Chickory strutted to the decayed stump in the middle of the yard. The wise tree's knobby roots usually housed squishy white bugs, but the intense searches of the flock had ended all the offspring. The barren wood was little more than dry rotted fluff. At least they had eaten some compost—Robert had helped them get inside, with *Fayne's* help, of course.

As though thoughts could summon, Fayne appeared from around the stump and stalked straight towards her. A chill snaked through her feathers and she tried not to look directly into the unnaturally bright eyes of her friend. Every time Fayne appeared, trouble nested in her feathers—she knew things that shouldn't be known and spoke things that should never be spoken aloud.

"Strong Eggs, dear Fayne."

Fayne didn't respond with the customary *Piasa Blesses*, only stared. She looked like a funny raccoon, with bands of dark feathers down her body. Her odd appearance was made worse by the large scar where Woodfawn had ripped half her comb off, several seasons ago. They had hardly been more than yearlings then, but some memories never faded.

Chickory ignored Fayne's penetrating stare. "You haven't eaten enough yet, surely."

"We need t-t-to get inside the house," Fayne said, still not blinking.

"What?" She wasn't sure she had heard Fayne right. "Get inside the… what? What are you chirping on about? Did you have another one of those dreams?"

Fayne tilted her beak toward the sky and spoke aloud. "Dream. A series of thoughts, images, and sensations occurring in a person's mind during sleep. Hm. We will need help t-t-to get inside. Then we must

4

leave."

After this pronouncement, she wandered off as though Chickory wasn't there at all.

Fear wriggled like a worm inside Chickory's stomach, though it mingled with a surge of annoyance. Still, if she occupied the bottom roost, Fayne lived in the smear of droppings underneath, so lowly was she in the order of the flock. The two youngest and smallest birds needed to stick together, no matter how odd one of them might be. After all, as Piasa said, "The small and weak have the sharpest claws and teeth." Whatever that meant.

Maybe, Chickory thought, she should tell Fayne about the dead Hum by the fence, though an agitated Fayne would only bring more trouble. Usually Chickory could distract herself from unpleasantness by focusing on the flowers and the fat yellow sting-stings that trundled lazily from bloom to bloom, but Fayne's strange words *we must leave* thrummed like a hummingbird inside her breast.

Woodfawn strutted by and glared as though Chickory hid a sack of corn in her feathers. No, fear or not, she couldn't tell the others either. Not about the child or about Fayne. The nervous and hungry farm bristled with hostility.

Chickory abandoned her efforts to eat. She'd better try to stop Fayne from—well, from whatever had buzzed into her addled mind. She scurried around the corner of the house and into the front yard.

Fayne cowered on the front porch. Beside her stood the white feathered nightmare named Lacey. She pecked at Fayne and grabbed one of her long tail feathers and ripped it out.

"Sneaking around! Feather-blend! Wretch of a bird," Lacey ripped a beakful of feathers from Fayne's neck.

Fayne shrank lower but did nothing to stop her attack.

Chickory ran to them "Stop it, just leave her alone."

Lacey lunged down the steps with a mighty flap of her wings and slashed at Chickory with her clawed feet.

"All right! All right!" Chickory skittered away, but the distraction had been enough.

Lacey glared at them with disgust. "Scrawny, unwanted. Lucky there's still room on the roost at all." She strutted away with a final warble of rage.

Chickory waited until Lacey had rounded the corner of the house before she joined Fayne on the steps. "What did you do?"

Fayne's yellow eyes looked blank. "N-n-nothing."

That might be true. Fayne's mere existence was enough to inspire the wrath of the others. She was different and that was the worst thing any bird could be.

Chickory sighed. "Well, what are you doing up here? Let's go find some worms or something."

Fayne wasn't listening. She huddled near the door and pressed her head near the ground. Chickory followed and lowered her head too. The same smell of the boy, the horrid scent of diseased guts and unclean flesh, wafted through the cracks around the door. She jerked back. "It's awful," she managed.

"It's Lady," Fayne said. "She's deceased."

Chickory shuddered. "Gone on, you mean? I thought she must have. I think she was old, maybe, though the smell is not right. It smells like sickness."

"Yes, she d-d-died of an illness. Likely some mutated zoonotic virus from what d-d-dog told me."

Zoo-not…ic? Chickory blinked. A strange word with no meaning she could understand. Fortunately, none of the others were around or Fayne would miss more than feathers. "Dog? But dog is gone too. He's been gone as long as—is he inside the house?"

Nights had once echoed with the boom of his barks and his musky odor still clung to the fence posts, but she hadn't thought much about his disappearance, not really. Piasa instructed birds to mind their birds. Other creatures were Piasa's concern.

Fayne lifted onto the tips of her claws and strained her neck as far as it would go.

Chickory followed her gaze to the front window. "Do you see her? See anything?" Ridiculous hope surged through every feathertip.

Fayne bobbed her head. "N-n-no. The solar glare makes it impossible to see."

Hope turned to mud. Chickory might not know what *solar glare* meant exactly, but Fayne's meaning was clear enough. "Well, of course not. That's all right. Let's leave it for now. We can check back if you really want to, though I can't see why we would. Fayne? Don't be a cracked egg about it. Have you eaten this sunrise?"

Fayne stared intently at the bright blue surface of the front door. "We need to get inside." For a moment, it was almost like she could see *through* the door.

Fear flushed through the length of Chickory's feathers, down into her scaly toes. Then she shook out her feathers and snorted. Ridiculous. Of course, Fayne couldn't see through the door. "You're being addled. We can't get inside and besides, what for? Really, when's the last time you had a good lay?" She regretted her words as soon as she said them because Fayne hadn't laid an egg in—well, it had been a couple seasons.

Fayne didn't respond.

Chickory tried again. "We've wasted so much light already. All this time and we could have had a decent meal—well, of something." That wasn't entirely true, unless they dared to venture beyond the yard and enter the tall grass on the other side of the fence.

Fayne turned to her and her eyes gleamed, like the hypnotic gaze of a scaled death worm. "Dog is d-d-dying. We must help him. We will need him to come with us."

Before Chickory could ask why, Fayne hopped off the steps and hurried around the corner of the house. Chickory lowered her head, as Fayne had, and heard a low thin cry. The sound was muffled by the door but it sounded like a baby rabbit or even a chick. Piasa's concern or not, bird or not, a thorn of sadness hooked inside her stomach.

Chickory hopped down the steps and dashed after Fayne. Along the side of the house, Fayne strutted and her keen eyes searched the sky.

"What are we looking for?"

Fayne gave no reply. Perhaps she had "gone" as she sometimes did. The others often tortured her in these moments because when she went away, she didn't respond at all. Fayne jerked around and crashed into Chickory and they became a tangle of feathers and legs. Chickory jerked free and bristled with annoyance.

"You there, come down here," Fayne called.

Chickory's mind reeled with confusion. Then something moved overhead.

Four large rats perched on the edge of the roof. They didn't usually hang about in the bright sunshine of day and preferred the night hours, but maybe with no Hums or dog around, they didn't mind as much. The rats stared down at them and Chickory thought they might run away. Instead the sleekest of them hopped down to the window sill above their heads.

He squeaked in rat, then cleared his throat and switched to the common sound—"Er, what's that?" He bared his big yellow teeth. "You brayed?"

"We need to get inside the house," Fayne said.

This was too absurd for any bird, even a bird like Fayne, and Chickory tried to intervene. "Fayne, don't you think—"

"Mmm. That so?" The rat interrupted her. Rats didn't have roosts and maybe, for them, it didn't matter how big you were at all. "Hm. Maybe, just maybe. Really, you got one good choice. Buddies of mine worked up a bit of a hole down by the cellar. The traps and baits are long gone. 'Course, you're far bigger than my buddies." He squeaked with laughter.

Chickory cocked her head. "How do we—"

"Well, suppose we could assist." The rat scratched his chin with a pink hind foot. "But we'll need something in return. Isn't that how it always is?"

Fayne narrowed her eyes. "Right. And what do you want?"

"We need a big yum like you to keep the dog from having his way with us. A distraction if you like. He's a might hungry. You keep the dog off our backs, and we'll get you in right quick. Lead him out of the house, then do what you like." The rat's smile grew wider.

Chickory hissed a sigh. "But dog is—"

"Yes, all right." Fayne interrupted, apparently forgetting flock manners too.

The rat wagged his naked tail. "Meet us by the steps."

Stone steps led down into the cellar, which housed sacks of grain and corn, along with the knobby vegetables Lady would toss to them on Weeds-day. A small jagged circle had been eaten through the wooden door. The rat popped his head through the hole and flashed teeth again.

"Be right with you." He sunk his teeth into the edge of the hole and was joined by three rats and then four, five, and soon the hole throbbed with the tips of wiggling whiskered noses. Their teeth churned against the aged wood, a horrible grinding sound mixed with their excited squeaks.

Chickory looked away.

"Even rats have their part to p-p-play," Fayne said.

Soon they worked away enough of the edges to allow a full-grown hen entrance. Stale air wafted through the widened space. It smelled like a morsel of rotted flesh wadded inside Chickory's beak. "Fayne, I don't know if I can go in there," she peeped.

"It is the unknowing, rather than the certainty, that sets you apart.

When we leave this place, remember what it felt like to be b-b-brave."
Fayne ducked her feathered head and stepped through the hole.

When we leave... A hot flash burned in the deep white where
Piasa lived—in the core of all creatures—and she tried to recall the
strange and unlikely events that led to this strange and unlikely place.
She had followed Fayne through all the suns she could remember, since
their chickhood dust fevers, their first courtships, since their first laid
egg, and Fayne had always been this way. How many times had Fayne's
feathers been ripped out? How many times had she been forced to sleep
in the rain, banished from the coop? Robert always talked the hens
around eventually, but though the others might hate her, Fayne's
understanding of the world around them, even about things like dogs and
rats—well, she was much larger than just a bird. Really, Fayne
frightened her. That *was* it then. Really, she was afraid.

And still, afraid as she was, Chickory stepped through the small
rat-infested hole.

2 | Tucker

"Follow the order of wings and feathers;
Some must lead and others must devoutly follow."

- Practical Wisdom, for Chicks and Hatchlings

Musty dampness tickled her beak as she entered the thick darkness. The strong smell of rot mingled with long accumulated mouse urine, though the mice had long ago been displaced by their meaner relatives. The patter of their feet signaled the presence of the many rats who now lived there. Much more than could be seen. A loud squeal punctured the dark and then all was quiet again. Chickory had never been inside any part of the house, though the bigger birds in the flock sometimes tried. She had only ever lurked on the front porch or at the top of the stone steps, excitedly clucking for a delicious scrap of Hum food. Familiar but empty sacks littered the ground, and there wasn't a single speck of corn left.

Chickory trembled and took a tentative step forward. The soft earth of the floor felt cold against her claws. Light emanated from an ajar door at the top of a small stack of steps, which led back up into the house itself. Fayne was already halfway up. Chickory hurried to follow and shivered at the thought of being left alone with the rats. The horrible smell that had wafted through the cellar door, the same as the smell of the dead boy, grew stronger as she hopped up each step.

Fayne reached the top and forced her feathery body through the door, the hinges giving a soft creak as the door opened. The smell almost felt alive and it squirmed down Chickory's beak and into her stomach like an undigested worm. All that lived knew to avoid disease and here they approached it instead. Fear fluttered inside her breast as she stepped through the door behind Fayne.

They stood on strange ground, coated with fuzz like the puff flowers that threw their seeds to the wind. This was much coarser though and strands caught in the claws of her toes. Walls rose on either side, much like the coop they slept in every night, though larger in every way. What would Lady think, seeing them inside her house? Maybe she would flap her fleshy pale arms and tut-tut in disapproval as she chased them out into the yard. She would smile and shake her frizzy head.

But there was no sign of her, except for a few grey hairs tangled in the furry loops covering the floor.

Down the passageway, on top of a high ledge, sat a moldy mound that might have once been food. Translucent flit-flies swarmed around the lump and they gleamed in the light of a small closed window. Lady's removable hooves lay on the floor and one was smeared with a brown stain.

A loud whistle cut through the quiet. Chickory jerked with surprise. Lady was the only creature she'd ever heard make that sound, the sound she used to call dog back to the house. Yet, somehow, Fayne had managed to produce a sound just like the fleshy mouth of a Hum.

"How did you do that?" Chickory gasped.

The floor shuddered with the soft thump of footsteps. The fear that fluttered inside Chickory became a throbbing boom. Dog must be hungry, after all this time locked inside the house. Lady or not, he *was* a killer of some sort. The sharp teeth, Piasa's gift to dogs, promised this. She turned to flee back through the cellar and out the chewed entrance.

"D-d-don't go. It'll be all right," Fayne said.

The floorboards stopped quivering and dog uttered an anguished cry. He sounded tired, afraid even. Chickory turned toward the sound, which had dissolved into a low continuous whine.

Dog squatted miserably on his haunches and his dark brown eyes gazed mournfully from beneath a tangled flap. His fur was matted and filthy. They'd always had a polite relationship with dog, even as they dodged his attempts to herd them. They sometimes allowed him to snuffle their small chicks, but they had never missed his presence or talked with him. He was simply a part of Lady, part of the way of the caretaker. Did he even speak the common sound?

"D-d-dog. I am Fayne, from the other side of the door, and this is Chickory. It's time for you to leave this house."

As though his forelegs could no longer bear his weight, he slumped to the floor with a sigh. "No, I cannot leave, birdy bird," he groaned. "I must stay and meet my fate."

He spoke the common sound as well as any creature. Chickory hopped closer to him and tried to remember what Lady had called him. "You're—you're Tucker, aren't you?" Lady had named him, as Hums always named the creatures they love.

He rested his large head on his dirty paws. "Yes, the name given to me by the Mistress of the House and of my Heart."

The funny way he spoke of Lady puzzled Chickory, but all creatures knew dogs had strange beliefs about Hums.

Fayne cocked her head, then fluffed her feathers and looked impatient. "Dog. I mean, um, Tucker. There is no good to be d-d-done here, not anymore."

Tucker let out an anguished yowl. "You don't understand. I've, it's, I've done a horrible thing."

Fayne clicked her beak but said nothing.

His body trembled. "I've committed the ultimate darkness." Saliva dripped from his loose lower lip.

Fayne sighed. "You d-d-did what you had to. To survive. All creatures must eat or face starvation. Lady would have understood."

Sadness coiled in Chickory's stomach. The brown stains on Tucker's paws and muzzle, the dirtiness of his coat, these were the only sign of what had happened here. All creatures would do mad things to survive. Even in Piasa's word existed stories of birds who eaten of the flesh of others, driven by madness or cruelty or simple hunger. The fear of being eaten plagued all who lived.

"She laid down and didn't get up. I tried. I tried to wake her. Pulled at her blankets, she always hated that. But she never got back up and soon there was nothing left! I was cleaning her, licking her face. She always loved that. Her sweet sweet face. I licked and licked and licked and, oh—oh dear. Her face was gone!"

Fayne pecked him sharply on the nose. "Stop this."

He yelped and scampered back, bizarrely afraid of the small bird. He could easily crush them both, but instead he cowered. "She fed me, loved me, cared for me," he cried again. "There was no escape, no escape." He collapsed to the floor again and groaned.

Fayne's eyes gleamed. "T-t-then consider this your call to redemption."

Tucker gazed at her and the white of his big eyes shone like a slivered moon. "Redemption?"

"Yes. Lady… the um, Mistress of the House and your Heart, is gone, this is true. B-b-but now there is no one to feed us or care for us. Once, she did all those things and now there is only you left. She needs you to carry on what she b-b-believed in. Needs you to continue as our protector. The same protection she so willingly gave us all."

Tucker gave a small whimper and his matted tail thumped the ground.

A surge of excitement tingled in the tender flesh of Chickory's comb and spread into the tips of her feathers. "As Piasa instructed all Hums to do for the creatures of the earth," she said.

Fayne glared at her, as though this was not the time to speak of Piasa. "Tucker, you need to come with us and care for us. And in turn, we can care for and protect you too."

"Protect him? Protect him from fleas, maybe." Giddiness tickled the back of her throat. A few scrawny birds protecting a dog, a dog who had every ability to hunt, to wander, to survive on his own? Well, it was ridiculous. She could imagine the click his teeth might make as they snapped her neck.

But instead, his brown eyes glistened with some strange dog emotion. "I—I could do it. For my Mistress. She would want me to, I think." His tail thumped again, hesitantly, before it became a steady rhythm. He staggered to his paws.

Fayne gave Chickory a dark look and turned, descending back down into the cellar. Tucker shook himself and his matted hair flapped around him like tangled vines. Chickory followed Fayne and Tucker thumped down the steps behind her. She shuddered as his hot breath puffed against the back of her head.

As they descended, the darkness writhed with the shadows of the rats as they hid from dog. Chickory and Fayne crossed the musty cellar and exited through the hole into the blazing sunlight outside. Chickory sucked in the fresh air and the smell of sweet grass washed away the stench of the house.

Behind them, Tucker scratched and growled at the wood. "I

can't, it's stuck, I can't get through." His growls dissolved into whimpers and sad yips.

"Grab it with your giant canines, c-c-channel the wolfish forefathers of your ancestry," Fayne called and flapped her wings in encouragement.

Chickory joined the chorus. "Come on, Tucker! You're big, you're a big dog, you can do it!"

Dolly and Daisy, who had been drinking from the trough of water, stopped and stared at their commotion.

Tucker grunted and crunched the wood between his powerful jaws. With a loud splintering crack, he jerked it off the old hinges. Dolly and Daisy cackled in horror and ran. Tucker gazed out into the yard and blinked in the bright sunshine.

"Well, come on," Chickory clucked.

His huge black nose twitched as he snuffled the air and then he ran to the trough of water near the crying tree. His sides heaved as he lapped the fluid desperately. Saliva ran down his jowls and chest.

The sleek rat appeared at the unobscured doorway. He bared his teeth and looked immensely satisfied.

"There. You'll have the run of the house, I suppose," Fayne said.

"Right you are, bird. Lovely smell's been taunting us for days. Nothing goes to waste," he said and with a last fanged smile he scampered back into the dark cellar.

3 | Piasa, Wings of Just

"Piasa is the glory and the sacred; she roosts at the highest rung.
For all creatures are Piasa's chicks, she lovingly
hatched them, one by one."

- *Tales of Piasa,* for Chicks and Hatchlings

Tucker slept away the rest of the sunlight and rose only to mark the fence posts and lap more water. He didn't speak to any of them, only curled beneath the sagging branches of the crying tree and closed his eyes.

Chickory bobbed her head. "He's exhausted, poor thing. No creature can survive long without water."

Fayne settled herself between two patches of flowering milk weed and Chickory hunkered down beside her. Hunger buzzed in her stomach but she tried to ignore it. "Are you all right? You got dog out of the house. You've done more than I could have imagined possible."

"We should call him T-t-tucker. Helps to remind him who he is. I am as right as can be expected. You should t-t-try to forage, we will need our strength." Fayne stretched out in the patch of dry warm earth and fluttered her wings, cleaning her feathers with a layer of dust.

"What is it? You've been all out of sorts lately. Tucker can protect us and we'll be safer than we were before. Doesn't that please you? I'll be sure to tell the others what you've done."

"Chickory, you are a friend and certainly not a fool bird, but you are naïve. We face greater d-d-danger than before."

Chickory blinked. She didn't know what *naïve* meant, but danger didn't seem likely. Especially not now. "Danger? You can't know that and other than lacking food, we're quite safe." A shudder of fear passed through her. "Fayne… Is it, well, is it like the other times? Did you have a dream?" She didn't want to think it but her mind flooded with the memories of Fayne's strange pronouncements of the past—the way she had known of the sun season storms that came before, and even the death of Lady's mate, who had been struck down by an angry sky-stinger. She had known those things would come.

"Yes."

Heat spread through Chickory. With every vision Fayne came to possess, the others descended upon her with fury. "Perhaps—well— maybe don't tell the others, all right? Not this time."

"We have to. D-d-danger is coming. Hunters are coming. Here and soon. We have to leave and we must take the others with us."

"Hunters?" Chickory waggled her head. "Take the others...? Fayne! Stop this, please, just, stop. Have you forgotten so easily what happened last time?" Her gaze lingered on Fayne's mangled comb. There had been many such instances though. The flock had stripped Fayne's feathers and banished her to the outside. Chased her around the yard until she collapsed. Pecked at her head and neck until she bled. Robert could usually talk them around by lectures about forgiveness and the gentle way of Piasa, but every time it was a horror to witness.

"My friend, there is no choice. Any creature who stays here will die. The Hunters will destroy any who remain."

Chickory's throat tightened and she squeaked. "But why?"

Fayne's yellow eyes gleamed, though they looked blankly toward the horizon. "It is far too much to explain."

A flicker of anger mingled with Chickory's fear. "No, no, no. I have always trusted you, always heeded you, but this can't be. It just can't. What would you have us do? Where would you have us go? You have to stop this. Please. The others might drive you out into the forest or even… kill you. Especially how things are lately."

"That d-d-does not matter. If we stay, we die." Fayne tilted her head up, as though she spoke to a listening sky. "It is coming. I know you are afraid, but I know where we will go."

The warm sunny day felt cold. Chickory searched for a circling sky bird, but there was none. "Where will we go?"

Fayne turned her gaze back to the distant horizon and Chickory tried to see as she did, though all she saw was the gravelly river that curved past the neighboring farmland and disappeared into the unknown beyond it.

"We will go to the valley. And we will tell the others, t-t-tonight at the Ninith."

Chickory rose and ran, an anguished cry in her throat.

***

Chickory gazed up at the wilting blossoms of the sweet tree. The sun would kill them all and already yellowed flowers covered the ground like melted snow. Maybe no sweet blistered fruit would drop during the fade, when the air turned cold and pleasant. Though if Fayne had her way, they wouldn't even be here to see it.

She had fled and hidden here in the small grove, wanting to be far from Fayne, far away from every creature. The heat of the sun glowed against her back and she stepped into the full shade of the trees. There was no puff of air to cool the yard and the horrible smell of the house had spread, now that the door had been ripped away. Even the flowers could not veil the diseased smell, no matter where she went to get away from it. A shiver of unease rippled in her stomach.

"Bird! Bird! Hungry bird! Isn't it such a hungry bird?" A group of chatterwings, known for their gift of song, trilled in the branches overhead. One relieved itself and it plopped beside Chickory. She abandoned her hiding place beneath the trees. Not all birds made pleasant company, pretty songs or not.

Vague hunger rumbled inside her belly and her mind spasmed like a fish in a shallow pond. She skirted the far edge of the yard and followed the length of the fence until she reached the front gate, which faced the gravelly river. Lady had driven her roar horse up and down the river, Tucker usually riding in the back. Sometimes she returned with sacks of food, grunting as she loaded them into the cellar, one by one. Just like the vanished Hums, there hadn't been a single roar horse for—well, it had been so long—and now Fayne wanted to leave. To travel the river and go wherever it was Hums and roar horses went.

The very thought of leaving the farm made her ill. Fear needled her breast like a nest of sting-stings and burrowed into the living knot that pulsed beneath her feathers. She looked again at the pebbly river. It disappeared as it crossed the fold where the sky touched Piasa's earth and beyond were killers and probable death. Though if the Hums did not appear to bring corn and knobby vegetables to the farm, then they might be alone. Forever.

She shuddered. Alone until whatever it was Fayne said was coming, arrived.

Fayne planned to tell the others at the Ninith, though the calm of the ritual wouldn't last once Fayne began clucking. The night probably wouldn't end until she was plucked of all her feathers, one by one, or was driven out into the dark forest. She'd be eaten surely. Chickory had begged her not to speak, not to tell the others of her terrible plan, but once Fayne declared she would do something, it would happen.

Chickory felt heavy and weak. So she forced herself to do what had always worked before: distract herself. She returned to the flock and spent the rest of the day being as a bird should be. She scratched new nests in the coop and helped Woodfawn fight off a sassy vole. She foraged in the pathetic remains of the compost pile with Dolly and Daisy and eventually, she felt, well, better.

As she scratched in the fermenting plant clippings and listened to the twin's rambling chatter on the appearance of flowers and Robert's courtships, she decided to be a better bird. Maybe try harder to follow the way of the flock, to accept her roost, and fulfill Piasa's gift of henhood. Though that would mean no more Fayne, no more listening to the storm inside Fayne's confused strange mind. Maybe it meant Fayne wouldn't have any more tail feathers, but at least the dizzy fear and confusion would end. That alone would be worth everything.

"You're becoming just as addled as Fayne," Dolly trilled.

Daisy tittered. "Indeed, contagious as buggy legs!"

Chickory cackled too, but in the deep place where a bird could hear Piasa whisper, guilt swirled with the pulsing glow of her terror.

As the sun passed its highest perch and strutted towards night, guilt had eroded and become anger. Fayne was to blame for all of this. All the strange events of the many past sunrises—how could any bird know so much? The sky turned muddy with streaks of orange and pink. The time for the Ninith had arrived. Woodfawn puffed out her breast and strutted up the ramp and into the coop. The others approached.

Crushing panic seized her.

She ran from the coop and bristled from head to claw. She was dying, she must be, the sting-stings were inside her, they got inside, their needles deep inside her innards. Stinging and stinging. She ran to the crying tree and collapsed beneath its sagging branches.

"Bird? Chickory!"

Warm and wet. A tongue slathered her feathery body. The stench of Tucker's breath washed over her. For a while, there was no sound but her terrified squeaks and the gentle *swish swish* of his long tongue as he washed her feathers and head.

Maybe she could be an egg again. Just go back inside, rebuild the shell, and return to living a life in a small safe world.

Time passed. She slowly became aware of the warmth of Tucker's body curled around her. He snoozed and his breath fluttered the loose skin of his lips. The panic had passed and she had returned to her mind. The sting-stings were gone and the sky was almost dark. The Ninith would start soon. She stumbled upright, dazed and feeling very old.

Tucker opened his eyes and nosed her until she almost fell over. "Are you all right, bird?"

"Yes. Well, I think. Maybe. Tucker?"

"Yes?"

"Will you go with us? When the time comes?"

His tail drummed against the hard soil. That seemed enough.

By the time she arrived back at the coop, Woodfawn was already perched on the top roost. Robert sat on a separate roost from the others, but his was halfway down, beneath Woodfawn and Lacey's usual spot. Rosie and Georgia hissed at Chickory as she passed their nests.

Woodfawn waggled her head in disgust. "You stink! Like dog and pond scum."

Chickory ignored her and settled on her familiar place on the lowest roost. The others trickled in and found their usual places. Lacey flapped up beside Woodfawn and they squabbled for the best spot. They nearly knocked each other off the perch before Woodfawn finally made room.

Fayne did not appear.

A surge of relief spread through Chickory's feathertips. Maybe she would never come back and they would never have to talk about leaving the farm ever again.

"Piasa thrummed to the world below—*qwah qwah, qwah qwah*," Rosie said, joined by the others. Their clucks melded together into one voice.

Outside, a dim silhouette approached. Every yellow eye glared as Fayne entered the coop and hopped up beside Chickory on their shared roost.

Woodfawn bristled at the interruption and continued the story: "Piasa walked the great earth, carving the valleys and erecting great mountains. The ocean roared from the tears of her efforts, splashing into the deep void. There was balance, there was peace, but there were many." Woodfawn's voice warbled like a deep bubbling stream. Though abrasive and hostile, she was one of their finest storytellers.

"The Hums hummed up from the world below – *ooah ooah, ooah ooah*," the others continued.

"The Hums grew fast, vast, and swift. Clever and sometimes cruel. They turned their eyes to Piasa, begged for rain, for sun, for plentiful gifts. They were always hungry and always greedy," Woodfawn said.

Now Chickory joined the familiar chorus. "*Take my seed, spread it forth, take my people, spread them forth.*"

"Piasa told them with thundering sky, 'you are caretakers of the Earth, you must serve the Earth before I will serve you.' The Hums cried for they feared Piasa would be angry. 'What should we do? What can we do?' they pleaded, hunger in their bellies and throats."

"*Serve them, shelter them, care for them, warm them, cockerel, hen, chick, and all.*"

"Piasa smiled and was not angry. 'You will care for the birds of the sky, beasts of the field, and all creatures will be your charge. And in return they will give you their gifts, their eggs, and in the end, their lives.'"

"*At the end let them return to sustain you, sustain you.*"
Chickory shivered.

"And it was so. But the Hums were greedy and became killers and ate *all* the eggs. They did not know how to care for life. Piasa thundered again and they cowered in fear, but Piasa was not cruel. 'Life is precious, you must protect it. Only in need will you take life and your own will be forfeit for the ones you have taken. Return to the Earth,' she told them."

"*At your end, return to the earth and sustain them, sustain them.*"
"Piasa shook the Earth and parted the soil, swallowing the many who had not obeyed. But as each Hum died, worms wriggled in their

flesh and their bodies became dust. They grew into plants and trees, fruits and roots. The birds of the sky, beasts of the field, all creatures, feasted upon this new life and balance was restored." Woodfawn bowed her head.

"*Blades of grass, blood of the flesh,*
One feeds the other to feed the other to feed another,
Piasa, Piasa—shield us wings of Just," the flock murmured.

It was Chickory's favorite story, one told throughout chickhood. The memory comforted, a reassurance of their purpose—the unity of Hums and all creatures formed a continuous and balanced way of life. It was Piasa's way. A way that should not be changed by addled birds or dangerous ideas. Though without Lady, how the way could continue at all, was unclear.

As though Fayne knew her thoughts, she said, "I have something I must t-t-tell you all and I feel now the t-t-time to d-d-discuss it."

The somber flock stared blankly in return. The story still warmed the coop with stoic peace. No one clucked a reply.

"Um, yes, we all know food has b-b-become scarce."

Woodfawn snorted. The sting-stings of panic buzzed inside Chickory again. The confidence Fayne had when they spoke in the privacy of their friendship always evaporated beneath the scrutiny of the flock.

Fayne took a deep breath and continued. "It brings about the reality of our situation. Of what must happen. The truth is we must leave."

Chickory's anguished sigh disappeared beneath Georgia's enraged squawk.

"Leave? *Leave?* Please do, go *now*, if you can! Piasa's grace. This is our home, our place of Origin. Leave? We must stay! Unless you propose we leave our eggs too?" Her white crown feathers lifted and her comb quivered with rage. Georgia was an often-hysterical white hen who squabbled with others for the best nesting space whether she had eggs to lay or not.

"Right! What would you have us do?" "How could we?" "Should we?" "Never!" Daisy and Dolly rambled over each other.

"We must leave," Fayne said again. "Go and find a n-n-new home. T-t-there is, um, there is a valley." She spoke to the deep layer of soiled straw that covered the ground.

Woodfawn flapped off her roost and stalked toward Fayne.

"Piasa would be furious with you."

Chickory hopped off their rung and scurried in front of Woodfawn. The knot beating inside her breast now thudded in her ears. "No! Wait! Fayne is right." The words surfaced as though they had waited there all along. Even Fayne stared at Chickory in surprise.

A grumbled murmur spread as they turned their glares upon Chickory.

"I mean, look. It's peculiar, yes. Strange to think of leaving our home, our farm. But she's right, isn't she? We're half-starved and even Piasa can't know whether our chicks will survive the seasons to come. Killers could come upon us, *will* come upon us. Stories of Piasa tell of creatures who fought to survive. They used their cunning, their bravery, their many gifts to fulfill the true way of the world. Though we are meant to have Hums to share in the way, I think… well, I think Piasa wants us to survive."

Robert cocked his head. "This valley you speak of. How far is it?"

Nervous silence simmered like the rumble of a sun season storm.

Fayne met Robert's gaze and for a moment they stared at one another. "It is a very long way."

"But you *do* know the way, don't you?" Chickory asked.

Fayne fluffed her feathers. "I do. I d-d-do know the way. But we must leave. Immediately. At sunrise."

Georgia panted nervously. "But the Hums will return, they will come for us and all will be as it was."

Chickory swallowed against a lump in her throat. "No. No, they won't. They would have come already. They wouldn't have left us. Lady is… well, she's dead."

Georgia shot from her perch with a hysterical cackle. The flap of her wings stirred up dust and dried droppings as she battered herself against the walls of the coop.

"Stop, oh no, please, you must listen!" Chickory ducked and squawked as she tried to avoid the flail of Georgia's body.

The others rearranged themselves and hopped from roost to roost as they moved out of Georgia's frantic way. She finally landed on a rung and her feathers stuck out in odd directions as she panted and hissed.

Robert hopped to her roost and pressed his large body against hers. "Don't be afraid, Georgia, we're all here together. Piasa watches over us," he crooned. He preened one of her displaced feathers.

Georgia quieted, her eyes still glazed with a panicky fright that overrode all sense.

Fayne glanced at Georgia, but she did not move or make any sound at all. "I am afraid we have already wasted precious t-t-time. There is, um, there is d-d-danger coming."

Woodfawn bobbed her head. "Wait, you wait. You said the Hum was… is dead. Well, I don't believe you," she said.

"You could check the house for yourself or ask T-t-tucker."

"… or are you afraid of the big bad dog?" Chickory asked, shocked at her own boldness.

Rosie waggled her head in disgust and Woodfawn growled a warning.

"No, stop this. Fayne is right," Robert said. "The Hums next door are also dead. There's a dead boy at the fence and none of us have seen any in far too long. The only explanation is they've gone on, as Hums sometimes do. Such is the way of Piasa. We should not concern ourselves with this."

Chickory chirped in agreement. So he *had* seen the boy for himself.

"Yes, yes, t-t-they have gone on, b-b-but we must leave." Fayne trembled. We should have already left."

Georgia jerked her head up. "I don't believe you either. I've already scratched a nest and it's ridiculous, I'm not leaving, you can't make me, and the rest of you are feather heads too. Piasa would be furious with your strange ideas. You're hardly even a bird! Hardly a bird! We have our place and it's here!" She hopped down from her perch and nestled atop her own clutch of eggs.

Robert rustled his wings and gazed down at her. "I won't be coming either. Rosie's also bedded down with a nest and it just wouldn't be right to leave her, or any of us, behind. There are other ways. We can begin to forage outside the yard, slowly expand as we clearly need to. I've been looking among the silver trees and there are no fox burrows or raccoon nests there. There's no rush to leave. The coop is safe and if you stay, dog is here to protect us again. These are good things. Things *you* have done, Fayne. For the flock." He cooed the last like she was a newly hatched chick.

Fayne stiffened. "But t-t-there *is* d-d-danger. T-t-there is, it is coming—I can see–I—I—" She stopped.

"What danger? Can you tell us what this danger is exactly?"

Robert stared at her intently, but with no sign of scorn.

"I–I do not know, exactly… what… Well, I will be leaving. Whoever wants t-t-to can, the rest of you will surely d-d-die." Fayne abandoned her perch and shoved past Woodfawn as she rushed into the darkness outside.

Woodfawn rustled her wings. "Goodness. Such a fuss. As is said, 'a fussy bird is a burden to all in the world.' I'll be sure to rip the longest feathers out. Tuh, but that can wait until sunrise."

"She certainly forgets each lesson as soon as it's taught. Save some for me, though she's hardly got any left," Rosie said.

They tittered with laughter.

The air tasted sour and Chickory paused at the coop entrance. Anger surged through her and the sting-stings hummed loudly in her ears. "Have any of you stopped to think, even for an instant, that maybe *Piasa* speaks to her? Maybe she knows what she knows because she's meant to? How furious is Piasa with those who do not heed her call? 'Those who fly too high or swim too deeply will hear my words, even at the last.' Isn't that what it means? That some will hear, even if it—" Her anger swelled into anguish. Anguish for her dear friend, betrayed by all and loved by none. Except her, maybe. "Even if that costs her everything."

Robert called after her, but she fled out into the darkness after Fayne.

There was nothing more to say to any of them.

4 | First Steps

"Piasa created all the birds and creatures of the world,
Giving some of them cunning and some wisdom,
But giving them all the courage to live."

- *Tales of Piasa*, for Chicks and Hatchlings

The swollen egg moon hung heavy in the sky and made the world bright and alternately full of shadows. A moon bird hooted and Chickory scanned the bright sky and treetops for some sign of the bird. But it was far away in the meadow, hunting. Insects chirped in the tall grass beyond the fence and musky frogs called for mates.

She found Fayne huddled beside Tucker, who still slept beneath the crying tree. As she approached, Fayne let out a mournful peep. Chickory's innards squeezed at the small sound, the sound chicks made when they were afraid. She nestled in beside her and preened some of her dark ringed feathers.

"They will all d-d-die." Fayne's yellow eyes reflected the bright white of the moon.

"You can't be sure, there's no way to know. Not for sure. You've been wrong before."

"I know. I know."

But what it was Fayne knew, Chickory did not want to know, so she said nothing.

Tucker's faint snores rippled the quiet of the night and Fayne's body relaxed and her breathing slowed. She had found sleep and Chickory was glad.

Her own mind would not settle, heavy with the ominous words that repeated in her mind: *we must leave.* The words choked like heavy pebbles in the fleshy pouch of her throat.

Sleep would not come so she abandoned the attempt and wandered over to the trough to sip the mossy water. Even with Tucker's frantic drinking, there was still plenty of water inside, slowly refilled by a drip from the hand pump above it. The egg moon disappeared as Piasa obscured the star-eyes with the down of her feathery breast. Though Fayne had once told her it wasn't feathers that filled up the sky, but cay-louds. Wait, no, it had been *clouds* she had said.

Chickory gazed at the wide black holes of the house windows, which normally shone with the reflection of the sun. Fear tingled in her feathers. Lady's corpse was still inside, rotted and half—

A white shadow passed the window.

She couldn't move, her chest collapsed and wouldn't breathe. Something had moved inside the house. A white shadow. A white gown. Lady's gown. But she was dead; Fayne said so, Tucker said so. She was gone. Gone. GONE.

"Chickory?"

She tried to turn but couldn't, paralyzed by sundown.

Fayne came alongside her and peered into her frozen eyes. "Is it *thanatosis*? Did something frighten you?"

Confusion filtered through and the fear evaporated. She gasped a wind pouch of air. "What? What are you clucking on about?" Her whole body felt soggy and limp.

Fayne looked toward the house. Nothing moved in the windows, no white shadow stirred. "Why are you out here alone? It is not safe. Especially not t-t-tonight."

"What's than-a-tis-tis-? Or whatever you said." She wouldn't tell Fayne about the shadow. Too much darkness already swirled in her friend's mind.

"You were stuck, could not move. The central nervous system's instinct is to run away or fight back—but sometimes we just stop instead."

Her strange words, again about things Chickory did not understand. "Yes. I was stuck. Thought I heard something coming."

"There *is* something coming."

Chickory nearly froze again, but shut her eyes and imagined a wide field of corn. *They're just words.* The feeling passed and when she opened her eyes, Fayne had stepped closer to the front porch.

"No, don't. Let's go back, try and sleep," Chickory said.

"You are right. We will need to sleep. Time is slipping away, too fast to catch now."

Dismay tingled in Chickory's comb—the others would stay and discover just how true Fayne's words might be. "I hope not. Do you think—should we leave Tucker here? To protect them?"

Fayne's eyes, usually hard or blank or gleaming with keen knowledge—well, now they shimmered with sadness. "He would not be enough to protect them and he would die too. I had hoped… no matter. All our choices have b-b-been made." Fayne backed away from the house and without another cluck, wandered back toward the crying tree.

Chickory followed, though she glanced back, wondering if a white shadow watched them go.

***

Chickory shivered to shed the thin layer of dew from her feathers. The sunlight brightened the distant fold of sky and soon Robert would announce the morning. Tucker's body emanated warmth and the small rise of Fayne's breaths pressed against her side. From here the coop looked small and dark, but inside Rosie and Georgia were bedded down on their nests of eggs, probably cooing as they slept. There was no greater sight than a mother hen. Chickory ached with sudden longing for the flock, for the comfort of the roost.

But that was over now. The moment she left the coop and entered the darkness, everything had changed. Whatever it would come to mean, she had made her choice: she would follow Fayne, no matter where it led.

A mourning bird hooted in the stillness, sad but serene. Red and yellow longbeak flowers perfumed the air, and they would soon bring hummingbirds to the farm. She wouldn't be here to see them sip daintily from the narrow bellies of the blossoms. She would miss all the sun season glory; the flowering of the large beebee bushes, the sweet trees and their sticky fruits that would fall during the fade. Lady had brought her to this farm, newly hatched and barely standing. This place was her home, the only one she had ever expected to have.

Fayne opened her eyes. "We should go." She rose and stretched each scaly shank, and flexed her twiggy toes. She looked calm and sure now. Stuttering or not, fool bird or not, Chickory would have to trust her.

"Aren't you sad to be leaving? Are we mad?" The words felt like stones, heavier with each breath.

"It does not serve the purpose. We will go t-t-through the front gate and follow the road."

"The road? The… gravelly river?"

"It is called a *road*, Chickory."

Tucker jerked in his sleep and a great snort rippled his jowls.

Chickory pecked at an oversized ear. "Let's go, you mangy creature." Even in her anxiety, she felt a swell of affection for the large beast. He had become an extension of Lady, a reminder of being watched over. She had watched him pounce on an absentminded sparrow, but he would never turn on the flock, she knew that now. A peace existed between them, even though there was no Hum to call him back to the house. Piasa designed those sharp curved teeth and his appetite for flesh, but Tucker would keep them safe.

He jerked awake and shook himself. Dirt and flakes of sloughing skin choked the air. "Are we leaving now?"

"Yes. Time is short," Fayne said.

He peed on a fence post and the yellow fluid steamed in the cold morning air, a last reminder to any killers who might pass by the small farm.

Together the three of them headed toward the front gate, traveling the opposite side of the house, away from the coop. They did not need to discuss any more and it was better to part this way, without hateful words and more glares.

They passed the blue house, once a source of pleasure, of food, and of delightful company. For as strange as Lady was, as all Hums were, she had understood Piasa's wish for them and never allowed the flock to experience hunger or needless pain. She had loved them; she named each bird and stroked each feather. In the window, cobwebs shimmered in the early light.

They moved quietly and *we must leave* bobbed inside Chickory's mind. The words cast the farm in an unpleasant light. Perhaps it would be a relief to be gone for it no longer felt like their home.

They passed the wire coops where large white rabbits had lived.

Morning flies buzzed around the towering piles of droppings beneath the cages. Chickory pecked at some spilled specks of their green pelleted food and Tucker stuck his snout against the bottom of one of the wire floors.

"There's fuzz butts still inside." He wagged his tail in wide sweeps and it knocked Chickory on the head with each pass.

The rabbit inside gave a terrified squeal. "Oh Frith, spare us. Go away Elil. leave us!" it snapped in the common sound.

"Fayne, wait, won't you?" Chickory peered up at the huddled mass. Long yellow claws poked through the holes in the floor. The other cages held the slumped bodies of the other rabbits who had died as they waited for Lady to return. The bodies were decomposing with the careful attention of flies.

Fayne sighed. "There is nothing we can do for them. We must make use of the d-d-day. It is too dangerous to linger any longer."

Chickory cocked her head. "We're just to leave them? Aren't they trapped, like Tucker? Shouldn't we try?"

Tucker whined and licked the wooden leg of the cage. He turned his mournful brown gaze to Fayne, who only stared in response. "The fuzz butt is in terrible condition, they are. Half dead." His whine grew louder.

The rabbit grunted and thumped the wire floor with a powerful hind foot. "I'll thank you to mind your own, leave us to Frith's bidding."

Chickory flapped her wings hard and launched herself upwards. She grabbed the wire door with her claws and hung there a moment, trying to stay upright, before hopping onto a small lip on the side of the wooden frame. She teetered on the edge and peered inside.

The large white mother crouched among her decayed litter. Their small bodies twitched as shiny white maggots wriggled in the flesh. A few of their bodies were half eaten, likely by the mother herself. The sight of the bugs squeezed Chickory's stomach with hunger.

The mother glared at her with shiny red eyes and her sides heaved with every breath.

"We'll try to get you out. Then you can run, go find a new home, like us." Chickory looked at the latch that kept the door shut.

"El-ahrairah's tricks would do me no good now." The mother thumped the floor and disrupted the horde of flies who promptly landed again.

Chickory glanced down at Fayne, who was scanning the yard and the road beyond. "Is there any way we could open this?"

Fayne sighed. She strutted back and forth and eyed the door latch. "It would be impossible. You lack the lateral-most pollical needed to operate it."

"I'm lacking a-what?"

Fayne gave an exasperated hiss. "You don't have *thumbs*."

"Who needs thumbs when you've got teeth!" Tucker attacked the cage door. His white teeth rattled against the wire.

The rabbit screamed in terror as the door buckled.

"Yes, Tucker, keep biting!" Chickory flapped her wings in encouragement.

One of his curved teeth hooked the wire and it caught against the frame. He reared back and shook his head with such force the whole cage rocked as though it might fall over. The aged wire bent and the door nearly folded in half. He jerked again and ripped the small wire frame off the hinges. He dropped the door and wagged his tail. Yellowed teeth were bared, but in a joyful way.

Chickory steadied herself. "There, there, he's done it now. You can come out, you're free!"

The mother did not move and let out a moan. "It's no use. It isn't. Frith wills it."

"Frith? What's Frith?"

"It is t-t-their God… their, you know, their Piasa," Fayne said. "Will she come out? After all this t-t-trouble?"

Chickory peered in at the mother and tried to look kind. "I don't think Frith has abandoned you yet. Isn't it likely it meant for us to find you?"

The mother stared, but still did not move.

"Well, should you want, you have the way out. I wish you all the luck Pia—I mean, your Frith, can bring you."

The mother grunted. "Frith watch over you too, bird."

Chickory fluttered back to the ground, her stomach like a lump of clay. Some creatures were just naturally very afraid.

Tucker whined deep in his throat. "The fuzz butt isn't coming out."

"Perhaps she is waiting for us to go. You *are* quite terrifying. For a dog." Fayne strutted away toward the front gate.

Tucker wagged his tail again and followed.

They arrived at the gate and Robert's screechy morning call echoed several times across the farmland. The sunrise was bright with early pink clouds. Together they stood at the edge of the road like placid stones. A sparrow chattered above them and dove after a buzzing dragonfly.

"We need to go." Fayne shifted from claw to claw.

Chickory could not breathe. They were about to leave the farm forever. They could not turn back, could not go home. There was no more flock to follow.

Then–

"Wait! No, wait!"

Chickory's heart swooped like a glorious swallow in flight. Daisy and Dolly ran toward them and behind them followed… Woodfawn. They panted and bobbed their heads as they approached.

"Good, so good of you to come." Tucker whined and wagged his massive tail.

Woodfawn approached, looking cautious, but once it was clear Tucker wasn't going to pounce on her, she waggled her head in disbelief. "Will it eat us in our sleep? As is said, 'killers wear many skins and eyes, beware all with pointed teeth'!"

Tucker laid his ears back and his tongue lolled out between his teeth, which were very pointed after all. Moisture shimmered in his brown eyes.

"His name is Tucker," Fayne said.

Woodfawn puffed out her chest. "And he's coming with us?"

Chickory preened a snag of fur on Tucker's foreleg. "Of course. Lady would want him to. But, look, it's so clean feathers of you to come. What made you, you know, decide?" Fear tingled through her, fear that the very mention might cause them all to come to their senses and flee.

Dolly and Daisy twittered. Woodfawn bristled, already looking irritable.

Dolly shuffled nervously. "Well–"

"We got to thinking," Daisy interrupted.

"The two of us really–"

"Should stick together and find more food!"

Daisy gave a coquettish wag of her tail feathers. "And maybe there might be some roosters in this valley?"

Woodfawn snorted and looked only at Chickory. "Perhaps Piasa does guide this creature, tuh, strange as she is. After all, a bird with doggy guard is something indeed." Woodfawn clicked her beak with wry smugness. "And really, who can stand Georgia?"

Chickory felt like singing.

Fayne rustled her wings and looked uncertain, as though she hadn't expected anyone else to really appear. "Are the others furious? T-t-they must be."

Woodfawn bobbed her head dismissively. "Hunger and fear addles the most admirable creature. Perhaps they'll scurry after us after Robert's had a good crow."

"No matter," Fayne said. "We need to hurry, now, and with all the haste we can muster."

Tucker gave a playful yip. "We follow you, birdy bird bird."

They all looked at one another uncertainly. Roost order said Woodfawn would decide, as the biggest and oldest, but none could deny Fayne would lead this journey, wherever it might lead.

"Let's see what kind of creature you really are," Woodfawn said with a low hiss.

Fayne squeezed through the front gate and the others followed. Tucker trailed at the end of their line, sniffing the ground and pausing now and then to scratch at a biting bug.

Chickory allowed herself one backward glance as she squeezed through the gate. Together they emerged onto the open gravel road, where Piasa, or maybe even Frith, watched over them now.

5 | Neighbors

"Go alone at your peril; Piasa created the flock as the
almighty embrace, to protect those, who alone,
could not protect themselves."

- Words of Piasa, Second Clutch, Second Year

The road directed them toward the distant unknown, and being
outside the fence meant being exposed to the wildness of the
outside world. Dolly and Daisy jerked as a shadow passed over them,
but there was no sign of a hawk or eagle. The shadows that flitted across
the ground were of starbirds and sparrows, who twittered with interest at
the unusual sight of chickens who traveled with a large dog.

The scent of blue boomflowers filled the air and in the steep
ditch alongside the lane, tall yellow sunflowers swayed. Everything
twitched with life; sting-stings trundled over splitting buds and prickly
grasshoppers sprang across the lane. Woodfawn chased a few of them
but the exertion soon slowed her down.

"Ahh, 'forage is the hen's true call.' There is nothing more
pleasant than open air and fresh grass," Woodfawn proclaimed. She had
caught a shiny green beetle and looked quite pleased.

"Though Piasa didn't intend us for endurance and long travel it
seems," Chickory said. They passed a dusty field and Chickory gazed at
a shallow depression, likely filled with cool soil. How she longed to
nestle in the soft dirt and be comforted—her stalky legs ached.

"If you t-t-talk less and focus more, your pain might dissipate," Fayne snapped.

So they said nothing for a while. Chickory pecked at lone pebbles and nibbled at wisps of grass as she tried to stay close to Fayne and the others. Though there seemed to be no sign of larger creatures or sky birds, they could be clever, and with the tall grass on either side of the river, it was difficult to see. Remembering the danger was difficult after pecking the same patch of earth beneath the crying tree for so long. This was not the barren land of the farm. Everywhere delicious morsels waited to be found, if one took the time to find them.

Fayne scanned the overgrown landscape. "We cannot linger here. It is not safe."

Woodfawn rolled in a soft patch of moss. "There is nothing here except us. Won't you rest? This moss is quite lovely and besides, 'rest the weary legs and wings, for tomorrow requires much.' Piasa watches over us."

Fayne snorted. "T-t-tucker is more effective."

Woodfawn squawked and rose from her cool recline.

Chickory reluctantly left behind a pair of mating beetles, succulent and unaware of their stalker. "I would think rest includes the beak, Woodfawn," she said. "Anyway, Fayne is right. There's sky birds, death worms, killer dogs. Sorry, Tucker. And what about cats? There could be anything out there lurking."

Fayne turned away and resumed the pace. "And we must keep our pace at a steady clip. As far away from the farm as we can get."

Woodfawn hissed, but joined the rest as they bustled back onto the road. "Can't even be happy when one succeeds. Will nothing please you, fussy creature?"

"Maybe when we are at t-t-the valley or hidden somewhere safe," Fayne said.

Woodfawn glowered but kept her grumbles quiet.

A large crow exploded from a silver tree and circled above them. His black contemptuous eyes gleamed in the sunlight. Daisy and Dolly threw themselves down into the ditch and cowered. Woodfawn didn't move, stuck in Sundown.

"Brother Crow," Fayne called to him in the common sound. The curve of his beak signaled his sex. "How is the road ahead?"

"Stupids! Stupid is, the hens that go!" he cawed in return.

"What do you mean?" Fayne ran to keep up with his wide circles.

The crow growled with exasperation and swooped down to perch on a fence post. A long web of rusted wire still clung to the gray wood.

"Crow! Go away, Crow! Crow!" Tucker barked at the black bird.

"Tucker, be still." Chickory pecked at a matted strand of his fur. He fell quiet but a low growl rumbled in his throat.

The crow shook his feathers and fluffed them, looking disgruntled.

"Brother Crow, please, t-t-tell us how things are ahead. Are there Hums? Is there someplace safe for us to go for the night?" Fayne stood at the foot of the post and panted from the chase.

The crow gave a low hiss and cocked his head. "Stupidest hen at the front it seems? Leads them all to death."

Fayne looked stern. "What death? Explain yourself."

"They fall one by one, Hum by Hum, Piasa save them all. You see the truth, but cannot abide the proof. You shall see, Seer Hen, you shall see." The crow cackled and with a huge flap of his wings, lifted off again into the clear blue sky.

Fayne watched him go and soon the crow was gone over the distant horizon.

"What did he mean by it?" Chickory shivered though the day was quite warm. *We must leave* rattled inside her head like a loose pebble.

Fayne bobbed her head dismissively. "Crows are always cryptic. It is of their nature to be cruel." She continued down the road.

The rest, one by one, followed in slow succession, though it took Woodfawn a few moments to recover from her shock. The crow, a reminder the world was not all bugs and feasting, quieted them and they traveled in silence for a long while.

***

The sun was at its highest perch and they were beginning to slow, the heat against their backs insufferable.

"Come on, we must keep on, no, Daisy, get back here, leave t-t-that." Fayne commanded, bossing them as much as they would tolerate. Every attempt to forage was interrupted.

"How far is this valley? My stalks feel fit to collapse."

Woodfawn paused for another one of her extended rests.

"It's not like we would be there by nightfall. Fayne said it's quite far." Chickory's cheer at the others joining their journey had faded. Woodfawn was tedious, even at the best of times, and now was not the best of times.

"So in lengths of sunrises, as you're being so vague and avoiding my question?"

"Let's worry on just surviving the first sunrise, shall we?" Chickory said.

Woodfawn growled. "You don't know, see, that's the problem there. None of us know what's in Fayne's head except what she sees fit to share. So quickly you came along and swept us all into it, and you don't even know how long it's—"

Fayne stopped and Woodfawn almost ran into her.

Fayne let out a sudden cackle. "Grain. Grain!" She burst into a run.

They hesitated only a moment before sprinting after her. Fayne's cackle was the call of food, the flock signal when a feast had been found, so irresistible even Woodfawn joined the joyous cackling. Tucker followed close behind them as they bolted down the long gravel road that led toward the neighboring farm. The land spilled out alongside their own, but Chickory had never dared to travel so far and there had never been any need. The large farm house, so much larger than Lady's, loomed before them. They dashed through the wide-open gate and, yes, the smell of dark fragrant wheat and sweet corn perfumed the air. Somewhere close. The grain smelled like home, like shelter, like life, better than all the caterpillars in the farmland. Hunger clawed at Chickory's stomach, her mind filled with nothing but the delicious bounty await—

"Stop!" Tucker snarled from behind them.

They all staggered to a clumsy halt. Chickory's feathers quivered with the strength of her hunger and now sudden fear.

But Tucker wasn't speaking to them. The fur along his spine rose in an aggressive ridge and an unfamiliar snarl snagged his lips. He rumbled with a primal rage that shivered throughout his entire body.

Two black dogs ran to meet them, eager tongues slathered over their pointy white teeth. One had a white blaze down its face and the other had mottled patches of red and black fur. The neighbor's dogs, known only by the chattering bark sometimes heard from the safety of the coop. The smaller dogs stared at Tucker with nervous grins.

The small red dog yapped and wagged his patchy bald tail. "What good fortune, shall we share? It's been a long time since we've had such good luck! Why do you follow them? There aren't any Masters left. No one to say 'bad dog!'"

Tucker advanced on stiff forelegs and his snarl grew louder. "These ones are mine, they go with me. They are *not for eating*."

Red dog snorted and pawed the ground. "Then you're a bad dog of a different kind. Here you are, still obeying the dead. Come on, buddy! There's plenty to feed us for days, good food is hard to find," he yammered.

"The Masters left us behind to care for them. They would have taken us with them otherwise." Tucker looked between the two dogs and whined. "Where are your birds?"

White face yipped and grinned. "They were gone long ago, we ate them for days. You look as though you could do with some eating yourself, pup."

Tucker snarled again and saliva dripped from his open mouth. "You ate them?"

"They are gone, this is ours now! To feast, to journey, to hunt. Have you forgotten the call of the moon? The whisper of the running blood? Has the wolf left you entirely?"

Tucker shook, hackles still raised. "The wolves have been gone far too long. We answer to our Masters, not the moon."

"So say you!" White face snarled.

Red dog danced forward a few steps. "Soft as a pup's milk belly. Well, enough!" He dashed toward Fayne.

Tucker bellowed and charged, a smear of furious flesh. He dropped one shoulder and collided with red dog, who tumbled and howled with pain. White face abandoned his crouch and charged Tucker with a throaty roar.

Tucker rose to meet him and they smashed together. Spit foamed at their bleeding mouths as teeth gnashed and punctured flesh.

The flock cackled and cowered, trapped in the midst of the fight. Fear crept up Chickory's stalks like cold season frost. Her stomach churned with panic and none of them ran, frozen in Sundown. Dolly tucked her head beneath Daisy's wing. The clash of the killers swallowed them in a sickening clamor of sound and blur of motion.

"Watch out!" Tucker cried and almost trampled Fayne.

White face sunk his teeth into Tucker's scruffy neck and they fell. Red dog pranced between them and pounced on Woodfawn, her wings crushed beneath his paws.

The air exploded with feathers and a screech of terror as Fayne launched herself at red dog. With this sudden bold motion, Chickory followed without real thought, flinging her feathery body at the dog. Fayne slashed at his muzzle and stabbed at his wet eyes with her pointed beak. Red dog jerked away. Chickory collided with the side of his head and kicked at the flesh beneath the flap of his ear until red dog released Woodfawn with a howl of rage. He reared as he tried to escape his prey's unexpected attack. He snapped at Chickory and his teeth raked over the side of her head. Heat pulsed through her and sound blended together in one cry, followed by a squeal and wail of terror.

The landscape melted and Chickory fell into uncertain darkness.

6 | Recovering

> "Fear is a healthy sense; it protects you, guides you,
> And best of all, keeps you out of the tall grass."
>
> - *Practical Wisdom,* Third Clutch, Second year

Dolly's voice: "She's waking up—Great Piasa, she's awake!" Chickory stared up into the wide yellow eyes of Dolly and Daisy.

"Move aside, move aside," Woodfawn growled as she shouldered into view. "Ah, back just in time to count cracked eggs."

Chickory staggered to her claws, heavy on her trembly stalks. The neighbor's farm stretched around them and she shuddered, though there was no sign of the other two dogs.

"Ease, be of ease." Woodfawn preened one of Chickory's crown feathers. "They've gone. They'd had enough of fighting birds." She gave a satisfied cackle.

Chickory looked around: Dolly, Daisy, and Woodfawn. Her innards heaved with anxiety. "Where's Fayne?"

"She's over there, watching over Tucker," Woodfawn said.

Behind them, Tucker sprawled in the dirt. His side heaved with huge ragged breaths. Chickory scurried to him as fast as her shaking legs would allow. All birds depended on Piasa to guide them, but this was Tucker, and Piasa or not, guidance or not, she feared for him.

"Oh, sweet, sweet dog are you," she cooed and hopped around him like a nervous mother.

Blood wept from a small white stripe of opened flesh and stained his neck. She had never seen their flesh laid open to the air, but knew their blood flowed from the same red river that ran through the flesh of all creatures. Though they all knew their fate when Lady took one of them from the flock, or when a bird was dragged off into the woods by a killer's sharp teeth, they had been sheltered from the worst of these things. Truly, Chickory had never seen anything more mangled than the gush of a large crawler's guts or the soft sticky innards of a stoneshell bug.

Chickory blinked hard and though she wanted to, she did not turn away.

Fayne stood on the other side of Tucker's head and preened the matted fur around his muzzle.

"Is he…?" It hurt to form the words.

"He will recover." Fayne struggled with a stubborn tuft, but did not seem overly concerned with the way his large furry body sprawled in the dirt.

"Then why is he lying here? And his neck, it's horrible."

"He is resting, exhausted. He was on his last legs when we coaxed him from the house. Hardly a full sun and running around like a fool bird… and those d-d-dogs." Fayne bristled and sucked in a breath. "Those dogs ran like cowards, crumbling beneath Tucker's might like dust in the wind."

Chickory was surprised at the strength of Fayne's words. She sounded stronger too, somehow. Different.

"We will rest here," Fayne continued. "Those dogs will not come back and we can seek out shelter in the barn. And of course, there is grain to eat and we should eat all we can. We might not have another opportunity. Will you lead the others? I believe there are bins of food inside."

"Aren't you coming with us?"

"I will stay here with T-t-tucker until he wakes. Leave me a morsel, will you?"

Chickory did as she was told and the others followed, their eyes sullen and sad as they passed by Tucker. No, they were no longer just a flock of birds. They were a flock of feather and fur, bound by unknowable fate. Did the others feel as she did? Did they sense the change, the shift in how they were to be in this new world? Was Fayne the wing of Piasa, here to guide them to follow her will?

Chickory pushed away her strange thoughts and focused instead on each tentative step she took toward the barn. Though the dogs had gone, her body prickled with unease.

The large barn door was ajar and when they entered, the smell of cows and horses washed over them, though none stood in the empty stalls. Mingled with the earthy scent was the sweet fragrance of food. A couple grain bins had been toppled from their stacks, their buttery gold contents and earthy chaffs of wheat scattered across the ground. Mice scattered as they approached.

"Piasa's bounty!" Woodfawn bolted forward and the rest quickly followed.

***

The sun passed in a wave of feasting and pleasant rest. The wheat and corn tasted of dust and though not fresh, each speck reminded Chickory of home. Though there had been insects and greens to eat at the farm and on the road, it had been many suns since there had been grain and dried corn. She ate until her stomach ached with fullness.

Eventually, after a long rest, Tucker had come inside the barn too. He nibbled a few mouthfuls of fresh grass that grew along the entryway and lapped water from an old trough. The whole flock had banded together and worked to remove much of the blood in his matted fur. Pecking, tearing, and preening were natural skills. Though his wound still oozed a little, Tucker hardly noticed. He even surprised an especially fat and lazy ground squirrel just outside the barn. As he crunched through the small, fragile bones of the fuzzy creature, Chickory shuddered. Everything seemed much more… violent now. The other dogs had been a good reminder.

"Can't we just stay here until we run out of food? We could even run back and get Robert and Rosie and Lacey and, tuh, I suppose Georgia. It's not too far." Woodfawn almost choked on her beakful of corn as she continued her gorge.

"No, we cannot stay," Fayne said.

Chickory bowed her head as she scratched in the dirt, afraid to look at the others.

Woodfawn glared at Fayne. "And why not? There is not a single solitary reason we shouldn't stay here. Piasa says 'grain is the sign of the caretaker's promise.' And here we are! Grain. I can't think of a clearer sign than that."

"Because we are not safe here, d-d-danger is still coming." Fayne met Woodfawn's glare for a brief moment. "And it is coming faster." She turned away.

"Safe from what and who are we supposed to be running from? Tucker can protect us from those mangy killers if that's all you're worried about," Woodfawn said.

"I can and I will. There's nothing to fear, birdy bird." Tucker wagged his tail.

"It is not the d-d-dogs."

"Then what is it?" Woodfawn squawked.

"We need to stay away from the—"

"Run! Oh, quick, hurry, run!" Daisy and Dolly burst through the open barn door. Their buff feathers stuck straight out from their bodies.

Right behind them followed the largest coyote Chickory had ever seen. He skidded to a halt and yipped as he realized their numbers. His mottled grey fur was patchy and red coloring traced the roundness of his eyes.

Tucker roared and ran to meet him.

Chickory, Fayne, and Woodfawn launched into the air. Feathers scattered as they landed on the rail of a horse stall.

"Ayooo—" the coyote switched to the common sound. "Ooo, peace. Seems I've stumbled into the wrong hidey-hole. Chickens with doggy guards? Nothing makes sense these days," he yammered and scampered backwards.

"You'd better take go on." Tucker positioned himself between the coyote and the flock.

The coyote plopped back on his haunches and scratched a mangy ear as though this were a casual visit between friends. "Right, well, I'll just catch my wind and be off. Those ladies gave me a bit of a run." He grinned at Daisy and Dolly, who peered out from behind one of the bins.

"No! Leave now, I will not—"

"No, Tucker, let him stay." Fayne flew down from her perch.

"Don't be insane," hissed Woodfawn. She glared at the intruder. "Sharp teeth!"

Fayne cocked her head. "Technically, it is called a coyote, also known as little wolf or more obscurely, is a member of the *canis*—

"Now is not the time!" Woodfawn squawked.

Fayne grimaced and took a step toward the coyote. "It is all right."

His teeth gleamed in his wide smile. Piasa's gift to the sharp teeth were jaws that fit together with fatal perfection, a snap that could crush a bird's head as easily as an over ripe berry. Chickory shuddered. Though it was their fate to someday die, there were finer ways to go than in the mouth of a coyote.

"What is your name?" Fayne took another small hop forward. She pecked at a kernel of corn, but kept her eyes on him.

"Latrans—say, you're a strange bird, aren't you? It's like you're not even afraid." Latrans tilted his head and stepped towards her.

Tucker lunged forward and his growl became a nasty snarl.

Latrans sat back again. "Hmpf, of course, if I had my own guard, I might be more wolf than scrapper. You might have a chance then, with your cur there."

"A chance at what?" Fayne said.

"Getting beyond the road. Surviving. If you stay here, well, they'll find you soon enough."

Fear twisted Chickory's already painful insides. "Who? Who would find us?"

Latrans snapped at a buzzing fly. "The people, of course."

Woodfawn burst into a raucous cackle. "The Hums? It's about time they show up, start doing their jobs. Our Lady went on and no one came. You say there are Hums about? 'Good are the Hums who caretake the earth.' Piasa's fortune, I say. See, Fayne? All this twittering and they're back!"

Latrans snorted. "Chickens. Full of meat and feathers." He shook his lanky body. "These people wouldn't feed you, care for you. Something's up all right, but I can't quite make sense of it. Dogs are all over the place, running loose, and there are strange stories on the wind. A fine bitch, just last sunrise, told me her Masters got sick, that mouth sickness they sometimes get. But they never came around. Just kicked off and died. First one and soon the whole brood lay dying all over the floor. One kit after another, four, I think she said. And not just her house, the whole neighborhood. Ach, but you can't follow every whimper and yip. You know how dogs exaggerate." Latrans grinned at Tucker.

Woodfawn puffed out her chest. "Well, stories of Piasa do tell of sickness that can spread. 'The cleanse of the evil—"

"Will you shut up, already?" said Chickory. A shrill buzzing filled her head.

"True moon, there's something terribly wrong in the people lands. I don't know about no 'cleanse' but they're roaming the streets. Half-crazed, confused, maybe. By my snout, if you see them, you run. Run fast as your wings, as fast as your *Piasa*, can take you. You'll be lucky if they kill you first. They might tear you apart, wing from wing."

Woodfawn flapped her wings and waggled her head. "Don't be disgusting."

Dolly and Daisy buried their heads in the coarse fluff of Tucker's haunches.

"B-b-but not all of them are gone. There are people still alive?" Fayne stood straighter and gazed at Latrans with her unnerving yellow stare.

Chickory admired her courage, her bravery, her absolute lunacy. To stand before a killer, to speak to him as an equal, was madness. Yet, there she stood, bold as a rat's tail.

"Well, the people, they're gone like the season of the mad deer. Running around, killing each other, and everything else in their way. Won't be long until they burn the whole earth down. No, you stick close to your cur, stay off the people roads. Mm. Maybe."

"How close are they? The humans you saw?" Fayne said.

"Howling mercy, right next door, saw one tearing through the back. Was just planning on running you down and taking off. Probably be here soon. Speaking of, I think I'd best be off. Good luck to you, your Piasa be good to you now." And with that, Latrans slipped out through the barn door.

"We've got to get out of here!" cried Dolly.

"But what about the others? Robert, Rosie, Georgia?" Woodfawn looked from Fayne to Chickory.

"It is t-t-too late; all our choices have been made. We run." Fayne bolted toward the entrance and the others flew down and followed.

As they burst out into the bright sunny day, Chickory cringed, waiting for the crazed Hums to fall upon them, but the farm still looked calm and empty.

Then they heard a screech. Down the gravelly road. A familiar voice, shrill, panicked, and full of pain. The sound cut through the day like the call of morning, but was abruptly silenced.

Scalding panic raged through Chickory and courage failed them all.

"Oh Piasa, preserve them!" Woodfawn squealed.

Together they all bolted into the tall grass of the opposite field and did not look back.

7 | Dreamer

"The shadow of the mind is a powerful thing; to soar and think is the gift
of birds. To go too high or dive too deep is to enter the land of
unknowing. Trust in Piasa, never in the mongering of
your own fearful mind."

- In Dark and In Light, Fourth Year, First Clutch

Chickory dreamed:
Sleeping sky stingers rumbled in the night sky above as she stood
in the middle of a long wide road. The invisible weight of the low clouds
made Chickory's feathers tingle. Houses with dark blank windows rose
on either side. The front doors were marred with red slash marks, like
blood and flesh pulsed beneath the surface of their walls.

The street was littered with the fallen, molested branches of
trees, and Chickory knew, in the way dreams always know, something
terrible stirred nearby.

At the far end of the road glittered bright lights, like the lights
Lady put up every cold season. She would grumble as she strung long
lines of blinking color across the edges of the blue house. These lights,
red and flower orange, winked and dazzled like swooping stars.

A humming buzz reverberated inside her mind. The street
wavered and bowed in the middle, then disappeared, placing Chickory in
front of a strange grouping of Hum-made structures. They groaned like
the thick bodies of roar horses, and they were all dotted with the

46

spinning, flashing lights. A strange sound filled the air, not the song of birds, or of wind through singing grass. It was the music of the fleshy mouths of Hums, smacking and moaning.

"What are t-t-these?" Chickory asked, but she didn't sound like herself and she didn't *feel* like herself either.

The structures roared to life. Their metal arms and legs twisted and whistled as they churned in mindless motion, like giant storks with broken wings. Dim passageways snaked between the (*carnival*) rides, but Chickory didn't know what *carnival* rides were; her mind was thinking someone else's thoughts or maybe it was the whisper of Piasa speaking to her, as told in the old stories.

Amid the shuddering structures, rose a huge red house. The soft billowing walls shivered in the wind like white gowns hung to dry. The mind that was not hers shuffled through images of games and strange dances. Hums dressed as animals and animals dressed as Hums—they hopped and cheered as they wore colorful skins that were not their own.

Fear tingled in her wingtips, and somewhere, deep in the place where Chickory was still herself, instinctual terror screamed at her to run. But the desire to see and to understand, was stronger. It guided her like silent hands and brought her closer to the red house. Unlike the rest of the cheery lights and animated amusement, this place lived in a pit of darkness.

A disjointed voice (*Lady's*) rasped over the moaning music and the strange words inside her mind translated faster than she could understand them. But it couldn't be Lady, she couldn't be inside, because Lady was—

(*IS DEAD*) The words inside her mind bellowed.

A deep groan shuddered beneath the ground and terrible cracks formed in the black road. Swells of imminent rain crept above them.

(*Yes, them*)

She was not alone.

The whispered disjointed voice became a deep growl and shining orbs peered out, like cat eyes in moonlight. Chickory could not fight the tide that pushed her forward like the surge of a flooded river.

(*Them. It.*)

The carnival slowed and stopped. The lights flickered.

Chickory tried to flap her wings but they barely fluttered. "No, no, no. Don't take me, don't take me in—"

The lights flared with heat, brighter than the sun, before they exploded, glass shards glittering in the light of a suddenly present moon.

A singular drop of rain landed on Chickory's head. Cold.

The red house yawned open like the fanged mouth of a death worm and a crowd of little Hums (*children*) stared back. Blood stained their clothes and the putrid smell of sickness (*of Lady, the boy, the sickness*) choked the air.

There, in front of the horrible things (*for they were not children at all*) stood Fayne.

"Fayne, get away from them! Run! Get away from them!"

But she did not respond or turn.

The children jerked at the sound of Chickory and they raised their arms, palms up toward the sky. The unseen force shoved her forward again. She dug her claws into the gritty gravel but they cut through the surface like soft sand. The sky shimmered, faint beetle green, and spinner-web cracks flashed across the dark bed of clouds.

A child with bright white hair opened its mouth and the others followed. A terrible unified scream slit the air, a deafening yowl of rage.

In the distance, came a bellow, not of beast or Hum or creation. The horrible sound drowned out the children's screams and beyond the rise of the red house, the clouds shifted, swirled, and formed their ether into a tentative wisp. The wisp grew, pulsed, and the braided force unhinged itself from the black field of the sky, stretching down and connecting to the earth.

Everything moved. The dead children slid backwards, back toward the seething vortex that howled and pulsed with a force only of Piasa. The living storm (*a twister*) towered above them and cast all in its shadow. The fabric house billowed like frantic flapping wings, then ripped away from its posts, a writhing fish in the force of the wind. The sick and terrible creature-children followed, their feet lifted from the earth by the greedy mouth of the wind tunnel. The punishing force ripped at their flesh, tearing them apart, before sucking them deep into its hungry belly.

Chickory flattened herself against the ground, to become small and heavy like a river stone. Stories of the oldest birds told of this.

Duck, hide, become the earth, become the soil.

She forced her own thought: *I am a stone.*

(*Birds of a feather, flock together*)

Feathers ripped from the blanket of Chickory's breast.

(*Some are born to endless night*)

I am a stone.

Chickory squinted up at the oncoming monster of thick blackened rage, watched helplessly as Fayne tilted her beak toward the sky, about to be swallowed up.

"Fayne, no, run! Please, just run!" Chickory squawked.

(*YOU CANNOT RUN*)

Chickory awoke and her body convulsed with terror, a squawk lodged in her throat. For a moment, she had felt her claws lift from the earth… but no, it was just the dream.

Crickets trilled in the tall grass, accompanied by the chirping whispers of the sleeping flock gathered around her. There was no storm and no wind at all.

Tucker grunted sleepily. "All right, bird?"

"Yes, yes. Go to sleep," Chickory croaked. Her whole body shivered as though submerged in a deep icy pond.

Tucker's groaning snores filled the air once again. Above, the sky was clear, illuminated in the light of a swollen moon, but no longer a full egg. A full egg moon could sometimes bring dreams and whisper the words of Piasa, but never, in all Chickory's seasons, had there ever been such a dream as this. The humming buzz of the dream still tingled in her feathertips.

Fayne twitched beside her. Chickory stared but she showed no sign of terror or horror. No sign that she too cowered in the path of the roaring funnel of wind. *A twister.*

Beyond the safe circle of their gathered flock, somewhere far away in the world, a soft moan floated on the warm night air.

8 | Natural Enemies

"Chickens, and all birds of the wing, can expect to find
that Piasa's world harbors far more enemies than friends."

- Practical Wisdom, First Clutch, First Year

Are you well?"

Chickory opened her eyes. Fayne stood above her, head cocked in a curious way.

"What? Yes. Why?" The sky was bright. She must have slept through all the others waking.

"Bad d-d-dreams?"

A chill snaked down Chickory's spine, though the air was quite warm.

The dream. A funnel cloud and unseen force sucking her toward all those dead—and towards Fayne. She shook herself and allowed the fresh air to ruffle in among her feathers. She breathed deep the smell of the damp earth. "Egg moon is all. I must have been tired. Where is everyone?"

"They found a colony of large *camponotus*. They are eating."

Irritation prickled through Chickory's body. "You know I can't understand you when you do that. They're eating *what*?"

"Ants. Those big ones, like the ones under Lady's house shingles."

Even as they stood there, beneath their claws, hummed the

vibration of life. Decayed leaves and browning ferns mingled with the rustle of bugs and stirring seedlings, all thriving on and below a light layer of pine needles. The tall trees cast them in deep shadow, and from where they had slept beneath the overhang of a linden bush, the forest felt almost safe.

"Oh. I could have a beakful myself. I'm famished."

"Come on, I will show you where they have congregated."

Fayne led the way out from under the snug concealment of the bush. Just outside the branches, a smooth brown egg sat on the dry ground.

"We'll have more left behind before we dry up," Chickory said, gazing down at it. The sight inspired sadness in any bird, a sign of life that would never be.

"Indeed. Our bodies will adapt and cease production as we go. Most of us have not been laying regularly for some time. Stress and malnutrition." Fayne said this as though she laid eggs too, but she had only laid a few after reaching full henhood. Soon her place on the bottom of the roost was guaranteed.

Eggs were meant for Lady, a gift of life for the caretaker, as Piasa had created them to provide. Any bird who could not follow the words of Piasa was not worthy of the care given. Pride swelled through Chickory whenever Lady slid her warm knobby hands beneath her to collect a warm egg. That Fayne could not experience this, made Chickory ache with sorrow for her friend. Though some of the hens would rather hatch fine feathered chicks, Chickory didn't mind so much. Usually Lady allowed Georgia or Rosie to raise a few broods and all was well, but here, this egg would be left to the killers of the world. No caretaker would receive this gift.

"Never mind. Return to the soil, little egg." Chickory turned her back on it.

"Indeed." Fayne led the way through the thick trees. Beyond the farmland, in these woods, furry sharp teeth thrived, only approaching the farmland in the dark for a quick meal. This was their sanctuary, their home, and it was clear why.

"It's like being in our coop almost. Though the sky is much taller here." Chickory gazed up at the blanket of green overhead. "Feels like being inside." There were no planks of wood or dry straw, but it felt like a home all the same. The continuous thicket provided endless places to hide, to nest, to den. Familiar somehow, and it tingled inside

Chickory's mind like a long-ago memory. Piasa's stories told of the wild birds they once were, journeying from the jungles of Origin. Maybe they could be wild birds once more, though they'd have to figure out nests and how to settle in.

Though, with no Robert, no male to help bring forth new life, theirs would be a solitary existence. Not the way Piasa had designed all things. Though if what Latrans had said was true, Piasa's way might be forever gone anyway.

Fayne peered up at the trees too. "Like being inside a hungry belly. Watch for sky birds. It is much harder to see clearly in the thick foliage."

Chickory followed her to the top of a gentle hillside, though the ground was so choked with ferns it was hard to see the land itself.

Been awake long?" Woodfawn cackled from the bottom of the slope.

The flock had gathered around a decayed log. Tucker stood alongside and his wet black nose twitched as he smelled the air. The faint *shisha shisha* of the ant's jaws cutting through wood and leaves could be heard even from their distance atop the slope. It was indeed a large colony of, well, whatever Fayne had called them.

Chickory weaved and ducked through the low brush until she reached the bottom and Dolly playfully nipped at her comb, though it was difficult with a beakful of crunchy ant. "We've all molted waiting for you."

"I slept like a stone," Chickory said and the words felt familiar somehow. She ruffled her feathers and fell upon a neat marching line of ants, snapping them up as they came. They tingled on her tongue as she crushed them with the sharp edges of her beak.

"I can barely stand myself. We'd better be eating all day and resting," Woodfawn said. "Piasa knows when we'll have another chance."

"Piasa has nothing to do with it." Fayne ruffled her feathers. "We must press on."

Woodfawn growled. "We should have our time, the time of the Mourning Call. For, well, for Robert and them."

Unbidden and unwanted, the memory of the terrible cry surfaced. The anguished squawk that had cut through the air. Latrans' tales of killer Hums. Images of flying feathers and pools of blood flooded Chickory's mind and her hunger vanished. She dropped a squirming ant before it could sting her. "I don't think I can eat any more."

"What? Ridiculous! Eat! Feast! Got to keep our strength up," Woodfawn said.

"Woodfawn is right. You must eat," Fayne said quietly.

Chickory looked at her, expecting her to say more, but Fayne was examining the trail of the ants. "The average *camponotus* can carry great weight and is one of the—" Her voice faded as she trailed away from them, speaking only to herself.

Woodfawn bristled. "What a bother. Always a strange one. Even how she first came to the farm with us. It's hard to remember chickhood, of course, but I thought I remembered something odd. Not hatched from any of *our* eggs, certainly." She wrestled with an ant who had gotten away and was crawling down her neck. "Well, she was right about this. I can at least be grateful Piasa whispers some useful truths into that twittering sparrow. Tuh, though talking to that *Latrans*? I doubt that mother-breeder knows ear from tail and I hardly believe any of those awful tales he told. Exaggerate, indeed!"

Chickory ate another ant, though the pleasure was gone. "It does worry me though. Back at the farm, with the dogs… what would have happened if we had lost Fayne? We'd have lost our way for sure or had to go back. How would we continue? We don't even know where we're going or whatever it is we're fleeing from. Everything's a jumble."

The others stared at her with wide yellow eyes and she regretted speaking these questions aloud.

Woodfawn grunted. "Tuh, none of this is as Piasa intended. Not the way she set forth for us all. What kind of birds go roaming about? Well, except for featherheads like sparrows and those fancy birds following the sun season. But what's happened to the order? Wandering Hums killing? Chickens fleeing their homes? Tuh, I don't believe half of it. The other half is Piasa's bidding, which we're not meant to know anyhow. As is said, 'strange ways lead to strange days, but all days lead back to Piasa.' So, we go on as best we can, I suppose."

"She knows though," Dolly chirped. Most of the ants were gone now. "What it all really means. Though I wish she'd tell us. Just so we know, you know?"

Chickory's innards turned to stone. "I'm not sure I want to know."

"Hmm? What's that?" Woodfawn glanced up from her foraging. A fat spinner wriggled in her beak.

"Never mind. Just eat. It'll all pass like falling feathers and rain."
Then Chickory left the others, who did not seem to notice her departure.

"Ugly bird! Ugly bird!" taunted a squirrel from overhead. It
threw twigs down at her and she hurried past its nest.

As the screech of the squirrel faded, she heard a tinkling sound,
like rushing—

"There's water," she said.

Tucker licked the back of her head, startling her. He sniffed the
air. "Yes, fresh and fast. A big river, I think. I came out here once, I was
just a pup, following my nose anywhere. Lady called and called though I
couldn't find her in all the trees. The sun was coming up before she
found me." He whined and his brown eyes glistened with the memory.

There, that loving bond between dog and Hum—A flush of
warmth crept through Chickory's feathers at the thought of Tucker as a
young pup. Long before they'd been chicks on the farm.

Fayne, having abandoned the ants at last, stood beside Chickory
and for a moment they silently listened to the distant sound.

"It's ahead somewhere, I think. We should keep moving,"
Chickory said.

"You are very right, my friend. We will cross the water. We are
headed the right way," Fayne said.

"I hadn't noticed the river until now. None of us did."

Daisy sprinted past them. "A stream? There will be water and
plenty to eat!"

"Wait, oh, wait for me!" called Dolly, running to catch up.

Tucker wagged his tail and followed as they all moved toward
the rush of the water. As they went however, Fayne stopped a few times
and tilted her head, then stared out into the heavy undergrowth. The
sound of the river steadily grew louder, becoming a roar that told of its
size. A sudden strange prickling sensation wrapped around Chickory's
throat, as though Tucker was breathing on her. But Tucker was ahead of
them now.

A killer watched. Unmistakable and the same, whether moon
bird or fox or other sharp teeth.

"Um, Fayne?"

Fayne did not seem to hear her, continuing to push her way
through the dense brush. The tall trees pressed in around them and large
ferns crowded them closer and closer together as they walked.

Daisy bumped into Dolly, who had come to a standstill. "Ack!

Watch where you're going."

"Well, if you hadn't stopped like a blooming fiddlehead…"

"Now you take that back!"

"Quiet. B-b-both of you." Fayne stared past them into the dense trees. "Our nerves are on edge enough without us fighting."

"We're being followed, aren't we? I can feel their eyes on us." Woodfawn scanned the overgrown brush surrounding them.

Tucker lifted his muzzle skyward. "We are. Though I don't know what it is. Too many trees and bugs. Not enough wind."

Dolly and Daisy cackled in alarm: "Oh my, oh my, oh no!"

"They'll have our throats, foxes, wolves, and—"

"HUMS!" They squawked in unison.

"Stop it! You will have us all falling to egg shell with your twittering," hissed Fayne.

Tucker growled, deep and loud. "Whiskered weasels."

A panicky tremor seized Chickory and she almost fell over. Clever and cunning, they had the speed and ability to rip a bird's head off and swallow it whole, without pausing for breath. "What do we do?"

Fayne bristled. "We run toward the river. There is a bridge. Once we cross it, they will not follow us there."

Woodfawn panted, her eyes wide with fear. "You're sure?"

"Fairly."

They broke into a run and Tucker crashed through the thick brush, trying to stay close, though the crowded ferns and thorn bushes made it difficult to stay together.

They had begun to spread out, trying to pick their way through the thicket, when Chickory understood. "Oh, rotten yolk! They're coming!"

Two large brown weasels burst out of the bushes.

One landed directly on top of Daisy and twisted around her like a furry death worm. The other hopped into Tucker's path and lunged, sinking small needle teeth into the wet flesh of his nose.

Tan feathers exploded around them as Daisy wrenched free. The weasel dropped a mouthful of feathers and snapped again, catching her by the wing this time.

"Get off, get off!" Tucker howled in pain and tried to shake loose the weasel hanging from the tip of his nose. He smacked the flexing attacker against a tree and it let go. Tucker threw himself upon the weasel, teeth flashing, but the weasel fled. Tucker bounded after it into the thick bushes.

"Get OFF her!" Dolly launched herself at the weasel and they disappeared in a flurry of feathers.

Chickory spun on her clawed feet, frantically searching for a way toward the river, a way to escape. Fayne pecked at Chickory's head. "Just move!"

There was a pained squeal, and Dolly and Daisy appeared from behind a cluster of thick horsetail. Blood stained their breasts but they still ran.

Chickory struggled to go. Sundown turned the world into new season mud, but to stop and be overtaken by panic was to die. Fayne shoved against her and pushed her forward through the brambles and tangling vines of forest ivy.

Woodfawn and the others disappeared from sight, swallowed up by the thick forest as they scattered. Tucker was nowhere to be seen at all.

Chickory and Fayne staggered through thick whipping branches. Brambles ripped at their feathers and snagged at their scaly legs. Then the brush finally thinned and they spilled out onto the sandy bank of the rushing water.

An aged bridge, constructed by Hums, crossed the rapid flow. Moss grew between every stone, like it had sprouted from the very soil becoming an especially sturdy tree.

Panic ticked in Chickory's throat. "Where are they? Where?"

"Just go, keep running," Fayne gasped. They staggered toward the bridge, winded with panic and running.

Dolly and Daisy burst out of the brush behind them. They stumbled and almost made it onto the bridge, before Dolly collapsed. She kicked her legs feebly.

Daisy strutted around Dolly in frantic circles. One of her wings sagged uselessly. "Oh no, oh no, oh, no. What to do, what to do, where is everyone? Where are they, Chickory? What do we DO?"

"Um, I don't—we'll wait a moment here, let Dolly catch her breath."

"It's not safe, it's not safe. Oh myyyyy, what if they're gone? What if they were eaten?" Daisy stared wide-eyed at the treacherous forest.

"I'm coming!" bellowed Tucker and he burst through a tangle of bramble upstream. His muzzle was drenched in bright red blood, a small chunk missing from the tip of his nose.

"Tucker!" Daisy ran to him. "Have you seen the others? Oh my, oh my, you're hurt. Dolly's hurt. What do we DO now? We should run, we should go, they'll be here, oh myyyyyy," her squawks became strangled screams.

Tucker hurried over to Dolly's limp body and snuffled her twitching body. "She'll be all right. If birds get spooked too much they have fits," he said.

Chickory found her voice. "Tucker, where's Woodfawn?"

"Oh here, I'm here!" cried Woodfawn. She appeared through the brush far downstream and ran toward them. "I had to run around the long way to dodge that horror scrapping with Tucker." She gasped and her feathery bulk shuddered with the effort.

"It is harder to take us in the open," Fayne said.

"Let's cross the bridge now," said Chickory. "Before they've a chance to decide the risk."

"Might not be as simple as you think," came a voice from behind them.

The creature looked like a badger. It was large and black, but there the similarities ended. The long nose and bristling whiskers betrayed its true nature: a weasel, but larger than seemed possible. His white face twisted with a grinning snarl. Perhaps a badger born into the wrong body.

"You would have quite the fight," Tucker stepped toward the badger-weasel and his body quivered with rage.

"Oh, you're the worse off already, you fine cur," barked the badger-weasel in the common sound. "You'll be missing more than pieces of your nose when Regulus is done with you. Admit it, you've never seen such a stunning creature."

Fayne stepped forward and stood between Tucker's front legs. "What is it you want?"

"To eat us, surely!" squealed Daisy.

"B-b-but you could have had any one of us. You had the surprise. None of us knew you were there, and we have an injured. You could have whipped through us and d-d-done quick work. There is something else you want, in addition to our necks." Fayne trembled as she spoke.

"Fayne, stay back," Chickory whispered, but Fayne ignored her.

The badger-weasel, or Regulus as he had said, barked a laugh.

"Well, I had thought there must be something quite strange about this traveling flock of birds, and you brought a dog even! You hide in the farmlands and never dare to enter the sanctity of our forest realm. But you now, *you* speak and behave as no mere bird. It is only good manners to explain what it is you are doing On Regulus' bridge and give Regulus good cause not to eat you… and maim your cur." He tapped his long claws against his furry chin.

Why the creature spoke of himself by name wasn't clear but Chickory shuddered.

Fayne narrowed her eyes. "And what b-b-benefit is there, spilling ourselves to a mangy weasel who will likely eat us either way."

"You don't think Regulus got this big, this fierce, and this cunning by just mindlessly chomping through every creature that passes by? A fellow has got to have more smarts than that. Got to stay on top of current events, local happenings, and such. And as it so happens, in Regulus' long life, there has never been such a group as this. So it intrigues him, tells him there's a story here. One he has yet to hear. And how he loves stories." Regulus bared his fanged teeth, and slid forward on his belly. He propped his slim triangular head on one paw and waited. He gave no sign of concern as Tucker snarled at him.

Dizziness Chickory could only attribute to prolonged periods of stress upon the bird mind, engulfed her. He wanted a story? A *story*? The ground tilted beneath her claws and she wobbled a little.

Fayne looked unimpressed. "And I'm to tell you this story with the hopes you won't kill us?"

"Well, suppose your story is compelling enough. Regulus might find it a shame to bring such a story to an end." He picked at his teeth. "But then again…"

"Right. Fine," Fayne said. "Our story is a p-p-plain one, for what is fantastic about the life of a chicken? Only when Piasa channels power through a vessel can a life become unordinary. And Piasa has—she sent me a vision, a vision of a world changed. The world of the humans is ended, death is everywhere." Fayne glanced at Chickory. "Um, and life can never be the same. But lo' she also showed me the vision of what we are now. Dog and flock traveling far away. She sent it to me that I should lead them to a far valley, where we can find a life far away from the humans destroying all creatures. Perhaps even weasels."

"The world of the humans? Piasa?" Regulus yawned. "Well, it is a story I—humph, Regulus has never heard before but you tell it with such brevity. Really no flair at all. Though you are just a bird, so what can he expect after all."

"We were also almost eaten by two very small, very unattractive weasels in these woods," Fayne added. "Almost succeeded in ripping out Dolly's throat. Fortunately, our brave canine was with us. He is sworn to protect us, an oath to the Mistress of the House and of his Heart."

Regulus snorted. "Mistress of the… dogs are strange awful creatures, aren't they?" He grinned at Tucker. "Humph. But two weasels in the woods, eh? Right, he knows them. Small, scrappy, hideous they are—"

"We'll take offense to that if you please," a squeaky voice said.

Creeping up the bridge were the two brown weasels from the forest. Blood stained their mouths and whatever they lacked in size, they had in bristling fur and bared teeth.

"Oy! What did I tell you lot about this bridge? This is my bridge, so shove off!" Regulus, abandoned all majesty and hopped upright, huffing with fury.

"Shame our feast felt this was an appropriate place to pause. But no matter, you can have what you kill, should be quick work between the three of us," squeaked the smaller of the two.

"I was listening to a story, you piss and sore inbreeds! Again, I say, feck off before you find my size has more uses than drawing females," he bellowed, abandoning all pomp.

Tucker snarled and ran from one side to the other, but how could he defend both from the encroaching killers? Chickory shuffled toward Regulus and the others followed her example. He was at least, somewhat, interested in something other than eating them. The better of two non-choices. But the other weasels saw their movements and advanced onto the bridge.

"No, no, no! This is my bridge!" Regulus howled. He charged past the flock and past Tucker's confused fury. His eyes blazed with murderous rage and his bristling fur made him look as large as a dog. The other two must surely flee, so terrifying he looked, but they didn't.

"Take him," snarled the larger one and they divided like a two-headed death worm. Their sinuous bodies rose to meet his charge.

Chickory did not watch. "Run! Run across the bridge! Run!"

Behind them, an explosion of screeches and anguished screams wrenched open the air. Regulus bellowed and one gave a terrible scream.

The flock fled, Tucker at the front now, his ears back and tail tucked between his haunches.

They reached the other side and Chickory dared one backward glance. Regulus gnawed the throat of the larger one, while the small one slashed at Regulus' back, slicing open his flesh with needling teeth and flexing claws. A black pool of blood spread beneath them.

"Don't look now, just run," Fayne hissed and Chickory obeyed.

9 | What's Lost is Found

"With Piasa, a bird is never lost; misplaced perhaps.
But Piasa will always place you exactly where
you are meant to be misplaced."

- *Words of Piasa*, Wings of Just, First Feathers

Robert, wait! Oh, oh, oh." Georgia hurried after him as he surged forward through the tall field grass. "How are we to find them? Mercy, oh, mercy on us poor birds. Poor poor birds."

Robert's mind surged with panic. He ducked under the low fence that encircled the neighbor's back pasture. They could get to the barn. If he could get them there, they could hide. Then find Fayne. Hide. Then Fayne. Hide.

Georgia rustled behind him in the grass, squawking with terror. Killers could be anywhere.

"Quiet now, just be silent," Robert whispered.

"Oh, oh, ohhhhh," she squealed.

"They went toward the barn. That much I could see from the perch. We must hurry, before they leave. Hurry, Georgia." He hated the impatience in his voice, how frightened he sounded. He should be brave and strong; he should have protected them.

And he should have listened to Fayne.

"Oh, poor, poor Rosie. Poor Lacey. Dear things, poor, poor eggs. Oh the *eggs*," Georgia continued, her cries a shrill signal to any killers who might be in the grass.

Rosie. His whole body trembled. He should stop, give it all up. Collapse, right here in this field. Let them come, let them free him of this impossible pain. The agony of being so horribly wrong about everything. But he couldn't do that, not now. First, he would—no, he *must* get Georgia to safety, reunite her with the others. She must not pay for his failure. Maybe he could give up and die then, but not yet.

"Wretched birds are we, Piasa loathes our horrible notions, that Fayne has brought the wing down upon us—"

"Georgia, enough! Please. I can't... I can't think if you carry on." His thoughts tangled and throbbed with alternating visions of the Hums who had burst into their yard. They had cornered Rosie in the coop, and their hands, dear Piasa, with their *hands*, they ripped—

But no. Robert forced the images away. There would be time later. Time for the Mourning Call. He had to focus. He would find Fayne, who had known all along of the danger that had found Rosie and Lacey.

The field was silent except for Georgia's moans and the buzz of insects, lazy in the heat. Robert ignored a colony of swollen ants crawling through the grass and made a straight run towards the barn. The others were there, they must be there. They *must.*

Georgia flapped and loose feathers blustered around them. "Oh, preserve us, preeeserve us!"

Nothing glinted through the veil of tall grass, no sign of a killer's approach. Except for… yes, just there.

Something moved through the tall strands. A moaning growling thing—the sound had hidden beneath Georgia's wailing but now it was loud and close. Fear spread through him and it felt suddenly impossible to move. *Not now, it couldn't happen now, Georgia needed him. No, no, no.*

"We need to run. Run, oh, run away." Georgia's clucks grew shriller again as she heard it too.

"Be quiet, quiet, *shut up,* Georgia." Because deep in his stomach, squirming like a drowning worm, he knew. The field was full of killers.

Georgia stepped back and he turned to push her along.

Something lunged through the grass and swiped at Georgia with clawed fingers.

"Oh oh oh oh!" Georgia cackled.

Robert shot into the air and flicked feathers in the attacker's face.

He squawked with fury. He would protect her, he would—

Maybe once it had been a Hum, but the thing staggering toward them was no longer a living breathing creature. Wrinkled loose skin sagged from the familiar angles of a Hum face, the eyes yellow like the guts of beetles. Fluid leaked from the ears. The horrible smell of the creature's *sickness* gnawed the air and choked Robert. He abandoned his charge and flew to the side. The creature jerked at the sudden motion and turned toward him. The thing was not like the other Hums who had come with rage in their eyes. This killer had nothing in its eyes at all. They were empty. Swollen bulging lips cupped around another wet moan and it rattled like the keening cry of a trapped fox. It lunged and slashed at the air with gnarled bloody fingers.

The shock of this walking skin of dead flesh paralyzed him. He couldn't move, couldn't, could never again—

"Piasa! Save us!" Georgia burst out of the grass a few steps ahead, a plume of white feathers scattering behind her.

The stinking creature jerked its head toward her commotion and staggered past Robert's limp body.

His mind reeled. He must move, he must stop the terrible thing from finding Georgia. It was his duty, his duty, his *duty*.

He blinked away a fly and release rushed through his feathers. He lurched forward into the grass, but angled away from the path created by the creature's shuffling feet. The thing moaned from somewhere in the grass, but Robert couldn't see it, could only hear its rapid urgent grunts. He did not have to be a killer to know the sound of hunger.

He scampered toward the barn and tried to shake the exhaustion of his panic. He burst out of the pasture and his claws slid on the pebbled ground. A large roar horse stood silent next to the barn and he dove underneath its gleaming red body, his chest croaking like the smelly frogs in new season rain. He could not see Georgia, but he also did not see the horrible creature. Pain twisted his innards. If the thing had caught her, if it had reached her, he might as well give himself over to the thing as well.

The wall of grass shivered and Georgia burst through. She tried to flap, tried to fly, and instead dropped like a pebble of ice. She lay on the ground and kicked her legs as though she still ran.

Robert scurried to her side. "Oh, here, I'm here now." He squatted beside her, bristling with fear. The groans came closer.

Her eyes rolled, unseeing, in the way twitchy stress always

captured her mind. At every summer storm or howling killer, she could collapse or become frenzied with panic. "It's all right, Georgia. That— that thing is gone. I don't hear it," he lied. "We need to get under cover. Under that roar horse. No one can get us there." He hoped she could not hear through the mist of her bewilderment and he preened her crown feathers, as though they were in the coop and this was the Ninith.

Georgia stopped kicking, but her whole body still shivered. "R— Robert? It almost got me. It touched me. Thought it was going to rip my head off. Like… like Rosie."

"I know, dear one, I know. But you're well, you've still got your wings. Come on now, let's go hide, together."

She struggled upright and staggered as she followed him to the roar horse. She collapsed against one of its round black legs, which used to turn around and around as it carried Hums wherever they wanted it to go. But without Hums, none of the roar horses could move.

Robert preened her askew feathers and carefully laid them back into place. It was all he could do and she calmed. She drooped her head and her breathing slowed. He wished there was a bird to preen him, to calm the pounding knot inside his breast.

The groans from the field faded. Perhaps some other prey had attracted the creature's attention. The quiet of the farm lulled Robert into a half-sleep, though visions whirled inside his mind. It had all started with the dead boy. Or maybe Lady. Nothing fit together and he was adrift, a seed sprout in a howling storm. The smashed nests, the oozing bodies of chicks that would never hatch, the snarling Hums… the spurt of blood as they wrung Rosie's neck until her precious head had snapped off. And for what? They had tossed her limp body aside. The Hums had forgotten their duty, they were killing again, taking all the life, as told in the Ninith stories, and the appearance of the dead thing in the field must be a frightful sign that Piasa had left this world far behind. Maybe it was a punishment set forth by Piasa, but stories told of her mercy and love, not of rage or vengeance.

From somewhere close by, a faint smell of corn and wheat perfumed the air. Robert's fleshy pouch squirmed with hunger and momentarily forgetting its panic and worry. "Can you smell that, Georgia?"

She untucked her head and gazed toward the barn. "In there… maybe."

"Do you feel well enough to go? Food would help us both."

64

She made no sound but rose from their nestled position.

He stepped out from under the roar horse and scanned the sky, pausing to listen for any sign of an approaching killer. "It's all right. Come with me."

She tentatively followed, favoring one of her clawed feet. The middle toe was bent and broken. They approached the barn and paused at the open door. A large overturned bin revealed soft yellow knobs of corn, scattered as though they had been scratched through by other birds. The sight gave him a surge of hope. Hunger clawed inside his stomach like he had swallowed an angry cat.

Georgia scampered inside and bobbed her head as she devoured the dry corn. Robert followed, but as he approached the bin, he smelled—

"Georgia!" He squawked, but too late.

The coyote burst through the open door and charged. Georgia screeched and tried to run, but the coyote pounced and pinned her down with a yip of excitement.

"Ohhhhh—no, no, no! Robert, please!"

"Oh ho! Fine feathered birds all across the land." The coyote grinned and yipped again. Then he jerked nervously and narrowed his eyes at Robert. "You don't have a dog too, do you?"

"Wait, WAIT!" Robert hopped out from behind the bin, shaking with fear. "Did you say dog?" The thought of the others, of Fayne, flushed him with courage. He must try. "Did you see others? A group of birds like us and a large dog?"

The coyote lifted one paw and looked down at Georgia. "Oh bother. You're with them, are you? Silly birds." With a grunt, he released her and watched mournfully as she staggered away. "Yes, they were here. Narrow miss it was. Should have seen it. Heard the screams from across the way and they took off toward the trees. Hums showed up here right after, looking for more of us. Well, more of *you*, I think. Not me though. They just kind of let me slip by. You birds are lucky, with quick feathers."

"Then Fayne has already taken them farther than I thought possible." Robert felt like singing, but remembered the coyote was a killer, and not to be trusted. "Um, yes, Brother Coyote, where did they go? Which way do you think? Do you know their destination?"

The coyote gave an amused yip. Perhaps "brother" had gone too far. But then he said, "Good grief, you are a feather head, aren't you?

I've got better things to do than track the flutterings of *birds*. They went toward the river, I think, turned hard into the trees out there, see the Wise Tree? Just past there. Yes, I've got better things to do than squat around and watch. Now I'll give you a running start, but then it's got to be fair game. Latrans has got to eat too." He looked stern and rather cross now.

Robert did not need a second warning. He turned and aimed for the distant trees littering the horizon. "Georgia, hurry, come on!"

Georgia gave one last terrified look at the coyote and staggered after Robert.

Latrans watched them disappear into the long grass and snorted. He rolled over and grinned a mouth full of sharp white teeth. "Head full of feathers, they are." The day had been a very interesting one indeed. All sorts of happenings, all sorts of people, creatures, fighting, and fleeing. He sprawled out on the warm floor of the barn, twisting his lanky body in the loose dust. Yes, it had been an interesting day and Latrans liked interesting days. His belly was full of fat mice and everything was all right. The dogs were gone and the people had moved on, so the land was his for now.

Of course, there was still that thing in the field… but it wasn't very smart or very fast really. As long as he stayed well away from it, all would be well. Hmpf. He hadn't seen one for a while, not since the people in town had slaughtered all those birds, heaping them into huge piles and setting them on fire.

Ah well. The earth kept turning and Yawyaw, the great wolf in the sky, would howl again with each new night. Local sparrows would do fine for his next meal and then maybe he'd go on, cut across the farmland and explore the city beyond.

He yawned. But all that could wait until tomorrow.

10 | Teeth

Tucker led the way into the overgrown field, creating a path through the thick grass. The bridge was behind them and they could no longer hear the hisses and yowls of the murderous weasels.

"They will not follow," Fayne said.

Chickory wanted to ask but she gulped air instead. Panic made it hard to breathe. The height and density of the field grass hid all from view.

"Can't we stop, for a bit, please." Dolly collapsed.

They halted their frantic run.

For a moment, there was no sound but Tucker's deep whooshing huffs and the hiss of panting anxious beaks.

Then a cricket chirped and the field slowly returned to life with the sounds of insects who had stopped moving with the crashing arrival of the flock.

Tucker sniffed Daisy and whined anxiously. "She's got to rest. We've all got to."

Fayne stopped several paces ahead and glared back at them. Chickory shuddered.

"This is a dangerous place to stop," Fayne said.

Chickory did not look directly at her but her glare still pinched. "We've no choice, Fayne, Dolly can't go any further."

"Very well, but keep close. No wandering. We must all keep close together in these grasses." Fayne bobbed her head and inspected the sky. Not a single cloud floated in the loft of blue.

The others clustered on either side of Tucker, and he slumped down with a snort. His pink tongue curled out between his white teeth and he licked Dolly's head. Daisy snuggled in beside them and preened her sister, her double yolk, her exact match in every way. Except Dolly's feathers were now matted with sticky dark blood.

Fayne stared up at the undulating tips of grass and cocked her head as though she listened to the whispering wind.

Woodfawn grumbled as she settled herself at the edge of their group. She moved with deliberate slowness and waggled her head in displeasure. She glared at Fayne for a few moments and then looked away.

The prickle of the flock's unhappiness spread through Chickory. She tried to still her mind, to close her eyes and sleep, but her mind refused.

The roosting order so carefully kept on the farm was not possible here. Fayne, the funny, racoon-marked outsider, was their leader, but even as they all depended on her strange knowledge of the faraway valley and what was happening in the world, this could only quiet feathered rage for so long. Stories told of the hatred nested in the hearts of birds; it could turn their feathers to sharp quills and turn them into killers too. She had seen it happen once, as a hatchling. A bleeding wound that would not heal and a stolen clutch of eggs. Such rage was like a dust fever, it would spread and everyone would be sick. Then one of them would be killed.

They did not even have a rooster to help temper this rage, to distract the others from their worries and fears. Robert could soothe any ripple in the flock's pond. It was his special way and they loved him for it.

It hurt to think of Robert. Of Lacey, Georgia, and Rosie. Left behind, dead surely. That horrible squawk and Latrans' warning. They had not had the Mourning Call and maybe now they never would. Not out here. The prickly unease and familiar fright needled at the knot inside her breast. She longed for the quiet of the coop, the warmth of the dry straw, the familiar chattering greeting of Lady each sunrise.

But Lady was gone. Robert, Georgia, Lacey, and Rosie—well,
they were gone too. They would all be gone, if not for Fayne. But
instead they were alive, afraid, and far away from home.

She longed for the simplicity of death.

The wind rustled its distant wings, and the breeze hummed and
whistled through the grass. The stalks rippled in the current. A voice?
No, it was the wind again, maybe the tall blades playing tricks, or what
Fayne had once explained to her was *barro-pressure*. Whatever that
was.

But it came again, faint and whispery, a low moan filtering
through the swish of singing grass.

She rose from her nestled spot against Tucker's flank. He slept,
curled around Dolly and Daisy, who had also lapsed into exhausted
sleep. Chickory shuffled past them and stood beside Fayne. "Do you
hear that?"

"Yes, he has b-b-been carrying on for a while now."

"He? Well, who's calling? You've been listening to it all this
time?"

"There is nothing to do, we cannot go off through the grass
running after every poor soul we come across," Fayne said.

"Well, good green! I think we should investigate," Woodfawn
announced. She came up behind them, her head also tilted toward the
sound.

"To what end? He will be dead soon, anyhow," Fayne said.

Chickory bristled and ran toward the sound of the voice.

She heard Fayne squawk at her but ignored it. She had to do
something, do anything but squat in the grass and wait for a miserable
end. Everyone couldn't be dead, surely there were still creatures, other
than killers, who still lived in these lands.

The cry sounded both near and far, the wind distorting the
distance and direction of the sound. Behind her, the grass rustled, but
whether it was Woodfawn, Fayne, or creeping sharp teeth, she did not
care.

"Oh mercy, white eye of the sky, lift me up." The voice
whispered, just beyond a triumphant spire of thistle.

She stepped around the prickly monstrous plant and wished she
had listened, had stayed away, had done anything but come here.

A young porcupine sprawled in a small depression of the grass,
crushed between the jaws of a crude Hum creation. It was a trap, used by

Hums who couldn't hunt as Piasa instructed, or too lazy or unwilling to care for creatures as Lady did. The old stories told of these things, but it was Fayne who had explained about the terrible thing called *metal*; the same stuff the roar horses were made of and stronger than any bone.

The fanged jaws crossed at the porcupine's middle, above its hind legs, which stuck out at odd angles. A large pool of blood dried beneath him. She shuddered as she approached. His mouth sagged open, his dark beady eyes glazed with shiny mucous. Death closed in around them, a feeling like suffocation in deep water.

He whimpered and flexed one paw, though he did not seem to know it. "Deliver me now."

Her legs shook. More blood, more death. The world was an endlessly hungry mouth. Maybe even Piasa was a killer. She who created all with her divine wings, she who hatched every creature, one by one. Chickory's body swelled with the stinging pain of her sorrow. There was nothing in their realm that could bring the porcupine peace. It was Piasa's time now.

Behind her, Woodfawn and Fayne entered the small clearing. Woodfawn hissed at the grisly sight but Fayne said nothing.

Chickory squatted down beside the porcupine, the prickle of his beautiful quills brushing gently against her feathers. They did not stiffen or threaten. His body had moved beyond all defense. She cooed softly, as she had done so many times for Fayne, preening her feathers and soothing her anguished cries. She knew of nothing else she could do, though this creature was not a bird and had no feathers to preen.

The porcupine turned his squinted face towards her, but he stared into the beyond. "The field, the world…so full of teeth."

Chickory stayed for a long time. Then she was aware of his passing and the stifling heat of death lifted, leaving only his limp body behind.

Woodfawn let out a low warble and left them without speaking.

Fayne shifted from claw to claw. "We should really go back to the others."

"Just go." It hurt to swallow. To breathe. To live. "Leave us alone."

And Fayne did.

The day darkened as the distant yolk of the sky disappeared beneath the height of the field grass. The blue above shimmered with all the colors of spring boomflowers.

"Piasa preserve you, Brother." She rose from her place beside him and stopped. Another sound filtered through the shush of wind. A moan, like the porcupine's thin cry of pain, but deeper, louder.

Maybe another hurt creature lay somewhere in this field. Sometimes they gnawed their way free and dragged their broken bodies into the woods to die in peace. She left the porcupine behind and stepped into the grass. Fear tingled in her feathertips, a whisper of warning: this was not a trapped rabbit. Not even an unlucky moon bird.

The moans grew louder and the grass parted. The hummingbird red of the sky illuminated the advancing creature.

The Hum, for yes, it must have once been one, shuffled toward her, its extended fingers smeared with dirt. It smelled of rot and death. It smelled like… *Lady's house*. The horrible stench that choked the whole yard, that festered inside where Tucker lay trapped and dying. The dead boy by the fence. But instead of dead, instead of sick and then dead, this Hum moved like a living *and* dead thing. She stepped back into the thick of grass and fought against the Sundown spreading up her legs. If she stopped here, if she could not run…

The thing stopped and turned its sagging face from side to side, like it searched for, well, for something. It moaned again, low and wet, spit dribbling from fleshy mouth parts. Though it lived in the flesh of a Hum, the flesh was mottled, discolored. A large split in the skin of its back oozed thick foam. Nestled in the torn flesh, a web of bone flexed and moved. The smell, the horrible familiar smell, burned her eyes. She stopped breathing. She did not need air. She waited for the very *dead* creature to pass.

A waking moon bird hooted from across the field and the thing moaned and staggered toward the sound. The sky was nearly black but an early moon provided some light and as the light filtered through the rustling grass, something glinted. A trap, like the one that had murdered the porcupine, was clamped around the creature's foot. A tail of metal dragged on the ground behind it. The staggering thing was much bigger than a porcupine and the trap hadn't been enough to stop it.

The creature wandered away from her, away from the flock, toward the distant hooting of moon birds it could never reach. A nest of death worms coiled around the thudding knot in Chickory's breast.

Moans blended again with the wind as it rustled through the field. She must get back to the others. Must warn them. If these things, these dead Hums, roamed the field, but no, surely there couldn't be any others, no more could possibly live. Piasa sometimes made mistakes, creatures not quite right. Even eggs could be born soft and soggy. Nothing was perfect. Like the chick who had hatched with bent legs that did not work. Lady took her away, still fluffy and yellow, and she was just gone. Life happened that way sometimes. This horrible dead thing must soon die from its terrible wounds, surely.

On the other side of the clearing, in the direction the dead thing had come, a rope swayed. It was tied to a worn wooden post and the other end disappeared into the grass. She didn't know what it was for but it was the wrong way. If she turned around and walked straight ahead, she should reach the place where the flock still waited. Her body trembled as she picked her way through the thick grass.

She tried not to think of the jaws clamped around the porcupine, around the leg of the dead thing, the merciless metal that brought life to a terrible end. She wandered, but it was too far, too long. Somehow, she'd gone the wrong way maybe. The field rustled and whispered around her and all the grass looked the same.

She surged forward and eventually the thick grass thinned and gave way to a small hill. No grass grew on the mound; holes and burrows pockmarked the sides of the hill, signs of a rabbit flock, but she saw no sign of any of the fuzzy creatures. She climbed toward the top, relieved to be out of the stealthy grass but terrified by the open space. She heard the moon bird again, but it was still far away. Would the sky birds of the night see her dappled feathers shine in the moonlight? Or would the grunting creature burst out of the grass and stagger up this hill?

She shivered and gazed from her perch atop the hill. The height gave her a wide view of the meadow below, the tips of grass silver in the light breeze. Beyond the field, she could see the bridge they had crossed and on the far horizon ahead, were more trees and the square silhouettes of dark houses. No lights twinkled in the distance. She tried to see where the flock had stopped for the night, but only saw faint glimmers flickering all over the grassy field like lightbugs.

But they weren't—she trembled.

The flickering light was the reflection of the moon on metal, the metal of the traps that filled the field from end to end. There were more of them than kernels in a feed sack. The entire field had been transformed into a waiting death, a death she had somehow avoided even as she surged through the grass. No creature could avoid this danger; certainly no porcupine or staggering creature or wandering bird. Why this field had been filled with such horror, Chickory could not say, but saw the rope was tethered to posts throughout the field and led to the other side.

The cold night air raked through her feathers. "The world is full of teeth," she peeped. But there was no one to hear her except for the stars winking in the sky and the teeth themselves, winking up from the world below.

11 | Leadership

"Be ever alert, danger is always present. Piasa's world is beautiful,
But it conceals treachery beneath every stone and behind every tree."

- Practical Wisdom, Second Clutch, Second Year

C hickory heard them before she could see them:
"For all we know she could be lying out in that field! What if a
moon bird caught—"

"There is no need to get hysterical, Woodfawn," Fayne said.

Tucker snuffled loudly. "It's true, Chickory will be with us
soon," he said.

"She probably could not travel in the night and hid until it got
lighter," Fayne said.

"You'll have us all dead before long," Woodfawn snapped.

"A distinct possibility."

Chickory pushed through the grass and stood before them. Wide
yellow eyes stared back at her.

"Thank Piasa's wings," Woodfawn sighed. "Where have you
been? We've all soiled feathers over you."

Chickory panted, uncertain how to begin. Her feathers were limp
with exhaustion and the continuous fear of the past few sunrises
drenched her conviction like heavy rain.

Dolly staggered upright. The feathers of her breast, though
preened thoroughly by her sister, were still crusty and stained with
blood. "Are you all right? You look absolutely terrified."

Chickory took a deep breath and finally said, "The grass, it's full of them. Those traps, this whole place is filled with traps. They're everywhere."

"Those metal traps? Like the porcupine? Oh no, oh goodness, no, no, no." Dolly swayed.

"You already knew, didn't you, Fayne? Is that why you said the weasels wouldn't follow us here?"

"The territorial preferences of the weasel meant—" Fayne paused as Chickory took a step toward her. "Anyway, yes, I suppose I did know."

"What kind of nightmare has this become? You would lead us into certain death and horrors, you're hardly a bird!" Woodfawn grabbed Fayne's wing with her beak, and Fayne hissed, snapping back. They lunged and slashed at each other with their clawed feet. Their agitated flapping rustled the tall grass around them and they scattered feathers in their scuffle.

"No, birds! No, no!" Tucker whined and plopped down between them.

Woodfawn screeched from her side of the furry divide. "This is absurd, this is *not* what Piasa would want. I'm going back to the farm. Weasels or not!"

"But *Rosie*!" Daisy cried.

They all froze. The screech that had come from the farm, well, it *had* been Rosie. They all knew though none had wanted to speak it aloud.

"There was no sense in worrying everyone about it. We must go t-t-through it. There is no other way around. The river wraps around one side and the other—well, we cannot go that way either." Fayne shook herself and fluffed her feathers.

"Yes, we can get through. But there's something else…" Chickory felt a sudden certainty she should not say it, that whatever she had seen, the dead thing stumbling through the field, well, it would be the end of the journey. No bird could face such horror and walk toward it willingly.

"We must be quiet." Fayne bobbed her head and finished Chickory's words, as though she knew. "There are many enemies and we would draw them to us if we are not silent."

Chickory shuddered.

"Why should we do any such fool bird thing? We could go back, live in the trees if we must!" Woodfawn's voice quivered.

"This field *is* the only way through and if we are careful, we should be quite all right," Fayne insisted, but looked at none of them and turned to step into the tall grass.

"Fayne, wait! There is a way through them. There's some sort of rope leading through the grass and it seems to avoid all the traps. Follow it and it should bring us to the other side."

Fayne cocked her head. "The humans must have strung it up so they could pass through the field safely," she said.

"Well, I came atop a hill where I could see the traps all laid out and the rope too. But couldn't we, why can't we just go around? Follow the fence—"

"No! We cannot. The alternative is far worse than you can imagine." Fayne's eyes widened.

"How do you know? You've never been here. Stop this foolish pretending," Woodfawn said.

"I can see it, sometimes at night. Sometimes when I'm awake. Look, we have come this far. We can get through this place and leave it far behind us." Fayne shifted from claw to claw.

The others cackled and hissed, their pitch bordering on panic.

Chickory flapped her wings, forcing the others into silence. "Stop, no, stop! We can't lose our heads now. I saw a way through, we can walk through the field, follow that rope, but we've got to be very careful and stay together. I remember the way and I will go first." She didn't want to but if the others fought Fayne, then she would lead, just for now. Through the field and on the other side they could regroup. Figure out what they should do. She focused on her memory of the path, the rope she had seen. The porcupine's death would not be in vain, as it marked one small clearing with one less trap ready to snap them up. Everything felt different in the daylight, but maybe, with Fayne's help, they would make it.

Fayne looked relieved. "Exactly as I said yesterday."

"Shut up, will you? I'm following Chickory." Woodfawn turned her back on Fayne.

"Just for now, through the field," Chickory said.

Woodfawn snorted. "No, I'll follow you off a ledge before I trust this horrid monster bird."

Chickory's heart pounded in her ears. "It can't be like that."

"And why not?" said Dolly.

"Certainly Fayne has proven to be—" began Daisy.

"Untrustworthy. How can we follow her?" said Dolly.

"You should—you should lead us," they said in unison.

"Because I don't know where the valley is. And, well, there's a lot of other things I don't know either. We're here because of her. If we hadn't left the farm there would be nothing to fight about, would there? Yes, Rosie and the others are probably—well, they're probably gone. We need her," Chickory said. "And Fayne *will* tell us what she can." She turned to Fayne. "Surely?"

"Yes, I—I can and I will, but let's get out of the grasses, shall we? This is not a safe place to pause and I do not relish telling it all only to have us killed the next moment."

"Right. Okay, stay together. I'll take the lead for now." Chickory stepped into the tall grass and headed back toward the porcupine's body, where she had seen the rope the previous sun.

They all followed and Fayne fell into line behind Woodfawn, followed by Tucker, who whined as the tall grasses swallowed up his stature and obscured the sky above them. The path to the porcupine was still clear from their previous walk and when they emerged upon the still body, Chickory looked away. Flies feasted and Woodfawn snapped up a few that buzzed too close.

"From here we go forward, the rope should be just here." Chickory shivered, because what if it wasn't? What if she had lost the way or the tricky darkness had lied? She took a few steps forward, into the thick blades. There, half embedded in dirt, the thick rope cut through the grass like a death worm, the fearsome killers who sometimes slipped inside coops and swallowed eggs whole. But the rope did not squirm or wriggle; it did not live. Indeed, it was perhaps the only way they would survive.

"Here, we follow this, out of the grass."

"Quietly." But Fayne needed not remind them. Even Tucker suppressed his anxious whimpers.

They walked toward the distant sun and the thick forest of grass whispered and rustled all around them. Chickory strained to hear any sign of the horrible moaning thing she had seen, but there was no sound or sign of it now.

The rope led them past the many lives claimed by the field of hidden teeth. Old decayed remains of birds and small furry creatures littered the flattened depressions where the traps lay in wait. One still imprisoned the remains of a fox, whose flesh had already peeled away from the empty eye sockets of its yellow skull.

Chickory did not know what would come, not the way Fayne did, but that dead thing… the *we must leave.* Was that the danger Fayne had sensed? She couldn't tell the others. The tense shudder of their wings, ready to take flight at any hint of danger—they all teetered on the edge of full panic. Woodfawn seemed determined to find an excuse to turn back. Fayne *would* have to explain some of this, to reassure the others somehow, but maybe she should keep some of the terrible details quiet. Not all knowledge was needed at the same time.

The grass thinned here and as they rustled toward what would hopefully be the edge of this terrible field, a chorus of moans filled the air, as though they had heard their approach.

Chickory froze and blocked the others behind her. "Stop, stop, oh, no, no, no." The memory of the dead thing flushed her feathery body with dread, and this did not sound like one, but many. Directly ahead.

"It is all right." Fayne shouldered past the others in their tight line and stood beside Chickory. "Allow me to lead now?"

Chickory could not protest because she could not move or cluck or breathe. The dead thing. The horrible wet eyes and sloppy wet mouth. She couldn't let Fayne go but she could not stop her either. Fayne, her reckless, fool bird friend, pushed through the grass ahead and disappeared.

12 | Dead Things

"To die is to return to the center of Egg – to the place all are
created and hatched. To die is no great sadness, only
a pause before hatching once more."

- In Dark and In Light, Final Clutch

The thick veil of moans pitched louder as Fayne disappeared into the grass. Her body created a soft rustling swish barely audible in the pulse of hungry sounds.

Chickory knew the thing she had seen, alone in the field, alone in the dark, that *dead* thing, was not alone. Like all creatures they had been drawn to their own kind.

"What is it? What's happening?" Woodfawn shouldered her large bulk alongside Chickory. "What is that horrible sound?"

"It's—I—don't know. They're dead, um… dead things."

"What?" Woodfawn waggled her head and her comb flapped with the jerky motion. "Dead things? What are you talking about? Where did Fayne go? Tuh! Fayne can't go on without us."

And before Chickory could stop her, Woodfawn pushed through the grass toward the groans.

"Watch out!" Fayne called from somewhere ahead. Woodfawn trilled.

Chickory's stomach surged with fear and an unbidden force shoved her forward, her scaly legs propelling her unwilling body to continue. The thick grass rustled around her, she couldn't see, and then she tripped over Woodfawn. A flutter of breath still ruffled the feathers on her chin, but as birds did in the grip of impossible fear, she had collapsed into a weak useless pile of flesh and feathers. Just ahead, the field ended, marked by an old rotted wood fence. Fayne stood facing the fence, her head lowered, as though she examined the ground.

A row of moaning, swaying dead things stood against the far fence. A couple of them jerked as Chickory appeared and extended their bleeding hands towards her, though they did not come any closer. Their feet, mangled oozing stumps, were caught in the teeth of traps, the same ones that filled this entire field. Each had one trap on each foot and the traps held them where they stood. That was why they had not attacked, they couldn't, and the metal kept them from—well, from doing what it was they wanted to do. One was smaller than the others, like a child, but also dead and moving. The round head had been cleaved almost in two and half of its face sagged and puckered like a squashed fruit.

Fayne's murmurs rose and mingled in the surge of lilting slurring voices. They reached for her, as Lady had reached for them, when she scooped them up to feed them oily sunflower seeds or a delicious scrap of dog biscuit. But these were killers, not caretakers. Though Piasa had created sharp teeth and death worms, it was impossible to imagine she would have created these creatures. They looked more like monsters in the stories of Piasa; like the Hums who killed and forgot the way, but corrupted further by a death that would not cease. This ceaseless death had transformed once curious eyes into wet sockets that gleamed with hunger.

"Fayne?" The cluck wedged in her throat like a splinter gobbled up in forage, her body heavy like a fallen wise tree. She wanted to sink down beside Woodfawn and die. To drift into the oblivion beyond, to return to the earth and become soil like in Piasa's stories. But these Hums refused to collapse and become soil as they were supposed to and this alone must signal the end of all being, the end of Piasa's way.

"It will be all right." Fayne's voice rose from a murmur and the pulsing moans quieted. Chickory forced herself to look, to see, and yes, even their movements slowed as their sounds faded into whispers.

Chickory trembled. "What are they, Fayne?"

"Danger! Danger! Killers!" Tucker burst through the grass behind Chickory, teeth flashing. His booming snarls roused the dead things again and they reached towards him, their groans becoming a unified bellow.

"Tucker! No! Stop, down, bad dog! Stay away from the
unliving!" Fayne flapped her wings and pecked at his forelegs.

Chickory blinked. *The unliving.* Fayne spoke the words without
hesitation, as though the words had waited inside her mind all along.

"Oh, no, no, what is this? Oh, Piasa! Save us!" Daisy squawked
as she came through behind Tucker. Dolly said nothing and slumped
down beside Woodfawn.

"Wait! Go back, wait!" Fayne threw herself at Tucker who still
barked and howled, pacing just out of reach of their greedy hands.

"Run birds! Run! Bad killer Masters, bad, bad, bad!" Tucker
frothed at the mouth and saliva spattered from his lolling tongue. His fur
bristled like porcupine quills and he looked larger, more frightening than
he had ever been, even on the farm as he chased away the killers who
roamed the back fields.

Fayne launched herself at his head and pecked him hard on the
nose. Tucker shook her off with a yelp, but took a few steps back. A
deep rage rumbled in his throat.

"Leave it, protect the others, go lie by them, they need you!"
Fayne panted too, feathers fluffed out from her body.

Tucker blinked and looked dazed. The growl still pulsed through
his body but the rage had subsided and he seemed to come back to
himself. He trotted to Dolly and Woodfawn and lay down beside them.
He licked Woodfawn's head, still emitting small growls and whimpers.

The dead things roared and writhed as they struggled against
their confines. Each buckled and moaned and the horrid sound made
Chickory's body ache with fear. *We must go.* Fayne had said once, but it
was true again. They *must* go. Run far away from whatever this was,
whatever these things might be, because simmering underneath her
panic, she knew this had been done on purpose. These things had not
accidentally stumbled into these traps. All of this had been done for
some purpose, a purpose beyond any she could understand, and the
intention burned deep inside her mind, more frightening than any
possible death or pain she could experience in this new way of the
world.

Fayne stepped closer to the seething line.

"Wh—what are you doing? Get away from them, Fayne, get
away."

"No, they will not hurt us. They cannot reach us. They are
trapped. We must get past them. Just wait, wait." Fayne swayed a little

as she spoke.

(*Quiet*)

The word plopped in Chickory's head like a cold fat raindrop, like something from a dream—a whisper of having happened before. But it felt different, it was no dream, and it was as though it spoke from a place somewhere else, somewhere outside herself. She shivered.

(*Quiet*)

The word plopped again, another cold droplet of thought. But the creatures, they *were* quieting. Their arms swayed then lowered to their sides. A few still chomped their mouths, slapping their wet loose lips together, but the rest looked…

"Are they—did they go to sleep?" This wasn't the right word but Chickory knew of no other way to describe it.

"They are. We can g-g-go now, they will not bother us if we hurry. I will stay here until you pass through and follow at the end. Tucker, get the others, take them out of the field."

Tucker whined, his former snarling advance seemingly diminished. "Bad? Those are bad Master killers. We should go, stay away."

"Yes, b-b-but they are sleeping. Be brave. T-t-take them and g-g-go. Wait for me in the field beyond. It is safe. G-g-go." Fayne didn't move but she sounded strained, tired, her stutter worse than it had ever been. (*Quiet*)

They needed to hurry. Why couldn't be answered, not now, but Chickory knew, somehow, they were running out of time. "Tucker, come on, let's, oh, let's get the others." She struggled to move, as though the word (*Quiet*) was a spinner, wrapping a tight funnel web around her feathery body.

Woodfawn twitched and Tucker nosed her firmly. She lifted her head. "Wh-what?" she said blearily.

"Come on, hurry." Chickory smoothed a few of her askew feathers and tried to soothe with an encouraging coo.

But there was no movement from Dolly. Tucker licked her beak and gently, as though he carried a delicate egg, he slid his jaws around her limp body. Daisy squealed as his jaws closed around her sister, but followed as he carried her double-yolk toward the fence. He hesitated, steps away from the dead things and gave a muffled whine. None of them moved, though one grunted and a thin trail of spit dribbled from its loose lips. Tucker slunk between two of them, his tail tucked under his belly, and slid under the bottom rail of the wooden fence.

"Come on, yes, we've got to go," Chickory said.

Woodfawn peeped and flapped a feeble wing.

"Look, it's all right, they're—they're sleeping." Encouraging wasn't working. Chickory aimed and with a hard jerk, ripped out a long thick feather.

Woodfawn squawked and staggered to her claws. "I can't, my legs are all wibble-wobble, I'll fall over."

"Come on. I can and so you can. You—you big bully fool bird."

Her eyes stopped rolling and she focused on Chickory. "What did you—you call me?"

"A soggy egg. Let's go."

Chickory led the way toward the fence, Sundown tingling in her own feathers. They could reach and snap them up with one swift motion, like the snapping jaws of a nimble fox. The air prickled with tense energy. Fayne continued to stare intently at the dead things, but her whole body twitched, as though the boom of a sky-stinger rumbled within her.

(*We must leave*)

Chickory forced herself not to look at any of them, willing herself not to notice how a few of them were starting to stir, the moans getting louder. She passed between the scabby oozing legs and the familiar smell of the sickness choked her.

"Chickory," groaned Woodfawn.

"Keep your eyes on my tail. Come now," she said, placing one claw in front of the other.

The child twitched and turned its gaze toward Chickory and Woodfawn. Smeared brown teeth clicked within the wet maw of its mouth.

Chickory stopped and looked back at Fayne, desperation clawing inside her breast. "You come too. Come now. Please."

Fayne did not look at her, just kept staring. (*Quiet*) "Just go, Chickory. I am close behind." (*Quiet*)

But the spinner's web of tension faded, the word no longer cold and wet, only feeble and faint. They *were* moving, beginning to shuffle their feet. The child grabbed at Woodfawn.

"Run, go!" Fayne commanded and a force shoved Chickory against the fence, as though Fayne's words were hands. Chickory's claws slid against the packed earth and she stumbled under the rail. The tall grass on this side of the post was gone and there stood Tucker, still holding Dolly in his mouth.

"Oh, mercy, oh, mercy. What has come? What has come?" Woodfawn sounded stronger and her voice lilted with terror.

"Just don't look back." Chickory's legs shook and though the grass was trim and short in this field, she felt no comfort. Woodfawn shoved past her and staggered toward Tucker. Daisy ran to meet her and bobbed her head as she paced in frantic circles.

Only Chickory turned back. The furry heads of the dead could still be seen just above the top rail of the fence and they bobbed and swayed excitedly.

"Fayne!"

Chickory waited but there was no movement and no sound but howling moans, enraged at being tricked, at being fooled. *We must leave.* But not without Fayne. "Fayne!" Chickory turned back toward the fence. She would not leave Fayne, not like this, not—

Fayne burst out from under the rail of the fence, her feathers bristling. "Run, you asinine bird! Do not stop, go, go!"

Relief surged through Chickory, dizzying as a sparrow catapulting through the blue sky. Fayne ran past them all and without another cluck, the others followed her desperate sprint.

13 | Left Behind

"Should a bird be fallen, crushed of wing or will, let them
not be forgotten, but leave them to Piasa, soaring
where none other can follow."

- In Dark and In Light, Final Clutch

The field, with its wide expanse of flatness, felt sparse and dangerous after the shadowed journey through the forestland and tall grasses. In every direction, all was visible until the next rise. Hum homes speckled the distant landscape. Though Fayne had called it a field, it was barely so, with bald patches of dust speckling the yellowed fuzz of overgrazed grass.

"Helloooooo," moaned a few of the cows clustered in a far corner of the pasture. They wagged their tails in unison and a few of them had shining bells around their necks.

Tucker barked a noisy reply and Chickory shuddered. The low calls of the cows sounded much like the dead things that guarded the field just behind them. Guarded. Yes, that felt true, the way Tucker guarded the Farm, the way even birds guarded their favorite nests. Lined up and waiting for any who would come to pass. And that word, *quiet,* the word that dripped into the mind and stilled the hungry creatures. Somehow, Fayne knew, and the possible answers hooked in Chickory's throat like a bramble of thorn berry.

"Watch out, watch out for the bad things, the sick Masters," Tucker growled. He snuffled the air with his big wet nose. Though

Chickory could smell the tang of insects, and even the urine marks left by the killers who had passed through this land, Tucker's nose, large and quivering, lapped up details far beyond what hers could detect. In the flat open expanse was the strength of the dog.

"Yes, we must avoid them, the sick ones. They are called the unliving," Fayne said.

"How do you know this?" Chickory asked.

Fayne ignored her and surged ahead, her eyes on the horizon. Though all looked safe enough, Tucker circled the flock and kept them moving as a scattered group, nosing them closer together if they became separated.

Fayne stopped abruptly and waggled her head. "Precipitation is coming. These altocumulus clouds will soon pass."

Chickory blinked and gazed up at the sky. The blue was mostly clear, dappled with a few stray clouds, like stray tufts of downy feathers. "What does alto—"

"Tucker, what do you smell upon the prevailing wind?" Fayne interrupted.

He whined as all of them stopped and circled them again. "The big mooers are females, they won't bother with us," he said. "I smell Lady. The smell of her sick. It's everywhere, all over, everywhere. I think it's their mouth sickness, terrible, terrible smell. And I smell a bird."

Woodfawn flapped her wings and scattered a few blades of dead grass. "A bird, a hen? Really? Oh, where, Tucker, where?"

"Over by the barn. I think it's all right. I don't smell anyone else around." But he whined again and the uncertain sound whistled deep inside his chest.

Without speaking, they drifted in the direction of the Hum house and the large barn. Chickory searched the sky as they went. Such open space was an easy land for hawks and eagles, but there was no sign of danger, and fear momentarily gave way to hope. She snatched up a crispy beetle shell and squabbled with Woodfawn over a slow-squish they found oozing over a warm stone. The despair of the tall grass and the echoes in her memory momentarily faded away, though she knew they would return.

"Feather, feather, egg, and weather." Daisy pecked Woodfawn's comb and ran away. It was a chickhood game and they chased each other, even as Tucker whined and tried to herd them into stopping. Hope bloomed in Chickory's breast. How wonderful it would be when, with bulging stomachs, they would return to warm roosts and the sweet smell of decomposing straw. Though, wherever they made their new home, there would be no Lady song as she shut them up for the night and enclosed them in the soft dark of the coop. Perhaps there would never be another coop at all. They might have to live as Piasa's chicks once did, nestled among the rocks and in the trees like the first wild birds she had created.

The light pleasant mood spread and even Tucker stopped whining, his anxious circles growing wider and softer. His tangled fur flapped in the wind and he stopped and rolled in a fragrant patch of cow dung. Chickory warbled with happiness, her throat tight, as though it had forgotten how to sing happy notes. It was a heavy happiness; Fayne's eyes still followed her every movement and the ever-present memory of Robert and Lacey and Georgia and Rosie—yes, they were gone, but just now, in this warm place under the blue, things were as they should be.

Fayne walked beside Chickory and their wings pressed together in a familiar way. "It is good to be away from there."

Chickory's feathers prickled with the intensity of Fayne's yellow gaze and she didn't respond at first, distracting herself with a few wayward ants. Or what had Fayne called them? *Campa...* ridiculous. They tasted faintly of rotted orange fruits.

"Yes, it is. But this is just the beginning, isn't it? The unliving... you know what they are, I know you know."

Fayne turned her gaze to the sky as though she too searched for sky birds, though she never really did, always seeming to sense whether killers were around or not. "You know more than you think for a bird. It will all be a disappointment in the end. For as much as I know, there is a lot I *do not* know. There are gaps all over the place. Memories I think I remember, but never quite the same. Time has changed it all. I fear the others will leave us once I tell them true. It is the only reason they have really followed. The secret hope I know all that is to unfold? Even you."

"You're wrong. I followed you because you're—well, you're my, you know—" But what she couldn't quite say. "We've been together since chickhood. I still remember your funny feathers growing in."

"And the first time Woodfawn pulled them out?"

A buzz of anger flickered in Chickory's breast. "Yes, that too. Being small is hard."

"So is being big. I do not think I will ever have quite proper feathers."

A gleaming green beetle buzzed loudly overhead. Chickory wanted to speak what was in her mind, but fear and that word *quiet,* wouldn't allow her to. So instead she said, "I don't know all you know. You're addled on the best of sunrises, maybe. But I believe you'll help us get to the valley. I think—well, maybe that's why you haven't told us everything. Of what you do know anyway. Maybe there are some things, awful things, we don't want to know. But it can't go on like this. You have to find some way to make them trust you or they won't follow. And they do want to, they need to. You have a responsibility now. You convinced them to leave. Now you must convince them to see this through."

Fayne said nothing and they walked together that way for a while, feeding and scratching in the dust.

The flock slowed as they drew closer to the house and barn. The last barn, occupied by dogs and Latrans, was still fresh in their memory. Tucker came out ahead of them and sniffed warily as they approached. The large panel doors of the barn were slightly ajar.

"The cows must have pushed their way through and escaped out into the field," Fayne said.

Tucker flattened his ears. "Their Masters have gone on too. That smell."

"Oh no, oh no no no." Dolly limped and pressed close to Daisy as they passed through the doors and entered the shadowed coolness of the barn.

Woodfawn cocked her head and peered down the long passageways on either side. "That bird, the one you smelled. Is it in here, oh, is it?"

Stalls formed the length of the barn and ahead was another set of large panel doors but these were closed and latched. Beyond would be the common ground around the house. The barn looked quite empty and there were no bins of grain or corn, spilled or not.

Relief glowed inside Chickory like new season lightbugs. "Might be best to go around outside. I don't think we can get through here," said Chickory.

"SCREEEE!"

A huge shadow passed over them and a huge bird descended upon Tucker's head.

Feathers exploded as Woodfawn, Dolly, and Daisy flapped out of the way, squawking and screeching. Chickory cowered for a moment and squinted up at the figure–perhaps a disgruntled moon bird rudely awakened.

Tucker barked and snarled. "Gerroff, gerroff!" He savagely swung his head and pawed at the attacker, but it had latched onto his ear. He reared, dropped to his belly, and rolled over. The bird let out a loud squeak and tumbled loose in the dirt.

"This is MY here barn and you all better shove off!"

The terrible screech had come from the smallest rooster Chickory had ever seen. His cream and tan feathers, maybe once beautiful, were straggly and broken, and hunger carved away any heft he might have once had. His huge size had only been surprise. Here in the dirt it was clear he could never have fought them off.

"Well, well, well! Is that a sparrow?" quipped Woodfawn from her spot atop a stall post.

"A sparrow? Who said that? I'll show you sparrow, come down here!" squawked the diminutive rooster. He glared up at Woodfawn and hopped with indignation.

Dolly wagged her tail. "It's just a little half-half cock. Some Hums keep them for dainty interests, but he's got spirit to be sure." The three hens burst into cackling laughter.

"And what brave chickens you all are," snapped Chickory. "Is that post quite high enough?"

Woodfawn growled down at her, but they all stopped laughing.

Chickory took a small step towards the bristling bird who glared at her with equal disgust. "I'm Chickory. Is this your barn?"

The rooster puffed out his small thin breast. "Clearly sparrow-minded, you are. This is clearly my barn, just as your lot is clearly *trespassing*!" He hopped and flapped his wings, puffing up his chest as big as it could go.

Fayne clicked her beak. "We are sorry. Never mind that we might be the last birds you ever see. Best we leave." She turned her back on him.

Tucker barked. "Yes, let's go away, far from this bad place."

The other three flew down from their perches and followed Fayne as she headed toward the open doors. Chickory also turned away but glanced back at the small rooster. He still glared and bristled but he bowed his head slightly as he watched them go.

She stopped.

"Are you sure you don't want to come with us?"

"You featherheads are crazy. Be killed, surely you will." His wings quivered and every feather stuck out from his small body. "Those Hums will tear you apart with their bare hands."

Robert. Lacey. Georgia. Rosie. A sliver of ice stabbed her wind pouch. "Is that what happened here?"

He hopped from one foot to the other. "Right, all of them. You can't outrun them. Those things, they're everywhere now."

"Things? You mean the… unliving?"

"And the living."

"Well, I don't think you'd be better off hiding here," she said. "We're going to a valley. A valley where we'll be safe and hidden. Won't you come with us?"

The rooster paused for a moment, his head erect and feathers shivering. Then fear passed over his dark orange eyes.

"No, I think it best I stay here," he finally said.

There was nothing more to say so she left him. But even as she followed the others, as they strutted through the field toward more of the distant unknown, she glanced back and wondered what would happen to the lonely bird.

And whether they would all come to suffer the fate of dying alone.

14 | As They Were

Robert, can we not stop?" Georgia's patterned feathers were dull and coated with dirt and her pace slowed with every step. A shelled slow-squish passed them, but they didn't even look at it. Their appetite had deserted them.

"No, not now. We go until dark. We can't afford to fall any farther behind." Robert tried to suppress his own anxiety, the fear, the knowledge it might be far too late, that they might never find them.

"But it's nearly dark now!" Georgia flopped to the ground.

He struggled to control himself. Impatience growled, greater than his hunger or fear. Mingled in his impatience was anger, and it devoured like the burn of a cold season fire. Had he been a leader, a true rooster vested with the importance of his calling, he would have sensed the danger, would have listened to Fayne.

Fayne.

He slowed and stopped. Hopelessness squeezed his feathery body like a giant spinner's web. How could they hope to find them? The trees cluttered the sky, and though it *was* nearly dark, he knew beyond the forest the sun would still be shining. Here, at the base of the tall sprawling trees, all was night. A moon bird trilled from somewhere and he jerked at the sound. He scanned the branches above them, but it was impossible to see and he was too tired to even properly shield Georgia.

"Robert?" She had righted herself and pressed close to him. She gazed up at the dark crown of leaves and branches. "Shall we find some place to hide? It's not safe—not safe at all," she peeped.

"Right, yes. Let's, um, here, over here." He plunged into a nasty tangle of holly. The spiny leaves ripped at his feathers like claws, but this would guard them against most killers. Except death worms or determined brown beasts with thick shaggy hides and large snuffling noses. But against the winged killers and smaller sharp teeth, this holly would protect them. He hoped.

They wedged themselves against the main trunk of the bush. A coyote yammered and the moon bird called again—everywhere stirred the sounds of forest creatures awakening. Night was their true realm.

"Oh, Robert." Georgia tucked her head beneath his wing. "Why can't it all be the way it was?" She moaned the cooing cry of lost chicks and desperate injury.

He had no response and closed his eyes to the world.

15 | Worldly Creatures

"Though all creatures must share the same earth, remember that birds are
the most precious of all Piasa's chicks and
must always come before others."

- Practical Wisdom, First Clutch, First Year

Chickory bristled as they neared the perimeter fence of the pasture.
On the other side of the pasture several cows shuffled over the dead
grass, nosing into the dust beneath. The momentary freedom of this safe
field faded with the reality they would have to leave it. Each feather
tingled with anticipation. Soon they would strut through the wide slats of
the fence, and the death, the horrid unliving, the barn, and the lonely
rooster, would be gone. Then they could try and forget, somehow.

One of the cows stood apart from the others and as the flock
wandered past, she broke into a gallop towards them. "Howsbyyooou?
Wait dere, just wait a moment." Her common sound wasn't very good,
but they could make out most of what she said.

"Bad! No, bad, bad, bad!" Tucker launched himself between the
flock and the approaching cow.

"No, leave it, it's all right! It's a mooer, not a killer!" Chickory
flapped her wings and threw herself at his head. The slap of her feathers
broke his strange focus. All dogs seemed to have it when they guarded
and they sometimes lost their minds for a while. He whined and gave
one last bark, but it was much more subdued.

The cow stopped and gazed at them, flicking her tail and

chewing her cud. Her face and most of her body was as pale as a cloud. Only her legs had splotches of black like the others. She showed little concern for Tucker. "Hello," she said again.

Fayne strutted up to the cow and ignored Tucker, who whined and pawed at the grass. "Hello, cow."

"Yes, hello. Sorry about that. It's been tough travel with many dangers," Chickory said. This hardly told the story, but it would take far too long to explain.

"Where you all live?" A strong smell of belch and fermenting grass washed over them as the cow spoke through her methodical chewing.

Chickory bobbed her head. The cow looked a little strange. The others stayed clustered at the far corner of the pasture, completely ignoring them, as cows usually did. In fact, this was the first time Chickory had ever spoken to a cow. "Uh. Well, we're going to a valley, far away from here. So we can find a safe place to be."

"A valley. Up norrrrt, is it? Huh. Past the field, is it?"

"We just came through a field, the tall grass?"

The cow's hindquarters rippled as she flinched and bolted. Tucker sprang to his paws and gave chase, barking savagely as though he had expected this all along.

"No, no, stop it!" Chickory chased after them and Fayne followed.

The cow ran closer to the fence and stopped abruptly. She resumed her chewing as though nothing had happened. Tucker stopped a few paces from the cow and whined. He backed away, his tail lowered.

"What happened? Are you all right?" Chickory panted from the run. Cow's legs were much longer than chicken stalks and they had covered quite a distance.

"The field cannot hurt you," Fayne said. She gazed at the cow with a gleam in her yellow eyes. "The unliving are trapped in there."

"Yes, yes, de field. Don't go in dere." The cow flicked her tail and gazed out at some far away horizon.

"You all seem to be safe in this field anyway. Though…" Chickory looked at the dry grass. The balding patches. The sharp corners of the cow's bones as they pressed against thin skin. "You might need to move on and find food somewhere else?"

"De grass is all gone."

Something was quite wrong with this cow. Maybe addled by

stress as so many of them were or even… sickness.

Fayne cocked her head. "Yes, the grass is all dead so what will you do?"

"You need to be careful. De other dings are waiting."

The sunny day grew cold, like plunging through the surface of an icy pond. "Other things? What other things?" A fearful buzzing filled Chickory's breast.

"Dey brought de gone ones and put dem in the field. Den dey went to wait. Dey will wait and den dey will kill."

Woodfawn, Dolly, and Daisy had caught up to them, but they waited next to Tucker. Dolly still limped quite badly and she stayed close to Daisy's side.

Chickory growled and irritation mingled with her fear. "Look, what do you mean? Who is 'they'? And why would they bring those, what did you call them? Gone things? You mean the, um, the unliving? The dead?"

The cow bucked and almost bolted again. Tucker snarled, but did not chase and the cow settled, though her flesh still twitched over her web of angular bones. "Dey use the gone to guard their land, to keep others from coming. But if you leave dis field, you will enter dere land. Dey will kill you."

Chickory flapped her wings. "But *who?*"

"De two-feet."

Fayne puffed out her breast and looked triumphant, though Chickory couldn't imagine why.

Chickory ruffled her feathers. "You mean the Hums? There are more Hums out there?"

"Everything all right?" called Woodfawn from her place beside Tucker. The playful mood of the day had gone.

At the word "Hums," a growl flickered in Tucker's throat. "Bad, bad, bad. Bad. Killers. Killers!"

"It's all right, Tucker. They're not here," Chickory said but the fear needled into the flesh of her downy breast. They're not here, *yet.* But they would be, if what this cow said was true and she had no reason to lie.

Fayne hopped a little closer and tilted her head again. "What is wrong with you, Cow?"

"Wrong? You should stay away. Maybe go back."

Something was happening. The air grew heavy and tense, like

the coming boom of a sky stinger. Fayne narrowed her eyes and the cow moaned deep in her throat. Tucker's growl twisted into a snarl.

Then the cow bolted again and this time Tucker followed. His barks became a high crazed sound, like the squeal of a coyote, as though he sensed what they could not.

"Watch out!" Chickory cried.

The cow barreled toward the fence, her hooves churning up clods of dirt and dead grass. The thick sturdy beams loomed straight ahead but she did not slow.

BOOM!

Her body seemed to become liquid as it smashed into the thick rails, her bones churning as the wood splintered. She reared back and flung herself forward again, cracking the wood along its center. She lunged at the now jagged edges, bucking and flailing as blood gushed from the tears through her stretched skin. The yellowed white of bone shone through the puddling gash in her side, ribs flexing as she charged once more.

Tucker sunk his teeth into her back leg and yelped as the cow gave a violent kick. He struck the ground and rolled upright. He stayed away and his hoarse bellows caught in his throat.

The slats of the fence were in shards, but they stubbornly clung to the posts. The cow paused and gave a last cry, before throwing her full heft at the broken fence again. The top rail gave way with a booming crack and the lower beam split in two. The cow staggered forward and an ugly fanged piece of the bottom rail caught the pink flesh of her supple stomach. The skin split like a rotten tree fruit as the wooden tooth dug deep. A gush of coiled worms burst out of the cow and splattered the barren earth with pink and green fluid. She sagged and crumpled, slipping in the growing pool, and then lay down.

"No, oh, oh, ohhhh—" Chickory couldn't breathe. The pounding knot in her breast squeezed so hard she thought it might stop, that everything might stop. Every feathertip was numb as though she had stepped into a cold season cave. The sun shone but there was no warmth, a breeze passed but there was no air.

Far away, Tucker still bellowed.

From the opposite side of the field, the other cows came. Maybe they would comfort her, be with her in death, like Chickory had with the porcupine, but instead they galloped faster. They moaned and groaned like they too were unliving, still moving on legs somehow alive.

96

A tremble spread through Chickory's claws and feathers. The cows were coming. Coming to kill, kill, KILL, they were dead too, must be, how—

The rumble of their pounding hooves passed and they did not even glance at the small group of birds, did not look at the foaming mouthed dog with slathering tongue and flashing teeth. They did not glance down at their disemboweled friend, for there must have been someone, at least one cow, who she could have called friend. They paused only to hop over the mangled bleeding body. Her blood splattered their forelegs but they did not seem to mind. They spilled through the fence and scattered like fluffy seeds in a high wind.

"They—they—" Chickory couldn't form proper words.

Fayne stepped closer and pressed her wing against Chickory's. Both their bodies trembled together like a single shake of the earth.

"They needed to g-g-get out. They would have d-d-died in here," Fayne finally said.

"But that cow, what—what was wrong? Was she sick?"

"Not a sickness of body. She knew. The others would have just died. Waited to die. Knowing is a sickness of the mind and she did the only thing to be done."

"Oh, Fayne, oh, oh. I just can't stand it. They didn't even… nothing."

"Perhaps they have their own Mourning C-c-call, or, um, something. We should go. We must go. And we must heed her words. But—" Fayne paused but Chickory knew what she wanted to say.

"We won't tell the others. About, well, what she said about the Hums. How can any of us bear it? I can hardly. Oh, it's horrible, this whole world."

"We must try. It is the only thing life requires of us. We must try."

"Like her?"

Fayne shivered. "Yes. Like all creatures do."

"The Land of Origin was strange and wild, a jungle and desert;
The land became a beast and the towering trees growled;
the desert sand became a Death Worm hissing
beneath Piasa's taloned feet."

- *Tales of Piasa*, for Chicks and Hatchlings

F or the last time, they are called *roads,* not rivers of stone." Chickory
pecked Woodfawn's comb.

"All right, all right, keep your beak dull! Well, the *roads* are
everywhere now."

And they were. The gravelly dirt they had walked on through the
farmlands had become hard gray stripes on either side of wide black
roads. Beneath the glare of the full sun, the stone burned with unseen
fire and the horizon wavered like a dream. The brown fields and pastures
had also changed and they shrank until they were just square yards
surrounding houses, not so different from the one Lady had lived in.
Some houses squashed together like fat hens on a small roost and didn't
have a yard at all.

The flock became a slow feathery mass as they all pressed close
together. Every step between them and the cow pasture and the unliving
in the field, was a relief, but new dangers presented themselves here.
Every yellow eye searched for signs of attack, for the sharp teeth which
could hide beneath the bellies of abandoned roar horses and under the
front steps of each house they passed. Chickory searched, not only for

killers, but for some sign of the Hums the cow had warned of. *Dey will kill you*—Chickory shuddered.

She leaned against Fayne and angled her a little way from the rest. "She said they would be out here, waiting. I haven't seen anything at all," she said quietly. Large square windows gleamed like cat eyes in the bold sunlight. She couldn't see inside but the memory of a white gown, of Lady's house, shuddered through her.

"Yes. I have no doubt they wait. They're cunning and have patience more than any other creature. It is the way they rule all beasts. We must carry our fear and allow no feather to be unnerved. When they come, we will be ready."

Chickory bobbed her head. "Ready for what?"

"To run, of course. But fight if we must."

"Don't be a fool bird, we can't fight Hums. They'd turn bang sticks on us or—or—" She did not want to know how Hums had made Rosie scream in such a way, but her mind conjured up horrible images. *Wing from wing,* wasn't that what Latrans had said? "Well, Tucker might be able to—well, you know."

"Yes, he will if he must. But our true strength is to abscond at the first sign of danger."

Abscond. Another strange Fayne word but she knew what she meant. "We can run only so far and so fast."

Tucker ran back and forth across the black road, sniffing and tasting the air. He limped a little from the kick the cow had given him. Dolly limped too, but she did not complain, and the changes of the land seemed to give them courage. Though danger still threatened from every side, this change at least signaled they were advancing toward the valley. Having left the farmlands behind, they had gone further than Chickory had ever imagined possible.

"Get it! Get it!" Tucker let out a series of excited howls and bolted after the streaking silhouette of a—

"Cat! Oh, oh, oh! It's a big yellow cat!" Dolly ran into Daisy and they collapsed into a tangle of wings and legs.

Tucker paused at the edge of a patch of dry grass. The cat had scooted under the stone of the house and disappeared from view, but his tongue lolled to one side and he looked pleased.

Chickory gazed down the street and froze. Ahead, on the doors of the houses, were red slash marks. Recognition buzzed and spread through every feathertip, threatening to swallow her mind like a raindrop on dry ground.

Fayne cocked her head. "What is it?"

"Those—the markings. On the doors. Well, I *remember* them."

"We cannot remember what we have never seen." But something prickled the air between them, an unspoken truth.

"It's like, we've been here before. Maybe. And you were with me." Certainty spread through her the longer she gazed at the red markings.

"Do not all creatures mark their territory? Probably deja vu. Nothing more. Your mind is piecing together other memories." But Fayne did not look at her and Chickory realized, with a flicker of horror, that Fayne was lying. Lying to *her.*

Like buildings had blood and flesh... Chickory could not shake the memory and the feeling grew stronger as they went. The only signs of life had been flying insects and the fleeing cat. Fat sting-stings bobbed among the blossoms of plants that blurred the edges of the land. Ivy swamped fences and draped across porches. Though they had not seen any Hums, remnants of their presence lingered. The red marks could only have been made by hands.

Scraps of paper and silver cans cluttered the road.

Tucker had padded back to them and chuffed the air, his black nose wriggling. "Smoke. There's a fire, somewhere."

Chickory's breast squeezed painfully. "Hums?"

"No, look, just there." And Fayne was right.

The remains of a fire smoldered inside the belly of a round metal can. Though the smell still lingered, no smoke or flame could be seen.

"The signs are old. Any Masters have moved away. No dogs," he said with a whine.

"Are there no good ones, left? Anywhere?" Daisy whispered.

Dolly uttered a tremulous cry and bowed her head. The ominous stillness filled them all with unease. This was a Hum world, but a dead one.

They traveled down a wide road where tall metal posts tottered in askew angles. Large roar horses sagged against some of the light trees and more and more of them cluttered the road, greater than any herd Chickory had ever seen. The ground glittered with clear pebbles that had fallen from the roar horses' eyes.

Dolly picked one up in her beak. "Oh no, no, no. Don't eat that. It's foul." She spit it out and they left them alone.

Fayne walked ahead of them and led the way through the confused crush of bodies. In some places the roar horses crumpled together in massive heaps, and the flock crept beneath the low bellies of the motionless beasts. Tucker swung around the outside as some of the tight passageways through the wreckage made it impossible for him to follow. He whined and barked continuously until they appeared safe on the other side.

"Oh, Piasa, what folly is this? What horrible place have you condemned us to? Soggy eggs and land of death. And to think, all Fayne's fault. Scaring us, getting inside our heads. 'Addled minds lead to addled hearts.' Hardly a bird! Hardly a—" Woodfawn tripped. She thrashed in a mess of fake worms that sagged from the bottom of one of the roar horses.

Chickory tried to push away the memory of the cow's split belly. "Serves you very well, indeed."

Fayne was ahead, but could surely hear them.

"Nightmare, utter nightmare!" Woodfawn panted as she struggled free. The same size that had allowed her to bully her way to the top roost now slowed her progress to a waddle.

Dolly and Daisy warbled in harmonizing notes of fear as they gazed up through spaces between the roar horses. The sky was turning dark gray and the air felt heavy and warm.

"It's like stories of Origin," Chickory said. Perhaps Piasa could put their minds at ease, though every sound was amplified in the quiet of the underbelly space.

"Like a jungle," Dolly peeped.

"Piasa had to travel through the jungle to the desert," Daisy added.

Woodfawn growled. "Tuh, yes, all the way to the nest of life." She flapped her wings and continued, "When Piasa arrived, she grew the forefathers of all birds from the soil of the deepest river. As their first test, the birds had to find a way to cross the raging liquid lifeblood that traveled through the split skin of the earth."

Chickory shivered. Creation, danger, and instruction pulsed at the heart of every Piasa story and though they could not have a proper Ninith here, on the move, the familiar notes comforted her.

Woodfawn's story trailed off as they emerged from under the last tangle of metal corpses. They neared the end of the main road and here a dam formed. There was a final monstrous yellow roar horse with a long thick body and dark windows all along the sides.

"It is a transportation vehicle for children. Sometimes adolescents, though one could argue adolescence in *homo sapiens* is—"

"Fayne, stop." Chickory shuddered and the others stared, wide eyed, at the chaos before them.

Leaning on top of the yellow roar horse was a Hum machine that must be a roar horse too, though it was covered with thick scales. It was almost bigger than Lady's house and instead of black tires, it had two huge legs with ridges all around them.

"Oh mercy! What is this horrible thing?" Woodfawn squawked.

Chickory took a small step back. "What is it, Fayne?"

"It is a military tanker," Fayne said. "They tried to make a barricade, to stop the other humans from leaving."

"Why can't you call them *Hums*. Such is a proper bird way," Woodfawn snapped.

"What's a military?" Interrupted Chickory, though she wasn't sure she really wanted the answer.

Fayne bristled her feathers. "A terrible thing. Killed almost as many as the sickness ever did. But do not worry. They left it behind. Seems their attempts failed, though they may have gone elsewhere." She gave Chickory a dark look.

Yes, elsewhere. Perhaps very close indeed.

"Monster roar horse for a monster bird," Woodfawn hissed, but none of them tittered with laughter. Their wide eyes brimmed with fear.

"Ohhhhh, no, no. So bad, terrible, awful." Tucker whined and scampered up the side of the yellow roar horse. The metal buckled and groaned as he ran across it.

Daisy hid behind Dolly. "Oh my, is that a de—what did you call them?"

Fayne sighed. "No, it is not unliving, just dead. Crushed it seems."

A putrefying hand extended from the doorway, the fingers swollen and almost as black as the road they walked on. The familiar smell of death mingled with the smell of the sickness.

Fayne took a sharp turn away from the street. "Come on, let us go away from here."

They all followed in silence, except for Tucker's continuous whine. It must cause him pain to see his Masters laid to waste, returned to the earth. Maybe dogs didn't have anything else to believe in except their Masters.

"Nightmare! What is this nightmare?" Woodfawn cackled.

They stood at the edge of a black pond of road. It stretched before them in dizzying length, wider than any water Chickory had ever seen. The world was not entirely unknown, for passing sparrows and traveling field mice told wonderful stories of the Hum's massive settlements, but seeing it was more than mere stories could tell. This one area was far larger than the entirety of Lady's farm. Heat rose from the surface like ripples on water and a few roar horses lay scattered and dead across the expanse.

The sky rumbled overhead and the gray darkened.

"We must get under cover. Somewhere," Chickory said, but where, she didn't know. Soon sky stingers would flash and boom high above and all wise creatures knew to find cover. But there were no trees or overhang, unless they turned back to the wreckage in the road.

"No, look over there," Fayne said.

At the far end of the huge expanse of road was a huge house, squat and square like their own familiar coop, but even from their distance it looked bigger than even the giant black pond that surrounded it. Maybe as big as a wide-open cow field.

"Fayne, are there Hums living there?" Chickory asked.

"No, it is what humans call a *store*."

"Yes, yes, I've been here before! With Mistress of the House and of my Heart!" Tucker barked happily and the sound melted with a rumbling boom from overhead. "She buys the grain and the foods and the smell-goods and the—" He stopped as though realizing Lady would never do any of these things again.

"Right. And that is where we will go, before the rain drenches us all," Fayne said.

"We'd better get a move on," Woodfawn said.

A fat droplet of rain splashed at Chickory's feet. "Well, yes, let's go."

Fayne looked intently at Chickory. "But not too fast. Just in case."

"Just in case what?" Woodfawn glared at her and then glared at Chickory. "In case of *what*? No, now, you just wait a minute!"

But Fayne burst into a run and left Woodfawn, and all her squawking, behind.

17 | Hunters

"Evil exists in all creatures and all who taste blood and flesh.
There must be some evil delight in the act of taking a life,
or no creature would survive.

- *In Dark and In Light,* Third Clutch

Wait, oh wait!" cried Dolly, as Fayne left them.

"Come on!" Chickory bolted after Fayne. Tucker let out a couple joyous barks and followed, galloping like a furry horse. He paused to sniff fragrant places, and urinated on a few of the metal posts that stuck up from the black surface.

Fat raindrops fell and they splashed the road and drenched feathers. Rain was the least pleasant of Piasa's gifts, grass or not, flowers or not. Though wriggly worms after a rainfall coaxed many creatures into the drear, standing out in the wet was for frogs and dogs.

Not for birds.

Woodfawn sprinted past her. "Gah, this blasted rain! Hurry, you rotten yolks!"

The road steamed as the rain pelted the hot surface. Far ahead, Fayne still ran, though Chickory didn't know how she could keep going. Her own stalks threatened to collapse from the frantic pace. She skittered under the belly of a red roar horse, panting and shivering from the wet and exertion. Birds were not runners either.

"Bird? You coming?" Tucker sniffed along the edge of the roar horse and whined.

"I'm coming, just let me catch my wind. Go watch the others."

He bounded away and knocked Daisy over with an overly enthusiastic bump of his snout. Woodfawn had slowed to a lackluster strut and her feathers and wings drooped from the weight of being soaked by the rain.

The sky growled again and a sky stinger leapt through the downy gray of the clouds. Chickory wasn't afraid of them but they all knew well what happened to creatures who were touched by the jagged flashes of light.

The rain slowed and the fat raindrops turned to a light mist. The sun season was full of days like this. Rain then none, sky stingers then wind.

Fayne already stood in front of the store, sheltered by an overhang. The entrance was crowned with bright blue language words, and a yellow circle with black dots. It had a round silhouette like the sun, though, Chickory wasn't quite sure how, it also looked like a strange Hum face.

Woodfawn was almost to the entrance and Dolly and Daisy followed Tucker's meandering pace, pausing as he did, seeming in no hurry to leave his side. Chickory forced herself out from under the roar horse and headed toward Fayne.

Chickory could hear Woodfawn's squawking before she reached them.

"Hardly a bird! What is this nonsense? I ought to rip every feather out of your soggy head, you terrible monstrous thing!"

Fayne gazed off toward the horizon, not looking at Woodfawn, who glowered and strutted around her in a maddening and aggressive circle.

"What's happening now?" Chickory said through pants.

Woodfawn waggled her head and glared at her, as though this too was her fault. "This beastly monstrosity doesn't know a single nit of sense. She wants to go in. Go in *there*."

Chickory looked at where *there* might be. The front doors were smashed and ripped from their frames and in the doorway was a corpse.

"It is just deceased. It will not move again and is not any danger to us," Fayne said.

The Hum lay face down and the arms stuck out at odd angles like it had been crushed. Blood had dried in a thick puddle beneath it, black in the gloomy light. The brown fur on its head was matted with blood and parts were caved in, mucus dried in the cracks of the skull. The visible flesh of the neck was rotted. Tangled around its torso was a blue gown, though it was nearly ripped in half.

Chickory peered at it and waggled her head in relief. "Yes, she's right. It's just dead. It won't hurt us. It isn't unliving."

Woodfawn grumbled and stiffened, shedding the accumulation of water from between her feathers by bristling from head to claw. Chickory shuddered the water off as well, though she was nearly dry already.

Tucker sniffed all over the entrance and growled at the dead Hum, but left it alone. Thin pieces of paper littered the ground and large colored pictures were splayed across their pages, fading into black and white words. He paused over one, gazing down at the crumpled page. "It's strange, there are many pictures of birds, just like you," he said with an anxious whine.

"What? How can that be?" Chickory came alongside him. The rising wind ruffled the edges and she held it down with the claws of her feet, staring into a reflection like on still water. There was a picture of a hen, one that could be quite herself if not for the fact she knew it wasn't. The comb wasn't the same and there was a streak of gold across its face, but still similar in every way. And she wasn't the only one. The front page was covered with many birds of different colors and sizes. "I wish I knew what the words meant. Why are we all here on these papers?"

Fayne glanced down at the paper. "It says 'the cull of 60,000 poultry not enough to contain Cambodian disease' and some other stuff about it spreading."

A shocked silence throttled the air.

Chickory struggled to speak. "You can read this?"

How was it possible? No bird could read this—never mind that, no bird could *read*. Never. It was not of Piasa's way. All creatures knew this to be true. A cold chill flushed through her feathers and it was not the damp of the rain.

"Monstrous," Woodfawn hissed.

"Look, I can read a bit of it. It is not too complex really." Fayne did not meet any of their incredulous stares.

"That's—it's—well, amazing. How, I mean, when did you know? That you could?" Chickory's voice squeaked with awe.

"Since always. Anyway, it does not matter." Fayne turned toward the entrance of the store.

"Oh no, you don't! What does this one say?" Woodfawn squawked and flapped her wings.

Fayne approached the page and then turned away.

"You wait! What is it? What does it say?"

"We do not have time for all this," Fayne said.

"Monster bird with secrets! Hardly a bird! Just a monster!" Woodfawn's comb quivered with rage.

"Stop falling to egg shell about it!" Chickory trembled, but understood, like about the Hums and other terrible things, that Fayne wasn't telling them for a reason. Must be.

Fayne stood at the entryway of one of the smashed doors and peered into the darkness. "Let us see if there is food to be found. We all need to keep our strength up. After all, avian emaciation can cause ocular or nasal discharge, conjunctivitis, even diarrhea."

Dolly and Daisy moaned with distress at Fayne's strange words and Woodfawn growled.

"Is it safe?" Chickory asked.

"Nothing is safe. But we have no choice. Or do you feel strong enough to carry on without food?" Fayne said.

Dolly and Daisy peeped fearfully and Tucker licked their heads in turn, slobbering down their pale feathers.

No lights flickered inside the building, and the entrance looked like the mouth of a deep cave. Nothing good lived in caves.

Fayne sighed. "I am going inside. Whoever wants to come can or you can stay here and wait for me to return. There has got to be some food here."

Hunger pinched Chickory's empty stomach. Foraging on the move was not enough and they had never traveled so far and so continuously. Tucker had fared better with small mice he had found along the way, but he too was tired.

"Well, I'm coming with you. She's right, we've all got to eat and we've made it this far. We can't all be done in with exhaustion and starvation," Chickory finally said.

"I'll stay here," Woodfawn said, and slumped down on a pile of the papers. Anger and panic had drained her. It was hard being a miserable rot of a bird.

Daisy and Dolly stared at each other uncertainly.

"We'll—well, I—" Daisy began but Dolly smoothed one of her feathers.

"It's okay, go with them. I'll stay here with Woodfawn and Tucker," she said.

"Let us go. I do not wish to stay here in the night," Fayne said, and led the way inside.

The deep and muddy darkness swallowed them up as they entered, and Chickory was momentarily blinded as they left the bright daylight. Her claws clicked against the slick floor and they sounded loud and unnatural.

She tried not to think about living in the darkness. Or of cellars. Or rats.

As her eyes adjusted, she could see overturned boxes and bags. Some looked like the ones Lady brought home in the back of her roar horse. Chickory's stomach growled. Corn and wheat also came in bags.

Empty boxes and metal cans littered the floor, covered with squares and pictures, but Hums had strange habits. Then she remembered, with a needling sting of awe and horror— "Fayne, what does this say?"

She paused and glanced at the huge box with the large picture on the front. "It is a contraption they use to maintain their lawns."

"Um, what?"

"The grass that grows around their houses. Lady did not have one and it does not matter. It cannot be eaten."

"Well, what about this one?"

Fayne glanced at the box. "Poison."

Fear ticked in Chickory's throat. "Poison?"

"Intended for rats and small vermin, though poisonous enough should any creature consume it. Even human children can be killed by small quantities."

The thought was so horrible Chickory decided not to ask about the other boxes.

Chickory followed Fayne between and around the obstacles. Behind her, Daisy panted and warbled nervously. Metal walls guided them deeper into the store. Strange smells filled the air and Chickory stepped over a mysterious puddle of liquid. It was not water, nor rain, nor blood. The pool smelled like—well, like a roar horse actually.

"Oil. Do not walk in it," Fayne said.

The rustle of their movements and click of their claws sounded like thudding footsteps in the absolute silence. They searched as they went but nothing smelled anything like food.

"Seems most of the supplies have already been eaten by others," Fayne said. They passed a wire cage of what looked like huge bright fruits. "Toys for children. Ignore them."

"Is this grain?" Daisy chirped. Small granules covered the floor but she picked one up in her beak and spit it out. "No, it's terrible. Don't eat those. Not food, not at all, oh my."

Fayne bristled. "Food meant for plants. Most of these are not good to eat. There may not be any food left."

Chickory's neck prickled and a tingle spread through her wings, down into her claws. "I think someone is in here."

The silent blackness pressed in on them like deep dark water.

Daisy cocked her head. "I don't hear anyth—"

"Quiet!" snapped Fayne.

A faint *swish swish* shuffled against the floor, whisper-quiet and nothing like the click of claws.

From the far darkness at the back of the store, footsteps approached.

Chickory turned toward the entrance, now a small glaring square of light in the distance. "Run, run, quietly, quickly," she warbled.

Fayne and Daisy squeezed in beside her. They moved together so closely their feathers tangled as they went, gasping for breath.

The swishing footsteps broke into a pounding rhythm. It—*they*—were running.

Chickory tried to run but her claws slid uselessly against the smooth surface of the floor. They had gone too far, the entrance was too far away.

"They're going to catch us, they're going to catch us," squealed Daisy and she nearly collided with a huge display of metal circles hanging from hooks.

"Split up, go that way," whispered Fayne.

Chickory careened into another passageway, blocked on both sides by metal walls. Alone, the darkness was worse, and her legs slowed in the grips of Sundown, stinging fear buzzing inside her breast. No, it couldn't happen. Not now. She'd die. She forced herself to move, thinking of Fayne, thinking of words, thinking of sunshine and pastures.

The footsteps approached and Chickory froze. "Oh help, help," she peeped, trying to overcome the Sundown, trying to quiet her mind, to move her claws. At the far end of the passageway, a Hum stepped out of the shadows, its shape distorted in the darkness. It saw her.

"BAWK-KA-KA!" A feathery figure flew down from the top of one of the walls, claws extended. Daisy landed on the Hum's head and slashed with her claws and pierced with her beak. The Hum shrieked and struck with its fists. One glanced off the side of her head and she dropped to the floor, dazed. Relief flushed through Chickory and with it, came freedom, but she could not leave Daisy. So she gathered her might, gathered her fear, and launched herself at the Hum's face, aiming for the gleam of its eyes.

She flexed her claws and felt the squish of wet flesh. The Hum screamed and smacked her away, but she used her fall and the flap of her wings to glide.

"Daisy, Daisy, come with me now!" Chickory landed hard on the floor a few steps away.

Daisy staggered upright and together they ran toward the entrance.

They heard a growl and explosion of snarling barks. Tucker sprinted through the entrance, ears flattened and teeth slathered with saliva. He leapt over them as they scurried under his belly and there was an immediate loud thud and scream.

"Where's Fayne?" Chickory gasped as they burst out into the glare of the overcast day.

Woodfawn's eyes bulged as she saw them. "What's happened?"

But without another word all of them broke into a run out onto the road.

Chickory glanced back. Tucker shielded Fayne, who ran a few paces ahead of him. Blood stained his muzzle, but it didn't seem to be his.

Three Hums stepped out from the dark mouth of the store entrance. They were stained with dirt and traces of blood. A tall female with matted blond fur on her head, raised one fist and around her arm were wrapped strands of—

Chickory's stomach heaved.

Wrapped around her arm were the remains of the many birds she had killed and around her neck she wore a hideous strand of decapitated heads. A length of rope skewered them through shriveled empty eye sockets. Claws and beaks decorated the Hum's waists and ripped feathers protruded from their heads. Their bodies decorated with the remnants of the dead. The maned female motioned to the other two male Hums and the three broke into a run. Toward them.

"They're hunters, run!" cried Fayne.

Chickory's body sagged like a rotting fruit. "Oh, run, run, run!"

"Chickory, no, stop!" Fayne screeched and Tucker yelped with fear.

"Oh no, oh no, oh myyyyyy!" Daisy squeaked and stumbled.

Chickory looked ahead and nearly collapsed as stark terror flashed in her mind.

A loud bellowing moan rose from the huge horde of unliving that shuffled at the far end of the road pasture. They emerged from between trees and around abandoned roar horses. None of these had traps around their feet and their bodies writhed with hunger, the same hunger all the unliving seemed to have.

And the unliving had seen the fleeing flock.

They were coming.

18 | What Cannot be Seen

"Wings give flight and freedom, but be wary of your height,
Should your claws leave ground, always have a landing in sight."

- Practical Wisdom, for Chicks and Hatchlings

No, no, no! Bad things! Oh, no! Birds!" Tucker snarled and howled as he ran a tight circle around the flock.

The horde advanced with surprising speed, shuffling on feet that did not seem to feel the ground, toes scraping against stone, drawing blood, and peeling away skin. With nothing to stop them or hold them back, their true nature emerged. A few at the front galloped, pulling ahead of the others, their loose slack mouths gleaming with saliva and blood.

"Run, turn around, run!" squawked Woodfawn.

They turned away from the horde, but behind them still came the hunters. All around the road pasture, unliving appeared and stumbled out onto the black surface, surrounding them.

The hunters loosened familiar long sticks from their waists.

"The Hunters have bang sticks! Hide, under here!" Chickory scurried under the nearest roar horse and the others followed.

Fayne shivered. "I am sorry, I should have sensed them, should have—have—"

"You couldn't have known. Even with, you know," Chickory gasped. The throbbing knot in her breast pounded in her ears.

Bellowing hoarse barks melded with the chorusing growls of the unliving.

"Tucker! You must go, run and hide in the trees!" Fayne flapped her wings but Tucker did not listen, running around the roar horse and snarling at the approaching danger.

From beneath the metal belly they could see the fast approaching feet: shuffling and stumbling on one side, nimble and determined on the other. However, the hunters slowed as they came, humming and grumbling as they spoke to each other.

Tucker's paws halted as he stood his ground and blocked the flock from the hunter's approach. He snarled and barked, taking a step towards them. One aimed a black bang stick.

Chickory scooted to the edge of the roar horse's shadow. "Tucker, no! Stay away from them! Run away!"

But maybe he could not, or would not, hear her because he took another step forward, white saliva streaking his jaws and chest.

The bellow of the approaching unliving overwhelmed the sound of Tucker's barks.

One of the hunters stepped back and another shouted. Then all three were yelling at each other, though it was hard to understand; any of the few known words were lost in the wash of commotion from all sides.

"They are afraid," Fayne said.

"Afraid? Well, we all are!" Woodfawn snapped.

One of the hunters stepped back and then they ran, ran *away* from the roar horse, away from Tucker, and away from the surging herd of the unliving.

The other two hunters hesitated, but the female with the bang stick shouldered the weapon and they turned and ran too.

"Tucker! Tucker!" Daisy cried. The unliving had reached one side of the roar horse, splitting and shuffling around either side of it, continuing in the direction of the store and fleeing hunters.

And in the direction of Tucker, who was just on the other side.
(*Come*)

The word was clear and cold, like *quiet* had been and it plopped into Chickory's mind like a droplet of water. She felt drawn to Fayne, drawn close to her side. All of them huddled together in the middle of the roar horse's shadow.

Tucker stopped barking. Any moment the unliving would come around the back and see him, they would tear him apart with their impossible numbers.

(*Come here*)

A loud anguished whine cut through the air and Tucker scrabbled under the roar horse, pushing with his back legs and wedging his large furry body between the tires. He barely fit but lay still, trembling and panting. The unliving shuffled around the back, where he had just been, and every side filled with the sight of oozing scabby feet. Some wore removable hooves, while others wore nothing at all. The smell of rot, of decay, of Lady's house, choked the air they huddled in. Chickory's breast squeezed and her beak burned like the scent could kill through breathing alone.

(*Quiet*)

That word again, clear and cold, a command but a comfort.

Chickory tried to speak but her beak opened and closed, heavy and slow like she teetered on the edge of sleep. "Fayne?" she finally said.

There was no response from any of them and as she dropped into a deep sleep, she wondered if her friend might be more than just a bird—maybe even a monster bird after all.

***

The horde had passed, gone on to wherever it was the unliving went. The flock shuffled out from under the roar horse and left the store and road pasture far behind, though how they awoke or traveled, Chickory could not exactly say. The dreamy sensation faded the further they went, and there was no sign of the giant herd or any Hum at all. Maybe they hunted the hunters now.

The distant horizon glowed with the roosting sun. Soon it would be night. They wandered deeper into the thicket of Hum houses that sprawled in every direction and their journey slowed and became a wander, without a sure or clear path.

Dolly jumped as a pile of dry leaves shuddered in the breeze. "Oh myyyy." She scooted closer to Daisy, who staggered unevenly. Woodfawn's eyes were unfocused and her steps grew slower and closer together. Chickory felt like a rotting tree, her flesh would surely start to disintegrate soon, and she wouldn't mind it so much.

Even Fayne, usually impervious to the pains of the flesh, looked downtrodden. She didn't snap or comment on their slow pace. Tucker trailed behind them, panting.

Chickory dropped onto the warmth of the road. "I can't—I have to stop."

The others collapsed in various positions of misery. Tucker plopped on the ground too and rested his head on his paws.

"What do we do now?" Dolly asked.

"Pray to Piasa death finds us quickly, so hunger can't have at us anymore," Woodfawn moaned. Daisy peeped.

They were quiet for a time. Chickory didn't bother breaking the silence; too exhausted to speak, to worry, to feel anything but the pain in her shriveled stomach and the heaviness of her mind. Exhaustion and fear and hunger carved away what little courage any of them had.

"I think I hear Piasa now," murmured Woodfawn. "Don't you hear it?"

"Oh, shut up." Chickory was half-tempted to peck her. "You hear nothing of the sort."

"No, I—I think I hear it too." Daisy craned her beak toward the sky. "It's calling us. Calling us to come home."

Fayne lifted her head and stared, not at the sky, but down the empty road that stretched into the far distance. "A human," she said.

Fear gave a small flutter in Chickory but she did not rise. None of them did.

Fayne staggered upright and shuffled toward the sound. Tucker rose to his paws with an anxious cry and trailed after her.

Woodfawn glared at Fayne's departure. "Where's she off to now? Another march to Piasa knows where. Surely, to our deaths."

"Yes, because the middle of the road is so much better. Come on." Chickory forced herself to stand. The others, one by one, drew themselves up too, even Woodfawn, though she chirped on and on about her aching stalks.

They followed Tucker, who followed Fayne, who didn't seem to care if anyone followed her or not. She led them across the crispy yard and stopped abruptly. The others gathered around her as she peered down a smaller side road that cut between two houses.

A tall Hum with no fur stood in the middle of the road. His gown was brown and stained with dirt. Clumps of paper stuck out from the arms and the middle of the tattered edges of cloth. His gnarled fingers curled like claws around the handle of a rolling metal basket, which he pushed in front of him. In the basket was—

Woodfawn bristled at the sight of the Hum. "Let's hurry past before he sees us."

"No! Don't you see?" hissed Chickory. "Look in there!"

Inside the basket was, well, it looked like food. A lump of what might be bread sat in the middle and colorful greens hung over the side, the sprouted heads of knobby vegetables.

"Are you *insane*? Fool bird and monster bird, what a pair! The Hums are all out to *kill* us or has Piasa blessed you with an empty egg for a brain? He could be a hunter or worse!"

Fayne stepped into the street. "He will not hurt us. He is blind." She took a few steps closer, walking in the shadow his lanky body cast in the fading light.

Tucker whined deep in his throat and his tail stiffened. He let out a small bark.

The man spun on his feet, like a sting-sting had bit him and his milky eyes rolled in his head as he listened intently. He muttered a few words and said one Chickory did understand: "Dog?" Most words sounded like droning hums but with great care and effort, a bird could learn a few of their words, pick them out from their often-incessant mouth-flapping.

He groped in his basket, his nimble fingers crawling over the food. He picked up the loaf of bread in one hand.

Chickory knew they should be more cautious, be warier, but hunger silenced her good instincts. Even Tucker looked carefree as he trotted forward and nosed the outstretched hand.

The Hum jumped, gasped, and then laughed, showing a row of blunt yellow teeth. "Dog-ee," he said again, along with a string of other humming words.

"He likes Tucker," Fayne said.

The Hum gasped and turned toward the sound of Fayne's clucks. He strained with eyes too murky for sight and scattered pieces of bread on the ground. Dolly and Daisy surged forward and Woodfawn scuffed them with jealous claws, savage with want. They fought, squawking and snapping, mere steps from the food.

"Stop it! Just stop!" Chickory squawked.

The Hum stepped back and his hands trembled.

"Stop it, you are scaring him," Fayne said.

Woodfawn and the twins glanced at him and stopped.

Woodfawn clicked her beak. "Scared? Him?"

The Hum spoke again, but Chickory couldn't understand.

Fayne hopped a little closer to him. "He is calling upon his god, *his* Piasa. He is afraid we will draw others to him… others who are dangerous," she said.

A strange energy hummed between them, but what was there to lie about? Fayne's way of understanding all the words, well, she could tell them anything she wanted, but surely she wouldn't.

"Birds," he said. He raised his hands towards the sky and bent forward. He clutched his stomach as he laughed.

Daisy surged toward the bread again and Woodfawn remembered their strife, kicking and snapping. Fayne leaped into the throng and slashed at Woodfawn with her outstretched claws. She gave a loud squawk and they stopped, panting with exertion.

A small trickle of blood dribbled down Woodfawn's shank and she danced away nervously. "Don't you be thinking to have at me, 'blood is the fury of all and the thirst of most.' Stay away now." She fluffed her feathers and looked larger and fiercer than ever.

They all knew the stories of birds that went mad with fury or hunger, tearing into each other until nothing was left but bones.

"Just shut up, will you?" Chickory said.

Dolly and Daisy fell upon the crumbs and warbled with pleasure. Fayne joined them and after a moment, Chickory did too, unable to resist the sweet smell of the bread. Even Woodfawn snatched up a few pieces, though she jerked her head and skittered away when any of them approached her.

The Hum wiped away tears of laughter and sprinkled more crumbs. He tore off a lump of the bread and held it out in his hand. Tucker whined and the Hum offered it in his direction. Only then did Tucker take the chunk gently in his mouth.

The Hum turned back to his cart. He hummed and chuckled again, and resumed pushing the cart down the road.

A tremble of unease spread through Chickory's feathers. "What's he saying, Fayne?"

"He is speaking to his god again. Humans do not believe in godly birds, only other godly humans, though the story of their god's son is a very strange one involving beams of wood and nails—"

"Should we follow him? He seems a bit, well, odd," Chickory interrupted.

Woodfawn flapped her wings. "Odd or not! What if the unliving come back? What if the hunters find us? He has food and we're all out of good fortune. I say we follow him. Besides, we could easily outrun him. He can't even see us!"

"He's not a hunter for sure, but Sam could draw others. Humans tend to live in flocks of their own," Fayne said.

"What? Sam? What do you mean? What is a Sam?" Woodfawn asked.

"His name is Sam."

"And *how* do you know this, monster bird? Oh, what a monster bird!"

"Do you think he means us harm?" Chickory asked, interrupting Woodfawn's questions.

"No, nothing like that. Anyway, Woodfawn, you are right, we are hungry and exhausted. We will take the risk. Night is coming and it is no good to be out in the open," Fayne said.

Woodfawn shut her beak and glared at Fayne suspiciously.

Tucker wagged his tail in silent agreement. They trailed after the Sam, as Fayne had said, following the sound of his rattling cart and murmuring voice.

***

They followed Sam until the sun was beyond the horizon.

"Where is he going? Is he out of bread? I think we should move on, leave him," Woodfawn growled.

"Be quiet, we've come this far," Chickory said.

"And besides, we are here," Fayne said.

Just ahead, a huge road looked like it had fallen from the sky. A field of smashed stone spread across the land, some chunks bigger than Lady's house had been.

"It was a bridge," Fayne said, although no one had asked. "It collapsed. See how it crumbled there?"

Chickory chirped as though she agreed, though she didn't really care about bridges and broken roads. She was too tired to worry about much of anything. A large piece of stone lay against another broken piece, and they formed a dark cave underneath.

Woodfawn glanced around, as though searching for an alternative.

Sam left his cart and crawled over the broken bridge. He stumbled a little but picked his way through the rubble to his hidden home and he ducked into the darkness without looking back.

The flock gathered outside and shuffled nervously.

"I'm not going in there with him, not in the dark," Woodfawn announced and preened one of her wing feathers.

Daisy bobbed her head. "You're the one who said we should follow!"

"But look there, he's lit a fire—" Dolly said.

"Oh, it's warm," Daisy and Dolly said in unison.

Annoyance surged through Chickory's exhaustion. "Let's go in. We're here, and where else anyway? There's not even a proper bush around. Though go ahead and crouch in that ditch would you, Woodfawn?"

The others only stared at her and Fayne said nothing at all.

Chickory's annoyance flared into hot anger. "Fine! You've all got soggy worm guts." She turned her back on them and hopped across the expanse of stone. Her claws slid on the steep angles of the rubble, but the glow of the fire lit her path and by the time she reached the entrance, the others had begun to follow.

Tucker bounded easily across the broken pieces and when he reached Chickory he licked her head. It wasn't quite the same as being preened by a proper bird, but Chickory didn't have the energy to stop him.

Tucker whined deep in his throat. "He's a good one, Sam is. A good Lord of the House he would be." He whined again. "But not of this house. Hardly a house at all."

Chickory fluffed her feathers and scooted away from Tucker, who had started licking her again. "We all make our nests where we must. Perhaps this is the only coop he could find," she said.

The small cave provided a deep but narrow shelter, not much bigger than their own coop had been. Sam squatted beside a fire and the light shimmered in his milky white eyes. Branches crackled in the flames and dark fragrant lumps sat in the middle.

"Are those droppings?" Chickory said as Fayne appeared beside her. The others were only a few hops behind.

The night air felt cold on her tail feathers, but the flat mounds burned low and produced a pleasurable amount of heat. The sooty smell reminded her of horses and of… cows. She shuddered and tried to shake away the memory of bloodied forelegs. Of sacrifice.

"Yes, humans are innovative. It is why they have come to rule this world," Fayne said.

"Piasa gives all creatures special gifts," Woodfawn panted, seemingly exhausted from her hop across the rubble.

Fayne waggled her head. "Or not Piasa at all. Just the way all things develop and grow. Evolution is more likely than a divine entity who watches over and judges all we do. *Much* more likely."

"The way all things—oh my, will you never cease? Death upon you and all your eggs," Woodfawn hissed.

"Woodfawn!" cried Dolly.

"We mustn't, oh no, we must not fight, not now," Daisy said.

Woodfawn puffed out her breast. "It is not our place to question the will of Piasa! She which has brought us life and purpose and—"

Fayne clicked her beak. "Will you think of nothing else?"

Chickory spun on her clawed feet, dizzy and agitated by their squabble. It was true, it had never been their place to question Piasa or the origin of the way. They had accepted what passed as inevitable, as part of the greater nest of life. Even death had its purpose: their life and death would bring new life. Not that they would sprout into blades of grass or turn into grasshoppers, but they would return to the—well, the spirit of these things. It was the spirit that mattered; the same spirit that had created Woodfawn, and her insufferable moods and temper; and even Fayne, with all her unusual and strange gifts.

Sam hummed again, familiar words tangling in Chickory's memory.

Come along, cheeky chicks. Come along. Lady's words floated like a living dream.

Tucker whined and stepped toward Sam and the warmth of the fire. "Let's go. He said to come." He wagged his tail.

"Yes, let's." Chickory hopped closer. Warmth washed over her feathers as she settled at the edge of the flames and nestled against the stone ground. Whatever Piasa was, or wasn't—perhaps that didn't matter anyway—maybe it was the unseen wing that guided them to this place. Their journey had been fraught with danger and still they lived. Lived through far more than any bird should. Worn and frightened maybe, but they continued to survive. Chickory's thoughts muddled into half-sleep. A feathery body pressed against her, Fayne's, and Tucker's hot breath pulsed over her head. The others all huddled in around them and they became a warm nest of bodies.

Maybe it was enough. Maybe all of this could be enough.

Sam pried open a silver box and scooped out brown pellets with his fingers. They smelled sweet and looked sticky with juice, but the bread still warmed Chickory's stomach so she did not move. He sucked his fingers and let out a loud belch. Daisy flinched, but did not fully wake.

"Why do you think he isn't dead like the others?" Woodfawn murmured. She sounded near sleep herself.

"Some of the humans are not affected by the sickness. He contracted the virus, maybe, then got better," Fayne said.

Virus. Chickory squeezed her eyes shut, afraid Woodfawn would lash out at her odd words, but Woodfawn didn't ask anymore. Her breathing had lapsed into deep rhythmic sleep.

"Can animals get sick with the virus?" Chickory asked, thinking of the odd cow.

"Not really. Not like that."

There was more to be said, but not now. Chickory ruffled her feathers to allow more warmth to radiate against her skin. Tomorrow's nest had yet to be made.

19 | Prophecy

"Listen only to the coo of Piasa in your feathery breast;
Creatures of the field know not the hushed whisper of godly wings."

- Tales of Piasa, First Year, Third Clutch

Chickory awoke—a Hum's voice floated in through the cave's entrance.

Fayne crouched low against the ground and glared at the others who also woke at the sound of the voice. "Quiet or we will all be dead."

Wide yellow eyes stared back, but none of them made a sound.

Sam stirred and let out a low grunt, but did not wake.

The voice hovered closer and hummed. Then it repeated one recognizable word: "Sam."

Chickory suppressed a squeal of terror. The cave air thickened and the remnants of smoke made it hard to breathe. Daisy tucked her head under Dolly's wing.

Fayne crept over to Sam and pecked at his tattered sleeve and at his bare fingers. "Wake up, you funny thing, wake up."

Sam pulled his hand back and jerked upright. He let out a loud blast of words and rubbed his face with the rough palm of his hand. The voice outside spoke again, but the Hum it belonged to did not enter. Sam staggered to his feet and hurried into the light outside.

Woodfawn gave an anxious bob of her head. "We need to run, while he's gone."

"There is no other way out," Fayne said. "There may be many of them out there, I cannot sense their true numbers. We wait. I think he will draw them away. He does not want them to know."

Chickory tried to ignore the woodpecker beat of her heart. "Know what?"

"They are afraid of us."

"What nonsense." Woodfawn waggled her head with ferocious disdain and looked as though she might let out a spiteful squawk.

Faint murmurs and hums continued outside and a jubilant shout of laughter made them all flinch. Tucker whined softly and gazed at the entrance. His tail thumped dully on the stone floor. Chickory focused on the tick of her heart, the feathers on Fayne's right wing—they were all a cluck away from panic.

The voice of Sam rose above the rest.

"What are they saying?" Chickory dared to ask.

"They are speaking about the unliving."

Chickory's breast squeezed with the memory of the massive horde.

"It seems we have entered a place of temporary safety. Humans have secured this land against the approach of that herd we saw," Fayne said.

If what she said was true, if this was a safe place for Hums, then there must be many of them living here. Together.

A visible shudder passed over Fayne and she ruffled her collar of black feathers. "Yes. Many humans."

The shudder traveled deep into Chickory, cold and prickling through each feathertip. Chickory hadn't spoken aloud and yet, in her strange way, Fayne had answered.

Sam reappeared. He flashed his teeth and pressed a finger to his leathery lips as he blinked one eye. In his arms he carried a brown sack, like the ones in his rolling cage. He set it down and picked up a shiny can and pried open the top with a pointed metal stick he had in his pocket. With a small cry, he tipped the can and they all quickly forgot their fear as golden kernels of wet corn rained from the sky.

"Oh glorious food!" Woodfawn chirped, forgetting to be a miserable bird as her beak flicked among the plump morsels.

Sam hummed and talked while they all ate, and he pawed through the bag and examined different cans inside.

Chickory strained to listen, to try and understand what Sam was saying, but he spoke too quickly. On the farm, she could tell if Lady was happy, if she was excited, or if she was sad, but these were things she could see, just by the way Lady flicked food on the ground, or the sound of her attempted chirps. A few of the words she had used to name them or call them to food was all that had mattered.

Soon the corn was gone, only a damp puddle of sweet liquid marking where the food had fallen. Woodfawn looked around and realized the feast was over. Her crown feathers prickled like a field thistle. "Here we are, another meal to run away from. It's ridiculous, really. Isn't that right, monster bird? We're to run away? To starve once again? How far is this *valley*? We've been walking for ages, with no sign. The houses get thicker, the Hums get worse, and you said we're in the middle of a whole flock of them! I don't think you know where you're going at all."

Dolly squawked, "Won't you ever stop? Even for a moment?"

Surprise flickered and the warmth spread into Chickory's claws. To not be the first to come to Fayne's defense, well, it was an odd feeling, but one mingled with pride.

Woodfawn strutted away from them.

"She's turning into an awful goose lately," Dolly chirped. "Fayne? Oh myyyyy, Fayne!"

Fayne lay upon the ground, her head arched back like a coiling death worm. Her wings flapped violently against the grey stone and a strangled cry gurgled in her throat.

In chickhood, they had all watched as one of the hens had become tangled in the wire fence and had broken her own neck trying to wrench free. Fayne looked as she had then, frantic and fighting against her own body.

"Piasa, preserve her!" Dolly squealed.

Even Woodfawn surged forward, panting and bobbing her head.

Tucker paced around Fayne's rollicking body. "Oh, bird, oh bird. What do we do?" he whined. He reached a paw out as though to roll her over.

Chickory flapped her wings. "No, just don't touch her! Wait a moment, give her a moment!" Whatever was happening in her friend's feathery body, they could not stop it.

Fayne's eyes fluttered, and after several moments her body ceased its frantic motion. With one last flap of her wings, she grew still and gazed toward the beam of light that poured through the entrance.

Chickory crouched beside her and pressed in close. She

smoothed each disturbed feather. "Are you all right? You're coming out of it, I think." Maybe her words could comfort, even as her blood surged with fear.

"The wind—the wind. I saw the wind," Fayne peeped, her voice weak and faint. As though she was near death though she couldn't be, she *must not be*. If they lost her …

"Hush, you saw the light. Only the light of sunrise."

"It is n-n-night." Fayne closed her eyes. It had been so long since she had stuttered that Chickory had almost forgotten what it sounded like.

Sam started to speak in a soft humming tone. He had sat straight and still, as though listening, his milky eyes flicking from side to side. Had he heard their struggle? Their panic? Could unseeing eyes still sense the true nature of things? He extended a hand and Tucker pushed against it with his wet nose, licking the thick crooked fingers.

Sam patted Tucker's head and slowly knelt on the ground. His fingers slid across the stone floor until they reached Fayne. A cry rose in Chickory's throat, he should not touch her, should not move her, but the sound never escaped her beak.

Sam's mouth parted and he sang. The words drifted like the colorful dying leaves during the fade. No two Hums ever sang alike and like the cluck of a hen or crow of a rooster, the melody told stories of who they were.

And Sam was beautiful.

His hands curled around Fayne and he lifted her into his arms, curling her against his chest. She did not move or make a sound, but he continued to sing and stroke her still body with his thick fingers.

They all watched as the beam of sunlight in the entrance grew long then short, and finally disappeared. The sun was above the cave now, but Fayne still slept, her breast rising and falling in a slow steady rhythm. Something terribly wrong brewed inside her. Beyond the pulse of her life source, something was growing. A gift? Knowing the words and *reading* the words of Hums, her dreams, her knowing… surely, a gift.

But sometimes gifts required something in return.

Sam's singing stopped and Chickory flinched. She had been dozing.

Fayne peered over the ridge of Sam's arm and she looked alert and focused. "Chickory, is everything all right?"

Sam carefully set Fayne down, allowing her to extend her claws and right herself before letting go.

A surge of relief pulsed through Chickory's feathers. "It's all right. Sam was watching over you, is all. You seem better. Do you remember anything?"

Dolly cooed, "Oh goodness, she's awake."

"You had us twittering like sparrows," Daisy said.

Woodfawn grunted and rose from her nestled position by the entrance, her concern seeming to recede as quickly as it had come.

Fayne shivered and gazed at the late sunlight outside. "We should go. Before the others come back for another visit."

Woodfawn grunted again. "As I predicted," she said. "Running away again. You don't seem well at all. Maybe you're just as sick as the rest of them. Best to give up your roost now and let a real bird lead. You don't know where the valley is, I'm sure of it. Tuh, this valley you speak of. I don't even think there is a valley. Your addled mind lays rotten egg after rotten egg and it's all begun to *stink*." Fury gleamed in her eyes.

Fayne blinked and walked past her, out of the cave. Dolly and Daisy followed, not looking at anyone.

A tremulous whimper bubbled in Tucker's throat. He gazed back at Sam and his eyes shone with something like sadness. Sam patted Tucker's head and rubbed his soft ears with both hands. He murmured words, some of the few that Chickory could understand: doggie, Sam, goodbye.

"Good-bye" was the word Hums often said as they boarded their roar horses and disappeared for a while. But this time, they were the ones disappearing.

"Come on, Tucker," Chickory said, swallowing the pebble of sadness lodged in her throat. Tucker licked Sam's fingers and wagged his matted tail. Though Tucker was their guardian, their sure-footed companion, no creature could deny the love he had for Hums and the sorrow he must feel at having to leave them.

Woodfawn clicked her beak irritably. "Absurd, utter nonsense," she said, before joining the others outside.

***

Leaving Sam's cave had not been an easy task. The collapsed bridge stretched a long way and it was difficult to find a place they could all cross together. Beyond the ruins, houses clustered along the black roads, which crisscrossed like spinner webs across the land. They traveled in the shadows and skirted under the bellies of roar horses where they could. A small group of Hums walked past, down another road, though they talked so loudly it was easy to hear them and hide. They did not look like hunters. At least, not like the hunters they had seen at the store. No bird heads or claws decorated their bodies and they looked very much like Lady had. One even carried a basket under one arm, though it was impossible to see what was inside.

The houses also looked cleaner than the place with the red door marks. The grass was short and no litter cluttered the streets. Here the roar horses lined the sides of the roads, rather than herding together in the middle of them.

For a long while they walked without seeing any Hums at all. No laughing or voices on the wind, no real movement.

A mottled brown rabbit shot out from under one of the low-lying bushes.

"Fuzz butt! Fuzz butt!" Tucker surged after it, barking with glee as he chased the bow-legged sprinter.

Fayne clicked her beak, but did not call to him. "I know what I am to do," she said instead.

Chickory cocked her head. They walked side by side and their wings rustled against each other. "Oh? Like in one of your dreams?"

"Like a dream but not. It is not for you to worry about. Not yet."

"Let me worry about my worrying."

Fayne sounded stronger, surer than she ever had on the farm. Underneath this blossoming courage though, Chickory sensed there was far more Fayne did not dare to say aloud.

Fayne bobbed her head. "Do you think they will follow? All the way to the valley?"

"What else can we do? Don't listen to Woodfawn. I don't think the others would ever really follow her. She's so miserable. Besides, we've come this far, haven't we? Can you say what it was? I mean, what did you see? When you were sleeping." The strange episode—Fayne's flopping body—well, no one had wanted to speak of it. "I know something is happening. You're changing. Somehow."

"It is not always as it turns out. The things I see, they come to me, but sometimes they grow wings and leave. Sometimes the thoughts fly away completely and my mind is empty. But you won't leave… will you?" Fayne looked at her.

"Of course not, but what do you mean 'leave'? How can thoughts leave from your mind? You would tell me, wouldn't you? If something bad were going to happen?"

"I do not quite know the end," Fayne replied.

A loud crack echoed in the distance followed by a sharp yelp of pain—Tucker's yelp of pain.

They all scattered, skidding under roar horses and hopping into shaggy bushes.

Chickory peered out from under a bench. Her claws tingled with surprise and she struggled against Sundown. "Tucker? Tucker!"

Again, the distinctive cracking pop, followed by others, sounded from somewhere down the road.

"Tucker!" A sliver of ice stabbed her stomach and tore at her insides.

Dolly and Daisy peered out from a thick stand of bluestem. Their pale bodies were bright against the dark stalks. "Do you see him–"

"Oh heavens–"

"Is he there?"

No, no, no. Not Tucker. Not now, please, not now. That cracking sound was the sound of bang-sticks. The sound that split the silence of the back woods behind their farm. The sound they hid from because it is the sound of Hums who do not raise life, only take it.

At the far end of the black road, Tucker appeared. He staggered on three legs, one of his front paws dragging against the rough ground. From his shoulder to his toes, blood flowed and spattered in a trail behind him. Foam curdled at the corners of his mouth like a sickened creature and his pink tongue hung loose between his teeth.

Chickory ran to him.

Tucker yelped as she came, "No, birds, run, run on. Bad things, oww, ow, owwwwww."

Chickory ran alongside him, as he still staggered at great speed. "You're hurt, oh, you're hurt badly. We've got to hide you, get you under cover."

The others emerged and ran to them.

Tucker staggered away from the street and headed toward one of the houses, turning down a small side passage. Then he collapsed on the ground and moaned. His sides shuddered with rapid breaths and each one bubbled into a thin whine.

128

Fayne peered at Tucker's wound and pecked away some of the sticking fur, which exposed an oozing hole.

"There's metal bits in there. The banging sticks spit them at you," Woodfawn said.

Chickory looked at her in surprise. "How do you know that?"

"A fancy bird—shot down last summer, right next to me. Thought Piasa was welcoming me back. But some of the bits missed, fell on the ground. I almost ate one but it didn't smell right," she said. "You've got to get them out. They kill from the inside."

Chickory peered at the hole. Thick dark blood hid anything that might be inside. "Get them out? But how?"

"I'll do it," Woodfawn said, though she sounded reluctant. "'Preserve the egg and the wing and the breast' Piasa tells us. But Tucker has preserved us all along. Tuh, I'll get them as I'm the one who knows what they look like, I suppose."

Fayne said nothing but her yellow eyes shone with silent approval.

Woodfawn bent over Tucker's shoulder and with a sharp jab she buried her beak into the wound.

"Ow, owwwww, no, owww," Tucker yowled and feebly licked Woodfawn's head, but she ignored and stabbed again with her beak.

Chickory ducked her head beneath one of his soft ears. "Quiet now, lie still, you must try. She'll get them out. You'll be all right, you will. But be still, be still now."

Woodfawn slashed again at the tender flesh, which sheared wider with each stab. Blood ran down her beak and spattered her dappled breast. She looked like a killer, a horrible murderous bird that ate flesh, that would kill its own to survive.

From deep in his cavernous chest Tucker bellowed and flexed his head back against the stone foundation of the house. They watched Woodfawn strike again and again.

Blood pooled and somewhere in the distance, bang-sticks continued to fire.

"The shared end for all is not in glory.
Only a sudden quickness, an ending of the flesh.
But of the heart, there can only be the light;
the light we all see when at the last we close our eyes."

- *In Dark and In Light,* Third Year, Third Clutch

The moaning bellow of the passing herd swallowed all sound.
Chickory stifled her panicky breathing and allowed Sundown to overtake her. In this moment, stillness would save them. Dolly's boney wing dug into her side as they all stood on Tucker's back, like perching on a furry roost. He cowered beneath them, and his body shivered. Stagnant water puddled around them and a swarm of biters flitted around their heads, but none of them snapped at the juicy bugs. None of them dared.

The horde of the unliving blocked the fading sunlight that would otherwise have reached the bottom of the roadside ditch, so the flock crouched in darkness. Thorny brush shielded them from view, but if the unliving saw or heard them they would have to run, and Tucker, well, he moved at such a slow hobble now that running would be impossible.

Everything smelled of Tucker's blood. Could the unliving smell? A deep cramp pinched Chickory's stomach at the thought of their slathering mouths and heaving nostrils. Hums were not the best at smelling and these shambling monsters were less than them.

Surely.

Tucker's blood not only matted his fur, it streaked Woodfawn's face and breast, crusted on her lacy white feathers. She had been able to dig the metal pellets out of Tucker's shoulder, but there hadn't been time for a proper preening or even a flutter in the dust. The distant bangs had been Hums firing on the approaching herd of the unliving.

After most of the pellets had been removed, they had staggered away from the clustered houses. Wide fields lay bare on either side of the road, the grass short and yellowed, and they had come across another herd of the unliving. Or was it the same herd they had seen at the store? They had thrown themselves into the ditch, the only place to hide.

As the unliving thinned out, more light shone upon their cramped hiding place. A few stragglers struggled to keep up with the others. One had only one leg and it scurried forward on all fours, managing an odd jerky trot like a three-legged horse.

"Most have passed," Fayne said. The words sounded strange in their silent huddle, as though they had forgotten speech.

Chickory's wings and stalks ached. "Spread out now, we can make room. Move, will you?" Instant relief surged through her as Dolly stepped away and hopped off Tucker into the deep mud.

Fayne gazed at the sinking sun. "We will sleep here tonight."

Woodfawn waggled her head. "In a stinking cold ditch? Have you no true and noble sensibility at all? As Piasa told, 'all of the wing shall perch freely in all manner of tree.' We should roost in those silver trees over there. Much drier up there too." She puffed out her breast and looked pleased with herself.

"And when hunters or the unliving surround us, how will we escape? Winged we may be, but none of us soar as eagles or hawks. And," Fayne glanced at Tucker, "not all of us can flap into a tree."

"You won't have your satisfaction until we are the most miserable dead sort!" Woodfawn flapped her wings and disturbed the branches of the thorn bush.

Fear prickled in Chickory's feathertips. "Stop it, they might not all be gone yet."

"Let us rest and sleep as best we can. Tomorrow we must travel," Fayne said, ignoring Woodfawn completely.

"But the bangs, there are so many. They will come. Find us," whimpered Tucker.

Chickory preened a bloody mat of fur. "What did you see?"

Tucker grunted and rested his head on his paws. The whites of his eyes shone in the red light of the fading sun.

"The fuzz butt ran past a whole lot of them—a fence with holes. The holes all had bang sticks in them. Bad food was all over the ground, smelled bad."

"Seems it was a trap," Fayne said. "Perhaps to lure the unliving or herd them in a particular direction, away from the settlement perhaps."

No one spoke. What Fayne said might be true, but it was impossible to say for certain.

Tucker groaned and shifted in the mud. There was little any could do to comfort him, so they resorted to the physical way of birds. Dolly and Daisy squeezed in on one side and preened his bloody matted fur.

Chickory tucked in on his other side and surrendered to the wet. Exhaustion and pain radiated through her feathers. Her claws had begun to chafe against the grind of the seemingly endless rivers of road. She curled her nails into the soft wet mud. The coolness felt wonderful, though that same coolness would become a bitter chill in the night. They would need each other's warmth.

Woodfawn squeezed in beside Daisy and Dolly and Tucker curled his tail around her. He closed his eyes and his breathing deepened with instant sleep. Fayne settled in beside Chickory. Though they were all ragged with fear, it was comforting to press breast to breast, no sound but the rustle of feathers and the breathing of quiet company.

A rumble of thunder sounded in the distance.

"Those awful things, those metal balls," Daisy said, ruining the peaceful mood. "Bang, bang, bang! How awful! Awful hunters, awful *Hums*."

Woodfawn clicked her beak. "Yes, yes, awful. But let's not get feather rot about it. Look here, we haven't had a proper Ninith in ages. Piasa will forgive us our long absence, and we should have one, just to lift our spirits," she said.

Fayne snorted. "*Piasa* has no eyes on our world. Or any world."

"Still, it might be good, take our mind off things," Chickory said quickly. Though she couldn't see Woodfawn, she could imagine her quivering rage. Now was not the time for Fayne, or anyone, to disagree so spiritedly.

Ninith, their nightly assembly of songs and stories, was a tradition they had shared for most of their hen life and it was as sacred to them as the morning call. *Robert.* The thought punctured like a pouch full of jagged rocks. Every sunrise had been marked by his call and every night, whether roosting or nesting in the coop, was marked by the Ninith. Since they had left the farm, there had been no ritual, no passage of sunrises marked by crowing, and no stories. Focusing on survival had quieted them.

"Yes, yes! Can we tell about when Piasa created life's end?" said Dolly.

"Oh yes, that's a good one," said Woodfawn.

A flutter of excitement stirred in Chickory's breast. "Shall I tell it?"

"No. I will," Woodfawn said. "You've hardly a pleasant chirp and besides, I always lead. Let's not go changing *everything,* unless monster bird objects?"

A small silence followed. Excitement soured. *Don't open your beak, Fayne.*

She didn't and Woodfawn began: "Piasa decided it had been far too long since she had last visited her lands and creatures and one day in the sun season, she descended and was shocked by what she saw. The world was filled with all the creatures Piasa had created, but in her love for all living, she had not known the passage of time. Fields lay barren and the forests were stripped of their green leaves and edible gifts. The world was dying. There were too many creatures and they ate and mated and drank of the water—Piasa had given them all eternal life."

"Forever living with a forever life," clucked the others.

Fayne did not join in the chorus.

"Piasa was filled with great sadness," Woodfawn continued, "and she walked the meadows, tears dripping down her majestic moon face. She walked the floor of the great waters and to the top of the highest mountains. So much death and no balance. Piasa despaired for many seasons and finally came to rest beneath the last remaining Wise Tree. The fade had come and the leaves had turned yellow and were beginning to shudder from the branches. As the leaves fell, she watched them drift to the ground where they would decay and be gone, replaced in the new season."

"Decay, decay, to turn into new life."

"Piasa shot into the sky, dazzled with elation and joy. The solution! A great meeting was called, and all the creatures of her creation flooded in from near and far. She stood along the great shoreline so that all the creatures of the water and land could hear her speak, and she said:

'My great and plentiful creatures, you bring me such joy and such sorrow. I have granted you great gifts of flight, of sprinting, of swimming, and of jumping. But all is not well. To live for always means to take for always. There must come an end.'"

"An end to a beginning, a beginning's end."

"Thus Piasa created death for all creatures. Some became killers, with claws and teeth, some became clever Hums, who invented many ways to care for *and* kill creatures. But they too would die, returning to the soil to grow as new life for the creatures they had once killed. Eternal life could not be the way and some creatures had long lives, some had short lives, but all shared one fate."

Chickory shivered. The sun had gone, replaced by strong moonlight. She joined in the next chorus, *"To the sky with Piasa, to the sky we return home."*

They all sat in silence. Chickory's anxious fear had quieted with the story, quieted as it always did with the familiar telling of Piasa and the way all creatures were expected to live their lives.

Tucker, who had drifted off to sleep, twitched and woke, his ears erect. The ruff of fur around his neck bristled and he snuffled the air.

"What is it?" Chickory asked.

"Is it Hums? Please, no," Daisy peeped.

Chickory strained to hear, but only silence surrounded them.

Tucker whined, deep in his throat. "No, it is the others." He didn't sound afraid.

Fayne rose and peered up the embankment. "The others? Others who?" Then she let out a shrill squawk and scurried out of the ditch and onto the road. "Georgia! Robert!"

Chickory couldn't breathe. How could it be? How was it possible? Joyous hope surged through every feathertip and she flung herself up the embankment after Fayne.

There, illuminated in the light of the heavy moon, Georgia and Robert stood. The others followed behind her, but Chickory couldn't move or speak.

"Oh, Piasa, what horror!" Woodfawn cried.

Robert's once beautiful gleaming collar of emerald feathers looked black. Part of his red wattle had been torn from his neck and blood stained his fine breast and crusted his stalks. He held his head high, but his body looked stiff and most of his long arching tail feathers were gone.

Georgia did not look much better. On her back, feathers had been ripped away, leaving a large patch of the pale skin underneath. Several of her wing feathers stuck out at odd angles, matted together with blood. She slouched and lifted her left foot several times, one of the toes limp and broken.

They all stood in silence, as though unsure they were seeing each other. Then, without words, Chickory ran to them and the silence swelled into a chorus of clucks, coos, and happy peeps. The others surged forward too. Woodfawn preened Georgia and smoothed out her matted feathers as she tutted like a mother hen.

Daisy cried, "Oh, Robert, oh, oh, oh!" Dolly and Daisy both fell upon him, crooning sadly as they inspected his wounds.

Chickory's breast pulsed with such joy it hurt. They were a flock once more, reunited and whole. "Oh, Fayne, isn't it wonderful?" She glanced back.

Fayne stood apart from them. Her immediate animation, her initial excitement, had vanished.

Tucker staggered out of the ditch with a pained whimper, but limped to Robert and Georgia and sniffed them all over. Georgia squealed and cowered but Tucker licked her head until she quieted.

Daisy gazed past them, down the road. "But where's—where's Rosie? Lacey?"

A cold and heavy silence settled over them. Their absence was a certain truth, for Robert would have never left them behind.

Tucker panted heavily. "We should go back. It's not safe here." He whimpered and gazed out into the darkness.

They all moved as one feathery creature and slid back down through the thorny brush and into the ditch again. Tucker yelped as he struggled through the spiked branches and once at the bottom, he immediately laid down again. They all nestled together in the curve of his belly and their assembly formed a halo of warmth, even with the damp ground beneath them. Robert and Georgia were bustled into the middle so they could be reached by soothing beaks. They all took turns stroking their bent and broken feathers and settled them piece by piece. Well, all but for Fayne, though she had never been a social groomer and it was not unusual. She simply stared at Robert and her yellow eyes looked almost empty, as though she were just a feathery stone.

"We could not dare to—I had thought we had lost you all," said Robert. His voice, once smooth and sultry, trembled and cracked. "The Hums. They've all gone mad, haven't they?"

Georgia let out a thin warble of terror at the mention and she tucked her head beneath Robert's wing.

Chickory hesitated and finally said, "Sickness has changed living for the Hums and for all of us. Our only hope is to press on to the valley and hope for safety there."

Everyone looked at Fayne but she said nothing.

"The valley. Such joy to see that day, but I admit, I'm afraid of what the next day will bring us. This world is a terrible one." Robert shivered even with the warmth of the flock surrounding him. "We should have gone with you, Fayne. I'm sorry."

"There is no choice. We go or die in the attempt," said Fayne, as though she had not heard him.

A cold certainty squeezed Chickory's throat. "Fayne. I think it is time for you to tell us. To tell us, well, anything you know. There won't be a better opportunity and we've been reunited; a sure sign of hope. Hope is what we need." Mingled with her certainty was fear of what Fayne might say. Her answers might confirm the worst: that she didn't know anything more than what her dreams told her, that the valley might not even be a real place.

Fayne tilted her beak toward the distant moon, as though the light soothed. "You will not like the answers. But yes, answers are wanted, though I am uncertain as to whether it has any benefit for you all."

The words prickled through Chickory. Fayne sounded strong, certain.

"Just tell us," said Woodfawn, but her tone sounded uncertain, not hostile.

Fayne turned and stared straight at Woodfawn.

"Well, we will all probably die," she said.

21 | Knowing Too Much

"If your mind settles on uneasy things, questions with no answer,
remember the warmth of the roost, the love of the nest, and
the Egg Song. These truths will soothe any troubled breast."

- In Dark and In Light, Third Year, Third Clutch

Woodfawn's eyes bulged. "Die? What do you mean, *die*? Explain yourself, monster bird!"

Chickory trembled. This was worse than she had imagined, worse than the fearful whispers in her mind. Fayne needed to comfort them, reassure them, *convince* them there was more to live for and that this terrifying journey would lead to safety and a warm nest. Not more talk of their probable death.

Fayne shrank back against Tucker, as though trying to disappear within his matted fur.

This was Chickory's friend, not a… not a *monster bird*, no matter what Woodfawn said. She ruffled her wings and bobbed her head. "Explain that. What do you mean, we will probably, um, die?"

"The papers, you remember? At the shopping center." Fayne stopped.

Everyone stared at her blankly.

"The store? With the hunters?"

Woodfawn bristled. "Yes, yes, what of it?"

"The papers tell of a virus, a form of influenza, likely a mutation of a common one. Highly contagious."

"Influ… Con-tay.." Daisy cocked her head.

"Make sense, you damn horror!" Woodfawn tried to snap at Fayne but couldn't reach her.

Fayne faltered and her wide eyes shone with uncertainty.

Chickory forced her trembling beak to preen Fayne's neck feathers. "Go on, it's all right. Just explain a little more."

"The mouth sickness as we've called it, though really that's an oversimplific—" Fayne cleared her throat and looked away from Woodfawn. "Anyway, something happened to the humans and caused all this. Lady died from it. So did many others. The birds we saw in that paper, they are not us, but they were. They represented examples of us, of birds like us."

Woodfawn clicked her beak irritably. "Yes, yes, like seeing one sparrow and knowing all of them must look mostly the same."

"Yes, that. Well. So, the humans now seek us out and are systematically destroying us," Fayne said.

"Syst—em—a—ti—l… what?" Daisy tried to speak the words but stopped.

"They want to kill all of us. Every single bird," Fayne said.

Daisy panted nervously. "But why? What have *we* done? Any of us?"

Fayne sounded weak and tired, as though she bore an injury none of them could see. "It is difficult to explain. Some of us got sick and then we got better, but the sickness passed on to the humans. A lot of them are dead and those red marks? On the doors? That is a sign of the disease and the houses that were checked for the dead."

Confusion buzzed inside Chickory's head. "What about the unliving still walking around?"

"They must have come from this sickness, and the rest of the living humans will seek us out and destroy us. I think most of us have already been killed."

"We've hardly seen a single bird," Daisy peeped.

"Only a crow, but that was back at the farm, and smaller sparrows and such. Oh, and that rooster," Chickory said. It was true, there had hardly been any birds, even with all the farm land they had traveled. No chickens. No ducks. No fancy birds. Not even sky birds, except for the hoot of a moon bird. "They've really… killed them all?"

"Piasa instructs all creatures to 'maintain the balance, flex the wing.' Killing in such ways violates *everything*. Piasa would not allow this to happen!" Woodfawn declared.

"Piasa has nothing to do with it," Fayne said.

No one looked at her or said anything for a while. Singing bugs chirped in the tall grass. A squeaking bat swooped overhead. Chickory wondered whether she should ask about *quiet*, the strange way the unliving had calmed and allowed them to pass, but she mustn't ask. If they thought her a monster bird already, what would happen to them if that were true?

Fayne finally sighed. "They think we brought the sickness to them, that we are to blame."

Chickory ignored the buzz in her mind that begged her to be silent. "And are we?"

Fayne did not answer immediately and when she finally did, pain flickered in her eyes. "It is unclear, but I, well—I do not think *you* did."

Familiar fear resurfaced inside Chickory. "What will happen to us?"

"We *are* headed to the valley. The one I have seen." Fayne bobbed her head and her words sounded stronger, more certain. "We may die in the attempt but there is no other—"

"Or we will *survive* and make new nests, lay eggs, continue on." Chickory glared at Fayne, wishing she could peck sense into her addled head. "We must be careful, though."

"Yes. I believe those hunters are still tracking us."

Chickory sighed. Fayne did not inspire hope in any form.

Georgia let out an anguished groan. Robert cooed and nuzzled her neck.

"But it is a long journey still," Fayne continued. "Our survival depends on our ability to adapt. We have to think less like common birds and more like… well, like humans actually. We have to put aside petty beliefs," Fayne said and she stared at Woodfawn.

"'And those lost to the ways of the killer, the savage forgetting— will die a forever death,'" Woodfawn hissed. "That is not *petty*, that's the truth. Even you, monstrous as you are, are *Piasa's* creation. You're a cracked egg if you ignore that!"

Robert lifted his head and puffed out his breast as he had done so many times on the farm. "This has been a long night. Let's settle our feathers and sleep. I can't think a single new thought," he said. His voice sounded frightfully shaky and it was only this, the sound of his weakened voice, the reminder of the permanent sacrifice that had been made—of Rosie, of Lacey—that forced them all into silence. The warmth and excitement from the Ninith and at finding Robert and Georgia, vanished.

Chickory shivered. *We are all going to die.* Was that Piasa as well?

***

Chickory dreamed:

She stood in the middle of a cornfield with Fayne and the tall green stalks blotted out the sky. A choppy wind whistled through the leaves. *Had she been here before?* A loud boom clapped overhead and the ground rumbled with the growl that followed. A sky stinger leapt across the thick breast of Piasa's feath—no, they were *clouds.* Fayne had said that.

"Fayne, where are the others? We must find them!" The wind whipped her words away.

Fayne stood in dark shadow and made no sign she had heard her at all.

The wind howled and clawed through Chickory's feathers. The stalks bent and the leaves ripped away like stinging rain. Her chest heaved with fear as her claws slid against the ground, but Fayne still did not move, seeming unruffled, unaffected by the storm.

"Help me, please, help!" Chickory beat her wings against the terrible shrieking wind.

(*I am helping you*)

The voice rang clearly in her mind, Fayne's voice, amplified louder than the storm itself.

"Then move! Help me find the others!"

(*It is too late. The others blew (away, away, away) birds in the wind*)

"No! No, it's not too late! Come with me, we can go find them and lead them to safety! The valley!" The wind sucked at the curve of her wings and almost knocked her off the ground.

(*Don't you know already?*)

"Why won't you help me?" Anger mingled with her terror at being blown away. For deep inside she knew she must not allow that to happen. This was no sun season storm, the sucking force was a death worm of the sky—*had she been here before?* The cloud spiraled out of the gray clouds and rooted itself at the far end of the field.

A trembling, crying voice rose over the sound of the wind, "the Hums hummed up from the world below – ooah ooah, ooah ooah."

(*You already know*) Fayne's words felt angry and insistent as they clattered through Chickory's mind.

Chickory staggered against the wind.

(*Don't you already know?*)

"Take my seed, spread it forth, take my people, spread them forth." The invisible voice fragmented and became many.

Chickory could not speak, the wind pressed against her breast and made it impossible to breathe. Pressure thrummed inside her ears.

(*Know what?*) She answered in her mind, though how, she didn't know.

"Blades of grass, blood of the flesh!"

(*Where the others are*)

Desperation pulsed up Chickory's throat like hot flame. (*Where are they, Fayne? Where have they all gone? Come with me*)

"One feeds the other to feed the other to feed another," the voices continued chanting.

Fayne took a step toward her. Chickory squawked and almost leapt into the wind, into the storm, letting it rip her far away from this creature.

Because Fayne was not Fayne.

Hardly a bird at all.

Hollows glistened where eyes had once been, their yellow gleam pecked away. Blood stained her feathers, her stalks torn and bleeding where the scaly skin peeled away like tree bark.

Unliving, unliving, she is DEAD.

Fayne took another step closer and she smelled of sickness, smelled of Lady, smelled of all the unliving horrors.

Fayne opened her beak and whistled. (*We are all dead here*)

She sprang, unfurling her wings and extending her claws. Chickory ducked and flattened herself against the damp soil. Claws raked her back. Fayne's body whipped away in the screeching fury of the pounding wind, becoming a mere dark speck of feathers. She disappeared inside the pulsing death worm cloud.

The storm gave a final deafening roar.

Then, abrupt and terrifying, the dark clouds loosened and became mist. The dark gray turned to white and the clouds raced away across the blue backdrop, leaving Chickory standing in bright sunshine.

The knot inside her breast pounded. Everything smelled of fresh new season rain. No smell of death, no sickness at all.

A soft buzz of voices whispered above, "Piasa, Piasa – shield us wings of Just."

Chickory jerked awake and the last fading notes still rang inside her head. For a moment, she could not remember where she was. Darkness pressed in on her, hadn't there been sunshine? The soft sounds of the breathing, snoozing bodies tucked against her slowly brought her back. The others slept like stones, Tucker's body still curled around their flock in a protective embrace. His hot breath exhaled over her, smelling sour and familiar, a comfort in the night. At the edge, Fayne also slept and her wings faintly twitched. Chickory shivered and hoped the storm had not found her as well.

22 | Journeys

"Trust none but the musk of the earth's soil,
the rise of the everlasting sun, and the strength of Piasa's grace…
and perhaps the swell of sun season apples and delicious corn."

- Practical Wisdom, Third Clutch, Fourth Year

Sunrise filtered through the low clouds and droplets of dew shimmered in the early pink light. The landscape looked refreshed and new, but Chickory merely grunted at the sight.

Waking up in a ditch meant the journey was still not over, they still had not reached the valley, and the coming day was sure to be just as horrifying as all the rest. How simple it would be to be eaten by a moon bird or cunning fox while in quiet slumber. Maybe she would return as a killer in her next life or simply return to the soil and become grass and trees, as Piasa promised.

The whole night had been filled with nightmares and Chickory could not shake the prickling sense of something—no, *someone* else inside the dream. She shivered.

Robert struggled to rise and he stiffly fluffed his feathers in the cold air. There would be no morning crow, not when the unliving might hear or the hunters might follow. Not today and maybe not ever.

"Still as pines and the sunrise half gone," came a peppery voice from atop the embankment.

Chickory peered up the steep slope. There stood the smallest rooster she had ever seen. In fact, it looked just like the tiny rooster they had left behind in a barn, in a memory that felt so long ago. But here he stood, his plumage ruffled with distress and poor temper.

"You followed us," Chickory said. She rose on shaky stalks, which ached from the cold ground and cramped ditch.

He eyed them beadily. "I followed to see whether you all had sense in your heads. Now I wonder whether I've lost my sense as well. What are you all doing down there?"

"Resting," snapped Woodfawn. "Not all of us have had a nice barn to hide in."

"Shame, I suppose, but you'd best be up. Hums are on the prowl," he said.

Dolly and Daisy jerked upright and their feathers bristled with fear. Tucker's fur ruffled in an angry ridge down his back and he growled deep in his broad chest as he struggled to his paws. He let out a sharp whine of pain and staggered up onto the road. Chickory followed, amazed at his speed and determination, even with the large scabbing wound on his shoulder.

He scanned the surroundings and snuffled the air, his battered nose twitching.

"I passed them around the last bend. Got ahead of them, looking for you," the rooster said. He looked as though he regretted having found them.

"Well, it's good of you to pass on the warning." Chickory called down to the others, "come on, we've got to get moving."

The others struggled up the steep muddy slope and gathered in the middle of the road. Robert and Georgia shuffled, but neither complained.

Fayne strutted away without giving any of them a second glance. "We will continue heading east."

"What is east?" The little rooster followed, as though he'd been with them all along.

Fayne glowered at him. "And who are you?"

"Name's Pip. Stupid name, of course. Hums come up with the stupidest things, naming anything that moves, slapping together sounds like it matters at all to any of us. Hah, but no matter to that!" he chattered.

He continued this way for quite some time.

They all shuffled forward, still bleary from lack of good sleep, but Fayne's pace increased until she was quite ahead of them. Woodfawn grumbled as she tried to keep up. The pace did not allow for foraging and Chickory's stomach ached. Did Fayne's stomach growl as theirs did? Did she feel anything at all?

The sun crossed the sky and the tall trees fell away, revealing stretches of meadows and tall grasses. The wind picked up and whispered news from faraway places, most of which only Tucker could decipher.

"Hums, they smell worn, not at all like the bad-soapy smell. They still have the bang stick though, but they're far off. Don't think the bang stick can reach us this far," Tucker whimpered and sounded unsure. He drew great drafts of air into the wet passages of his nose, but it also kicked up dust and he sneezed ferociously.

Houses reappeared alongside the road and they passed a large double house with a small front yard dusted with fluffy seed heads and sprightly yellow flowers. A red mark crossed the front door and windows.

"They condemned this place and left the sick inside," Fayne said, though no one had asked.

The smell also returned on the wind, the smell of death and the undertone of sickened flesh. Chickory knew what must be behind the boarded-up doors. Here was an entire settlement of the fallen and forgotten, like Lady, who had died alone inside her house. More fortunate than most because she had Tucker at her side. All the houses that stretched down the sides of the road had bright red signs on their doors.

A growl and bang disrupted the quiet.

"Oh, oh, oh! It's horrible!" Georgia cowered low on the ground.

"An unliving, just there," said Fayne. "It is trapped inside though."

In the window of one of the houses moved a shadow and a prickle of recognition Chickory could not quite place, stirred in her memory. The unliving, a female, maybe, smeared its palms against the window and they could hear its muffled groan. Streaks of blood and mucous on the glass made it hard to see for certain, but it did seem trapped.

In addition to the red slash marks, red words were scrawled across the front of all the houses they passed.

Chickory cocked her head and tried to understand the strange lines and shapes. "What do they say?"

Fayne didn't respond and Chickory hurried until she walked side by side with her. She glanced at the others but they were searching for specks of seeds and bugs. "I know you know."

"Do you truly want all these answers? It might not be best."

"Maybe not, but, well, someone must, yes? You can't be the only one. What if, well, what if something happened to you?"

"The words are warnings. This entire settlement was overrun and abandoned. They cleared some of the houses but eventually, gave up. Most of these houses have unliving inside."

"Will any of them return? To, you know, look for the others? They can't have all just left them behind. I know they're dead but… do Hums have no Mourning Call?" No one had come for the dead boy, the child lying dead against the farm fence, but the young, even among Hums, were not quickly forgotten.

"No. These things are gone to them already. I do not believe they still consider them to be a part of them. Not anymore."

Dolly and Daisy bravely lingered along the side of the road and attempted to peck at a few stray blades of grass as they traveled, but Chickory had no appetite. The street of houses filled with the unliving made her feel small inside, as though she were being crushed between the palms of the sky. Her spine prickled with unease. There was nothing to fear from death, according to stories of Piasa, but this was not the way of death as foretold. As caretakers cared for creatures, the creatures would then share their bodies with the caretaker. Someday the caretaker would become the very earth that sustained the creatures. This exchange of life promised a complete way of living and the thought that Piasa no longer guided the way felt surely impossible. But surrounded by proof made such thoughts hard to ignore.

"Here! Look here!" Daisy cried.

Dolly frantically scurried back and forth, snapping up a line of ants as they crossed the wide road. The others gathered, a flustered mass of snapping beaks and excited chirps. Chickory ate a few at the edges and gazed at a crack in the middle of the black surface. It looked very much like she felt, like her insides had been replaced with a large rocky hole.

"Come on, come on, we cannot stop here," Fayne said.

Woodfawn slashed Fayne with one of her clawed feet. "Shut up, monster bird."

146

Fayne waited alongside the road for a moment and then walked away, the distance between them growing wider. Chickory hurried after Fayne and one by one, the others abandoned the ants and followed. Woodfawn came last, though she growled and squawked with outrage.

The houses eventually faded into a larger swarm of buildings, larger than the houses but smaller than the store had been. The wide roads had been blocked off with wood and the ground was covered with crumpled paper and gleaming cans. A strong pungent smell, like rotting grain, wafted up from the warm surface of the road.

"Smells like beer," Pip chirped.

"What is beer?" Chickory asked.

"A Hum drink, like long aged pond water but they use plants to make it. My Hums used to give the leftovers to the cows. They loved it more than most, better than apples during the fade. Weren't all too bad, tried it myself a few times. That's the smell though. You know how Hums get, never satisfied with nothing plain, love mucking things up, changing around—"

"Yes, well, keep moving," Fayne interrupted and she looked cross.

The strange bitter aroma of beer surrounded them, but there was no scent of any other food.

They passed by large metal beasts, made by Hums long gone from this place. Each was covered with colored light bulbs, like the twinkling magic of Lady's lights in the cold season. *Had she been here before?* Though she had never cared much about the eccentricities of Hums, this place looked frightening and very familiar.

At the far end of the street stood a large tent. The sides were stained and watery tracks of dirt smeared the fabric; there were large rips in the swooped top. The torn edges shivered in the breeze, as though alive with some enigmatic beating pulse.

"I think there are Hums in there." A strange urge pulled Chickory towards it.

Fayne blocked her path. "No, Chickory." She bristled and her fluffed feathers make her look larger and fiercer than ever. "There is nothing there, nothing at all. It is gone."

Georgia peeped and they all drew closer together, instinct making them wary of this strange place.

"Come on, just, go on." Fayne directed them away.

Chickory glanced back at the tent. A child stood at the entrance, blood soaking through the front of its white gown. Blonde hair rippled around its head like a plume of white feathers.

"There's a—a—a Hum! A child!" But when she turned back to look, to see it again, the child was gone.

Fayne scampered to Chickory's side and scanned the deserted landscape.

"I—oh, I'm sorry, I was sure I saw—"

"Silence plays tricks on the mind, rattles the heart," Fayne whispered. "Let us press on."

The others didn't meet Chickory's distracted gaze and she buzzed with anger at herself. She had let fear best her sensibility, allowed herself to be addled by stress and unease.

A strange buzz spread through each feathertip.

Tucker gave a low growl, then a soft huff of suspicion. "Something. There."

Fayne glanced back and her eyes widened. She shot into the air. "Chickory!"

The child stepped out from behind a tangle of overgrown brush and its hands closed around Chickory's sides, pinning her wings. Sharp hungry fingers clawed through her feathers.

"Oh, oh! Help!" squawked Chickory. She gazed up into the yellowed eyes and the child's breath washed over her head as the it brought her to its wet oozing mouth.

"Bird, no!" Tucker slammed against the child and knocked her to the ground.

The unliving released Chickory and grabbed handfuls of Tucker's fur. He yowled in pain as he reared and twisted in its grip, trying to get away.

"Here, no, here!" Chickory ran alongside the unliving child, just out of reach.

It turned toward her and lunged, squirming on the ground like a drowning worm.

Tucker regained his paws. "Run, run away birds! I can't— can't—" He limped heavily, barely able to use his front leg at all. The shoulder wound had opened again and it spattered the road with a dappled trail of blood.

Chickory scurried after him, but the child staggered to its feet and followed close behind. It extended its hands toward Tucker again.

"You must run!" Chickory screeched at Tucker, flapping her

wings. "Go, go, go!"

Tucker gave an anguished howl and his three good legs churned in unison until he managed an awkward gallop, out of reach.

The others fled ahead of them and the child still followed.

"We can't keep this up!" Chickory called to Fayne.

"We must hide, leave its sight!" Fayne gasped.

A large black crow swooped off the top of one of the buildings. "Stupids! Found the stupids again," he cawed down at them.

"Help us!" Chickory squawked desperately, but knew it would not, it would fly away, cruel and unfeeling.

Instead, the crow tilted his wings and dove down over the head of the unliving child, nearly grazing its matted hair with his claws.

The unliving grunted and swiped at it but the crow was quick. He circled around and swooped again, cawing with glee, before landing on the ground near the child. It turned and immediately lurched after the large black bird, snarling and snapping its hungry mouth.

"Go on, stupids! Long way to go yet! The valley awaits." The crow hopped and flapped, staying just out of reach. "Hah! Stupids human, stupids, stupids!" he crowed with glee as the child howled with rage.

"It's just a game," Chickory said, awed by the crow's lunacy.

"Then let it have its play!" Fayne ran down a smaller road and they all hurried after her. The child disappeared from view, still following the cackling crow.

Pip flapped his wings and came alongside Fayne. "Ahem! Hate to intrude on our cheery escape, but there's a small farm close by that might do for a look. Had some friends holed up there, fat sparrows, just in the rafters of the barn, been chattering about it, got loads of food stuffs it seems. I lived there as a young cock, before being brought to my other place—"

"Will you just go on?!" Fayne screeched at him.

"Yes, right! This way!" he crowed. He led the way, continuing to chatter as they went. "It's possible, with so much sickness around here, the Hums fled this part of the town and left things behind. Messy things they are, leaving stuff all about."

"Just lead the way," Robert said.

Pip glanced back at him, and they regarded each other. They had settled into an easy truce, uncommon between two roosters, but as tiny as Pip was, it was hardly worth pursuing for either of them.

Pip hopped off the road and scampered through the backyard of a particularly large house. Aggressive vines strangled the branches of a row of hedges. A miniature roar horse sat on the grass, forgotten, and in the corner of the yard was a box of soft soil that smelled strongly of cats.

"Cats," whispered Georgia and she shivered. A nasty cat had snagged her last sun season. Robert had harassed and distracted the cat long enough for Tucker to come running, but it had been a terrifying brush with death.

They shuffled closer together. Chickory's entire body thrummed with the pulse of her heart, the twist of her innards, but Tucker snuffled the air and snorted.

"Never mind the cats. Tucker won't be letting any get the jump on us, will you?" said Woodfawn.

Tucker wagged his matted tail in reply.

"Not far now," chirped Pip, hopping along as though oblivious to the eerie state of the abandoned houses and terrible smell of cat. The rest straggled after him, Tucker still limping.

A long fence traveled along the back of the yards and Pip followed it until he reached a small opening between two loose boards. He ducked through it and disappeared. The hole was too small to enter together and so they went one by one through the hole.

Tucker whined deep in his throat. "I'll have to go around. I'll be on the other side," he said to Chickory.

"Right. Mind yourself, we'll see you there," she said and stepped through the fence.

On the other side was a large yard, larger than most of the houses they had wandered through past. Though hardly a farm, there were a few empty rabbit coops along the far side.

"Look! Oh, my, just look at it," cooed Daisy.

A small chicken coop with a fenced yard lay barren in the opposite corner. The wire had been torn from its posts and feathers littered the ground, the only remaining sign of the birds that had once lived there.

Fayne eyed the high edge of the fence. "Seems empty enough," she said. "Where is this food you mentioned?"

"Should be just along here, they have a small building where they keep supplies, foods, and such. What fun I had sneaking in when I was just a puff of feathers," he said as he hopped across the lawn.

Dolly jerked at the swoop of a shadow, which turned out to be a passing butterfly. Woodfawn stalked it to a nearby flower and ripped it off its stem, swallowing the small blossom as well. Then they all gathered and followed Pip around the corner of the house.

"Here's the shed. Got all sorts of stuff," Pip said.

The small building appeared to be secure, the door still right in its frame.

Robert cocked his head. "How are we supposed to get inside?"

"Waste of nonsense, this feather head," Woodfawn hissed. "There's no way inside for a bird!"

Chickory gazed up at its good windows and shining paint.

Pip gave a chirpy chuckle. "Maybe not for a stout bird such as yourselves! But there's always tiny hidey-holes if you know where to look. Rats usually do, so I'll go first if you don't mind. Might know them from when I was around here."

Chickory shuddered as she remembered their own farm rats. Rats had little to fear from starvation.

Pip hopped around the exterior of the shed and cocked his head. "Aha! Be back in a wag."

They waited in silence. Chickory watched a slow thin white line cross the clear blue sky, like a soft slow-squish of cloud.

"What a sorry lot you find yourself in company with," said a gravelly voice.

In the windowsill of the shed squatted a large fat rat with a round face, nothing like the scrappy rats they had back home. It grinned and its chubby cheeks formed bulbs of well-fed flesh.

"They've had a hard road, they have. No good sense to hide. They're headed off to some godforsaken valley if you can believe it," said Pip, reappearing from behind the shed. "Still, times are changing, my barn was pecked over thoroughly and food is hard to find on the run. My friend Pappy here has obliged to share some of their rations."

Woodfawn snorted. "Rations? Seems they've had nothing short of feasting."

"It's very gracious of you, Pappy," Chickory said.

"Us wild things have got to stick together we do. People have lost their way," Pappy said. "Just last week, a few of us gone missing and come to find they're hunting us. Us! Eating us like common cattle, if you'll excuse the expression. Yes, the world is mighty strange."

"Then the good that can come of this must be our cooperation," said Fayne.

"Yes, yes, let's not waste more time with idle talk," said Pappy and he wiggled his small ears. "Swing forward!"

A small click came from the shed and in one smooth motion the door swung open, revealing a couple equally fat rats inside. They grinned and flashed their yellow incisors.

Nestled in the squat shed were tall stacks of rabbit pellets, dried corn kernels, and oily black seeds. The bounty spilled forth from chewed holes in the bags, the ground speckled with the delicious assortment of food.

"Oh, Piasa blesses!" squawked Woodfawn as she rushed inside.

Chickory could not move quickly enough as she tried to snap up every tiny speck of grain, any small mote of corn matter, greedily devouring all she could reach. The flock ate in a cheery way and the shed was full of soft warbles of happiness. Strength and warmth spread through Chickory as she ate, her stomach heavy as she stuffed it beyond its withered shape.

"Can't say there's a better sight. Happy creatures in happy feed," said Pappy, as he stuffed a knob of dried yellow corn in his mouth.

In the distance, they heard the chattering bark of a dog and for a few moments they ignored it, overwhelmed by food and good fortune.

Fayne jerked upright. "Tucker?"

Dolly and Daisy continued to peck away, still oblivious to the commotion taking place outside the fence of the house.

"Eh? What's that?" Pappy looked up and his squinted rat face distorted in a strange mismatch of glee and horror. Chickory turned to see, but was knocked back as feathery bodies collided against her.

"Run, oh, oh, oh, myyyy!" Dolly frantically pushed Chickory back toward the sacks of grain, trying to escape the Hum that towered in the doorway of the shed.

The Hum's mouth slapped and formed words. Not unliving, but an old one like Lady. In his hand, he held an empty sack.

Fayne shrieked and flew forward, extending her claws and snapping with her beak, but with one quick motion the Hum snatched Fayne from the air. His experienced fingers crushed her legs together and he twirled her until she slackened with dizziness.

"Run, attack, do something!" squawked Fayne as he stuffed her into his sack.

"Ladies, g-g-good fortune to you," squeaked Pappy. He squeezed through a small hole in the wall and disappeared.

For a moment, they all stared at one another. Then chaos erupted, as the flock screeched in unison. Feathers scattered the ground and dust swirled. Though the Hum was old, he still had speed and agility. He shut the door behind him and in quick succession snatched each one of them up, stuffing them into the dark cavern of the sack he carried.

"No, no, no!" crowed Robert, as he was rudely shoved inside.

Chickory evaded him until the end and slashed forward with her claws and beak as best she could. But within moments, the fight had ended.

The flock had lost.

23 | Warm Nests

"The blessed home of all birds, and especially chickens,
is the nest. No place is warmer or more secure than the
soft downy breast of mother hen."

- *Practical Wisdom,* for Chicks and Hatchlings

Fayne? Fayne, can you hear me?" Chickory whispered as she writhed against unseen feathery bodies. Her right wing flexed painfully beneath her and she couldn't feel her left wing at all. "Stop! Just stop moving!"

A panicked silence fell and the bodies stopped twisting. Chickory focused on the rapid breathing of their collective and tried to regain control of her whirling mind. The bag smelled of hay and dust.

"I hear you," came Fayne's muffled reply. She sounded far away, towards the bottom of their squirming mass.

The bag swung back and forth as footsteps thudded below them.

"Where is he taking us?" Woodfawn asked from somewhere in the dark.

"Likely to eat us, 'course," Pip squeaked.

"Best we can do is be calm." Chickory tried to slide her wings free and squirmed with the painful twist of her legs.

The bag plummeted to the ground. Their bodies clashed painfully and light poured over them as the mouth of the sack opened.

"Fly, fly, go if you can!" cried Chickory.

Together they pushed forward, a single feathered creature fighting for freedom. The bag fell away and they stumbled out into the bright light. Dolly shot into the air and collided with the wire draped across the sky.

"We're trapped, trapped!" she cackled as she struggled against the wire.

The Hum stood on the other side of the fence, grinning down at them. His nose was round and bulbous and his cheeks bright red. Chickory shuddered.

"We are inside the chicken run," said Fayne, looking around.

Feathers marked the ground and the wire that had been torn from its posts had been repaired, likely by the Hum who stood over them. How foolish they had been, blinded by the comfort of food. The run looked well-made and secure. Chickory's stomach twisted with fear. None of them had the strength or forward-most poll—what had Fayne called them? —*pollicals* to bend wire and splinter wood beams.

Fayne tilted her head as though listening. "Where is Tucker?"

"He had gone around to meet us," said Woodfawn. "You think the damned creature left us? Sure he did, as he should, damned dog, free as a lark in the new season. Leaving us here, we should have known, cursed foul thing he is." She stalked back and forth across the small enclosed yard and her feathers bristled with rage.

Dolly and Daisy huddled together and clucked mournfully. "P-poor Tucker. Maybe the Hum killed him."

The Hum rubbed his hands together and hummed words that Chickory couldn't understand.

"What's he saying?" she asked Fayne.

"He is happy we are here. He does not want to kill us all. I think he wants us to lay eggs," said Fayne.

The Hum watched them for a few moments and then retreated to the porch of the house. He drew a strange curved thing from the front of his gown and suckled the white tip as he lowered a burning flame into the bulbed end. A musky pungent smell filled the air.

"Lay eggs?" trilled Woodfawn. "He's bound to eat us, surely. None of us have laid an egg in—well—in quite some time! Running around like fool birds, no roosts, no coop. Ridiculous!"

"Then he has made quite fine nests just for eating birds," Robert said as he emerged from the small coop at the end of the run. "I think Fayne is right, he intends to steward us here and eat our eggs as Lady did. It would last far longer than eating us one by one, especially in our poor condition."

"Well, I shall not be laying any eggs for such a brute," said Woodfawn.

"I don't think any of us should plan on staying. It would be a long while before any of us could prepare nests," said Chickory. "Soon Tucker will come and we should be prepared for any opportunity to go."

Georgia slumped to the ground. "Do you really think he would return? What kind of dog thinks of anything other than his belly and warm scratches behind his ear." She swayed her head like a chick dazed by a high fall.

Chickory paced the length of the wire and worry pulsated through her feathers. "Tucker will return for us. He would do the Lady's bidding. And we are her flock. His flock now, a family, no matter how strange," she said.

"What a family we be," said Fayne quietly.

***

The next sunrise, they were roused by the sound of scraping wire and the Hum who clicked at them and hummed. He sounded happy, as Lady had when she greeted them.

"He's brought us food," peeped Dolly as she watched him from between the wooden slats of the coop.

"Hurry, let's eat. We'll need all the strength we can scratch up," said Chickory.

They waited until the Hum disappeared back inside the house before leaving the warm, dry coop. Though they had worried through the night, waiting for some sign of Tucker, eventually exhaustion had overtaken them and they had fallen into a restful slumber. Now hunger drove them forward and they fell upon the corn and pellets. The Hum had provided a magnificent spread of food and they ate until their stomachs ached and they could eat no more.

Robert strutted alongside Chickory and scratched in the grass with her. "Georgia didn't join us last night."

In the corner of the run, Georgia remained squatted on the ground. Beside her Dolly preened her feathers.

"No, she insisted on staying where she was. Think she's in shock, poor bird," Chickory said. "It's been a hard journey. Awful, really, in every way, and, well, Georgia has always been, um…"

"Yes. She has," Robert said. He lifted his beak and gazed at where she sat with Dolly. "You know, I never did thank you. For speaking up and bringing the rest along with you and Fayne. I don't know that any of them would have gone without you. How did you do it?"

Chickory didn't answer for a moment and nibbled a few blades of the tough grass that grew in the run.

Finally she said, "I'm not sure why I followed. It's just *something*. She's always been this way, always right about the strangest things. Remember the terrible storm the first cold season? We were just fluffs of feathers but even then, she saw it coming, had us hiding like loons. But she was right."

"Yes, she has seen before. I won't deny it, she frightens me some, frightens us all, I know. Are you sure this is the right thing to do? If what she says is true, and the Hum intends to feed us and shelter us, is it so wrong to wish for that?" He gave a small peep of dismay. "Or am I just a weak fool bird, wishing for the past? Can you tell me?"

Chickory didn't know how to answer him. Robert had never shared his innermost thoughts with her, not like this. Never had he expressed fear or doubt. Though they had shared in courtships and were companions for these many seasons, she knew him only as their rooster. Perhaps she had taken that for granted. Really, only Fayne had ever confided in her the strangeness of her inner mind. It wasn't really something you talked about with others. Some had eccentric ways, but it wasn't entirely normal. There had been an old hen, Engrid, who loved to tell the most fantastical lies. There were things like that, but between roosters and hens it was almost never heard of at all. And Robert had long harbored a strong preference for the other hens, not so much Chickory and Fayne, though he never neglected any of them. Really, he had a gentle, favorable nature.

"Things are different now, yes. Everything is. But, well, you're back with us and we've got to press on and do what we can. I don't know if we should stay or go. We might not even be given the choice, especially if Tucker doesn't come back." Sadness bloomed at the thought of that. "But we need you. All of us, we need you and every one of us needs each other. Or we won't make it."

"You're right. Of course, you are. It's hard to know what we are meant to do. I—I failed you all. No, now, don't look at me like that, I know I did. I should have listened. Should have been a better bird."

"None of that matters anymore. You can be a better bird now. We all can."

He bobbed his head in a silent agreement and they scratched together again, though Chickory really couldn't eat another scrap. So she turned over a pebble and examined the dirt underneath. No worms, but maybe the next sunrise.

Robert stopped. "Can we trust her?"

Cold fear flushed through Chickory's feathertips because she knew the answer to that and did not want to share it.

"There's only one thing I can say—Fayne brought us this far. Our instinct, staying on the farm, hiding, could have killed us all. Those Hums… how could any bird know that? Only Fayne could. For all her strangeness, she has an ability to see, maybe see even inside Piasa's fog of beyond. I believe that is a gift. How can we ignore that?"

Robert stared at her for some time, and then stooped his plumed head. "We cannot."

Chickory left him to his silent contemplation. Fear and confusion wiggled inside her. She went to Georgia and Dolly and squatted down beside them. She preened one of Georgia's neck feathers and Georgia flinched at her touch.

"Is all well? You were missed in the house last night," Chickory said softly.

"She hasn't spoken all morning," peeped Dolly. "I think there's something terribly wrong with her."

"She's been through such an ordeal, haven't you, Georgia? Haven't we all? She has a right to her quiet for a while. But Georgia, I hope you hear me, we must be ready. When the time comes, we must all go together. All right?" Chickory peered at her, but she appeared to be asleep, her eyes squeezed shut as though she were in pain. "Stay with her a while, will you, Dolly?"

Dolly chirped and Chickory rose, hot impatience in her claws. She paced the length of the wire netting. It kept them from leaving, more frightening than the open road had. Even on the farm they had always been allowed to roam freely, only gated out of Lady's garden and the compost.

And where was Tucker? She could not doubt him, but still, nagging thoughts of freedom lingered. Had he sought out a new life, free of their burden? It wasn't impossible to imagine him on the road again, sniffing out smells, chasing fuzz butts, and marking a new territory.

"They are wanting to stay."

Chickory hadn't noticed Fayne sitting in the dark shadow of shade beside the coop. Chickory went to her and nestled down in the coolness. "Some of them, I think. Robert can see how this would be good. And Georgia… I don't think she has it in her to continue. She's clearly been addled and I don't know that she'll go when the time comes. Maybe it would be best." Chickory was surprised at her own words, how she could speak so plainly about the others.

"She would slow us down, yes, to be sure. I do not think the man will do her any harm, or any of them harm, really. However, when the other humans come this way, they may find him and whatever creatures he possesses." Fayne stared out beyond the wire.

The beyond was shielded by the tall wooden fence that surrounded the larger yard of the house. The tops of houses and trees cluttered the view.

Chickory ruffled her wings. "Do you really think those… the hunters will follow us this far? Surely they've given up by now. What killer would travel so long for mere prey? There must be others they can seek out."

"Would they? You remember the papers in the parking lot? Those pictures of birds, of us, on the pages? That sickness is real. To many of the humans, destroying every last one of us is the only way they see to survive."

"And the Hum? Why would he risk having us here? If we're the sickness the papers spoke of?"

"He has survived this long, maybe his lymphatic cells are simply more advanced and he has immunity."

"Fayne…"

"Like chicks after a bout of dust fever. We never get it again after the first time."

Chickory thought about this, then said, "Do you think the others have… what is it, *immunity*, as well? Then why do they still hunt us?"

"Maybe they have nothing else to fight for. Or maybe they seek revenge."

A shiver of horror crawled down Chickory's spine. "Like the story of the Hum and the Tiger? But… Lady was never cruel and those are just *stories*. You really think they've completely sacrificed Piasa's way? Look at this Hum, he still wants the giving of life and taking of life. He seeks the balance. Isn't that so?" Chickory struggled, understanding like a ripe fruit just beyond the reach of a grounded bird. An important truth, yet it felt unknowable.

Fayne snorted. "Piasa. Well, if you insist on that, remember, she did not only bestow them with gifts. In any case, we must be vigilant. Ready to move at once and those who wish to stay ought to tell us so we do not waste precious time trying to ferry them along."

"Tonight we could ask, in the house," said Chickory.

"Do what is best. I feel a heaviness in my head and should rest here for some time."

"Are you all right?"

"Yes, but the pain often precedes a… dream. How I— Never mind that, leave me to it, only time can usher them in."

"Is it very bad?"

"It is… getting stronger, more powerful. At times I can barely keep it all inside," peeped Fayne. "But go now, there's nothing to be done about it." Fayne's chirp sounded like the cracking of cold season ice.

Chickory rose and wandered toward the others, but when she glanced back, she saw Fayne squeeze her eyes tightly shut. That same expression of pain Georgia had. The things she might see in her dreams… well, it was the only way forward and the only way they would ever reach the valley.

24 | A Heavy Heart

"Piasa gave the greatest cock the greatest strength;
to lead and to listen, to be kind and to have joy. And sometimes,
they will be called upon to sacrifice all."

- Tales of Piasa, Final Year, Final Clutch

Four sunrises had come and gone.

Robert stared through the chicken wire and tried to see beyond the tall plank fence that surrounded the modest yard of the house. He had paced the length of the run and had finally found a place where he could see the rise of distant hilltops. Other than that, the view was quite grim. The faint light of the sunrise glowed and a flush of warmth, of purpose, spread through his body. They were here, yes, and it looked safe, maybe.

There was no post or high point to situate himself, so he did what he could. He turned toward the sunrise, which would soon drench the world with heavy heat, and he opened his beak, tightened his wind pouch, and crowed.

It felt glorious to crow. The sound would improve eventually, but for now it was a thin screech rather than full and complex. Never mind though, he was out of practice. He crowed again, feeling immense relief. This was how it should be, the true way.

"Stop, no! You must not!"

Robert turned. Fayne stood at the entrance of the coop, her eyes wide and shimmering with fear. His stomach twisted. He hadn't *done* anything and his mind swirled with confusion and uncertainty. "W-what?"

She strutted down the ramp and lowered her head as though she might attack him. "They will hear you," she whispered.

His confusion and fear bubbled, but he tried to calm himself. She wouldn't attack him, not Fayne. "Who will hear? The Hum? Well, I don't think he'll mind."

"You complete self-centered pompous bird," she hissed. "They will hear you. You think they are gone? If you want to live to draw breath, you will be *quiet*." The heat of her words radiated from her feathery body like living flame.

Robert stepped back and a loud hum pulsed inside his mind. He waggled his head but the sound only increased.

"Fayne?" Chickory stepped out of the coop and cocked her head. "Everything all right?"

The heat and humming dissipated like early mist in the heat of day.

Fayne straightened and strutted away from them, returning to her usual corner in the shade of the coop.

Robert could barely breathe. Whatever had happened, whatever she had been about to do… fear coiled inside him and choked any crow that might have followed.

The others awoke and spilled out of the coop in a boisterous surge. They chirped and playfully scuffed each other as they spread throughout the run. Beaks flashed and snapped up grass, though they all waited and knew that the Hum would return to feed them.

"Isn't it wonderful, Robert? Oh, oh, oh, to have someone to wait on, a Hum to *feed* us and *love* us. Feels like my breast is full of flittering sparrows," Dolly chirped. She gave a coquettish wag of her tail and eyed him significantly.

"Y-yes, lovely."

"And I heard you! So magnificent, so strong. Ah, how I've missed you and your morning call. Just isn't the same without it," she said.

He wasn't sure he'd ever crow again, so he bowed his head and strutted away from her. He felt her gaze on him, but he couldn't muster the energy to respond.

The door to the house swung open and the Hum appeared. He wandered over to the side of the run and gawked down at them, watching the hens scurry about. That keen stare, the yellow slabs of teeth—Robert shuddered. The unliving might be *dead* but there was no mistaking that they had once been Hums, just like this one. Fear flickered inside him and he puffed out his breast and shook his remaining tail feathers. The Hum grunted at his display and turned, heading toward the shed.

Hum or not, there were bigger problems. Tucker still had not appeared and though difficult, Robert forced himself to think. He was unaccustomed to invention and found it rather disconcerting. How did Fayne do it so regularly? The practice was exhausting and his mind whirled. Fayne was no regular bird, he understood that plainly enough, and that understanding smothered like he had grown an extra layer of feathers.

He shook himself and the early air cooled his hot skin. The biggest problem he faced was whether to tell the others he had found a way to escape.

The Hum returned and sprinkled large handfuls of grain through the wire. The hens clucked and bustled around the yard as they eagerly snapped up the food. Well, all except for Fayne and Georgia. Robert's heart swelled with sorrow. Most of them had one type of injury or another, and some, like Georgia, had injured their minds. Daisy's wing would never be the same and though Dolly limped, it was improving. He watched as Chickory went to Fayne and nestled in beside her. He did not have to hear to know she cooed and comforted, as she always did, Fayne's constant and one true companion. Though hens and roosters might fit by design, Chickory's interest in courtships and in, well, *him*, had faded long ago. Sometimes it happened. Some hens preferred the companionship of other hens and it was quite all right with him. Even he sometimes longed for another rooster, another like himself, to be with. But as he watched Chickory and Fayne, unease prickled through his feathers—though Chickory was more a bird than Fayne, it was Fayne who led them. Fayne who held their fate in her claws.

Pip came up alongside him and shared the view. "Piasa bless it, what a beautiful sight. Fed birds and warm weather. The best of all things! Eh, your head filled with dust and motes?"

"Perhaps that's the problem after all," Robert said.

"I remember what that was like, always fussing over the right decisions to be made. My own hens—" Pip paused for a moment. "Well, my own hens were bloody inbred, took much watching over, they did. Refused to use their own heads for hardly anything. Practically had to squat on their eggs for them! Tuh, but I loved them, the way we must always love our flock. In spite of their feather heads, and our own feather heads for that matter!" He gave a sad chattery laugh. "Still, I wish I had been nicer to them. Looking back on it, I mean."

Robert didn't know what to say. They had lost Rosie and Lacey, but he still had the rest of them. He couldn't imagine his life without them. Couldn't imagine doing or being anything but what he was.

Pip peered at him. "So, eh, I know you've puzzled a way out of here."

Robert looked at him in surprise. "You've seen it too?"

"No, no, nothing like that. Call it intuition if you will. You're wandering around like you've swallowed a mountain of rocks. I don't envy your decision, not at all, but just want you to know that whatever you choose, I'll follow your lead. You've all reminded me of wanting to live. I think I'd forgotten that for a while. And that's a powerful thing, living. So, whether we fight to live here or fight to live out there, at least we fight." Pip bobbed his head firmly.

"Thank you," said Robert.

Pip left Robert to his thoughts.

***

Robert approached Fayne and a pulsating fear radiated from the tip of his comb down into his clawed feet. Whatever Fayne was, whatever she had been, she was the leader of this journey and he needed to tell her.

"I know how to get us out of here," he said.

Fayne opened her eyes slowly, as though the simple motion caused her pain. She peered up at him. "Oh? How?"

"Remember Lady's compost heap? The way it was gated in? Remember the wire and nail?"

"That was a long time ago."

"Yes, but you told me how to unhook it. How to get it open. I—I don't know that any of us would have figured that out."

She didn't say anything.

"Uh, so, yes, the door here is similar. Not quite the same, but almost. It's a hook with a different kind of metal loop. If I could scale the wire, I might be able to nudge the hook out of the loop. Like I did with the compost."

164

Fayne gazed at him. "It was the right choice, Robert," she finally said.

His feathers prickled. "You knew then, this whole time?"

"Yes, I did, but sometimes I cannot be the only one to decide. Everyone must share in the desire to keep going. The others were losing hope, losing faith. You returned, a sign of better things. But… we cannot stay here. Danger approaches even now," she said.

His throat seized like he swallowed frozen pond water. "Danger has stalked us all along. We must fight and run and, um, well, continue. To the valley."

"To the valley." Fayne bobbed her head. "Let's gather them," she said.

It took only a few moments to assemble the others. Georgia still refused to move from her crouch and finally Dolly left her side to join them at the gate.

"Look, there's, uh, no certainty this will work," Robert said. His skin prickled with heat and as they all gazed at him.

"What will work?" Woodfawn asked.

"I think I can open the gate."

"What? But, but *why*?" Dolly sounded incredulous.

"Yes, yes, why would you have us leave?" Daisy squawked. "It's wonderful here!"

Woodfawn turned her glare on Fayne. "Because monster bird says so. Isn't that it? Isn't that always it?"

They all burst into a loud squawking argument. The din overwhelmed Robert and he stepped back. Chickory and Woodfawn squabbled, snapping and slashing at each other. The heat of their anger and fear choked the air.

Fayne said nothing and he met her gaze. She bowed her head slightly.

"Stop!" He flapped his wings and hopped into the middle of them. "Just stop."

Woodfawn panted and growled. Chickory's eyes were wild with fear.

He swallowed hard against his own. "Yes, Fayne has said. But we all know, don't we? Really? To think the danger had just ended because we're here." He glanced around the small run. "That one Hum could protect us? From those things? Those," he forced himself to say it, "those *dead* things?"

"The unliving," Fayne said.

"But we've come so far already," cried Dolly.

"Oh, oh, oh myyyy, we're all going to die!" said Daisy.

"No, no we won't. Not if we keep trying. Not if we," Robert looked at Fayne, "not if we choose to listen."

They all turned toward Fayne, even Woodfawn, though her eyes burned with malice.

Finally, Pip sighed. "Don't seem much more to say about it. Think it's time we left."

"We've all rested, eaten. It's more than we could have hoped. But yes, it's time to leave," Chickory said and looked at Robert. "It's all right. Do your best."

Robert eyed the latch of the gate, which was positioned on the outside towards the top. He would have to scale the wire and use his beak to nudge the metal hook. Once, with Fayne's instructions and a well-fed body, he had the strength to open a compost gate, but his body was not as it once was.

He gripped the square wire with his clawed feet and slowly climbed. Using his beak to also grip, he found he could manage, but as he went higher, his body grew heavier and heavier. Below him, Daisy chirped in fear and Dolly shushed her.

He reached the top and rested for a moment. Somehow, he would have to let go of the wire with his beak and leave his legs to support his weight. He tested it and his legs quivered and he nearly fell, catching himself with his beak at the last moment. The hens cried out beneath him.

Woodfawn bristled. "Be careful up there!"

Robert struggled to focus. His legs shook and he knew he would only have one clear chance. Pushing up sharply, he stuck his beak through the wire. Every part of his body shook and tensed as he struck the latch.

He missed.

No, no, no. AGAIN.

He gave a mighty squawk and lunged once more. The metal clicked painfully against the tip of his beak. The hook jerked out of the loop.

A squawking cheer rose from the flock below and relief overcame his strength.

"Watch out, he's coming down!" shouted Pip.

Robert landed with a thud and the others crowded around him.

"Back, back, give him room," barked Pip. He glanced down at Robert. "All right?"

"Yeah, just fine," said Robert as he struggled upright. He was better than all right. He felt *wonderful,* as though everything had been restored to how it should be. Fayne was right. They were meant to leave this place.

The flock gave a collective sigh and Daisy and Dolly cooed. Woodfawn flapped her wings in approval.

Fayne drew close to him. "You have done well, Robert."

He stiffened and waited for the terrible hum in his head to overtake him, but nothing happened.

"Well done," she said and preened one of his feathers. Then she shouldered through the door and entered the yard beyond.

Chickory gazed at him as she passed. "That's a lot. Coming from her, it is."

Robert followed.

***

The others gathered outside the open gate, silent and wary. Dolly and Daisy hesitated and glanced back at the freshened coop where warm and inviting nests awaited occupants. Woodfawn glowered and clucked irritably. Even Chickory could not deny the powerful desire to stay and hope for the best. They could make a home again, be cared for. Someday, even have chicks.

Fayne ruffled her wings. "Are we all ready?" she asked.

They all moved without speaking, until they had almost reached the fence.

Dolly said, "Wait, where's Georgia?"

They turned, one by one, and saw her, still squatted in the dirt inside the run. She looked as forlorn as before.

A beetle buzzed overhead and a sparrow chased it across the blue sky.

"I don't think she can...come," Robert said quietly.

No one spoke but they all knew the truth of it. Pain had rendered her unfeeling, unknowing. A hen couldn't always come back from that, from the sickness of the mind. Deep down, all creatures were as fragile as fluffy seed heads, waiting to be scattered by a cruel wind. Georgia had been blown away.

"Let us go. The man will care for her," Fayne said.

They turned and followed the fence line.

"Watch for him though. He will try to recapture us," Fayne said.

From somewhere, they heard muffled barking.

"That's Tucker," whispered Chickory. They reached the end of the fence and turned the corner

The three hunters stared down at them. They blinked stupidly, looking surprised by the appearance of the birds. Around their necks and waists and arms were looped their vicious prizes. The dried heads and claws of their killings. In one sinuous leap, the female with death worm hair, whipped out a long spear. Her mouth contorted into a terrible black gash and she let out a savage scream.

"Oh no, run!" Chickory screeched.

"Hurry, go!" Robert called.

They scattered.

The female set after Robert and struck out with the deadly point of her spear, missing the mark. The other hunters took off after Daisy and Dolly, who cackled hysterically as they dodged in between bushes and over low-lying garden fences. Chickory dashed after Fayne and they hid under an overgrown hedge.

A loud voice boomed over the yard.

The hunters stopped and turned to face the porch.

The Hum, their recent captor, had a long bang stick, pointed, not at the flock, but at the hunters. He chattered a stream of angry hostile sounds.

The hunters shouted in return and pumped their fists as they pointed at Robert and the others.

"What is he saying?" Chickory asked.

"They want him to give up the birds, but he thinks," Fayne swallowed hard, "he thinks his God sent us to him. To care for."

The shouts grew louder and the Hum pulled on his bang stick, which made a click sound.

One of the male hunters held up both hands and their voices abruptly dropped to a low murmur.

"The man is threatening to kill them," Fayne said. "If they do not leave his land."

"But why?"

Fayne didn't answer and the female lifted her hands too. The

168

three hunters backed away from the porch and turned the corner of the house toward the road out front.

"We must run, before he tries to capture us again. The hunters will not give up so easily," Fayne said.

Chickory peered out from between the branches of the hedge. The Hum watched the hunters go, then lowered his bang stick and looked around the yard. He muttered faintly and headed for the shed.

Fayne slipped out from under the bush and ran down the side of the house on the opposite side of where the hunters had gone. The others left their various hiding places and followed.

"Hurry, hurry, go," Fayne commanded them and they rounded the front of the house together.

"Tucker!" Chickory ran towards him.

"No, wait, don't go near him!" Fayne cried.

Tucker lunged and fell back, tied to a post with a rope looped around his neck. Something was tied around his muzzle, his jaws clamped shut. He thrashed against the rope and she could hear his desperate muffled whines.

The hunters sprang out from the other side of the house and ran toward Chickory.

Fear swarmed through Chickory's mind and throttled her sense. Sundown loomed and she spun dizzily on her claws, unsure of where to turn, where to go.

A loud bang cracked the air and Chickory fell over with the shock of the sound.

One of the hunters screamed and stumbled back. The other two froze.

The Hum had appeared on his front porch and a small sliver of smoke rose from the nose of his bang stick. The air smelt sour and strange.

The hunters screamed and one clamped his hands against his chest. Blood welled between his fingers.

"Chickory, get up!" Fayne grabbed a beakful of her feathers and jerked them painfully.

Chickory stumbled upright, her head still whirling with confusion.

Tucker's eyes bulged and streamed with moisture as he lunged again, still bound by the rope.

"Do not pull, back up and twist! Twist your head!" Fayne trilled.

Daisy and Dolly sprang out across the front lawn and scurried down the road.

Robert and Woodfawn screamed, but Chickory could not see them.

"We have to move!"

"They're coming, oh, Piasa, they're coming!"

Fayne ran to Tucker and Chickory stumbled again. Her whole body felt heavy and stiff, as though every feather had turned to wood.

The road swirled in strange slow movement. Sounds warbled and grew shrill then faint.

Chickory staggered under the belly of a roar horse. *What's happening?*

Then she saw the herd.

The sound of the bang stick, as all sound apparently did, had called the herd to them. The thick savage swell of the unliving approached. They shuffled between roar horses, emerged from between houses, and filled the road like hungry ants swarming the corpse of a beetle.

She turned to see her flock, the hunters, the Hum—they all gawked and stepped back. All that lived feared the unliving, including the Hums.

The bang stick sparked with bright flame again and the loud crack of noise cut through the shouts of the Hums and the terrified squeals of the flock, of Tucker.

A few of the unliving fell, but the others walked over the bodies. Some stepped onto the bloody corpses, oblivious to their fallen, mindless but for one thing: hunger.

Tucker backed up and twisted. The rope pulled forward and slid over his ears and off his head. The hunters ran—well, two of them did. The third writhed on the ground and blood spread around him. The Hum on the porch disappeared back inside and the door slammed shut.

"Chickory!" Fayne paced frantically, yellow eyes wide and fearful.

But there was no time. The flock was too far now and the smell of the unliving, the roar of their desire, was close. Fayne gave Chickory one last desperate look and turned away.

Chickory watched as her flock, her Tucker, her everything, left her behind.

25 | Lost

"Mind the storms and terrible winds of the world.
A hen not in her nest, is a hen ready to be blown away."

- *Practical Wisdom*, First Clutch, Second year

They were gone.

Chickory watched as they fled into the houses beyond, melting like flakes of snow into the landscape. Her head still surged with confusion and she lay quietly beneath the roar horse. Fear drained from her body, even as the unliving surged past her hiding place. As long as she was quiet, as long as she was still, they wouldn't see her, wouldn't even know she was there.

Besides, they focused on the continuous sound of the groaning hunter who still twitched on the ground. She watched, limp and dazed, as the unliving fell upon him. They covered his body and fought for a mouthful of his flesh. Some became frenzied by the feast and took bites out of each other, though they did not eat the unliving flesh, letting it fall from their gnashing mouths.

Others broke off from the main herd and staggered up the steps of the Hum's porch. They banged at the door and scratched against the windows. One shattered and an unliving fell forward through the window. It draped over the sill and kicked its legs. The others crawled over its squirming body and tumbled through. Chickory shuddered as the body squelched and split, cut nearly through by the broken glass. It did not seem to notice, only moaned and tried to struggle inside the house after the others.

A series of loud pops came from inside, the muffled sound of the bang stick. The Hum screamed and the air was swallowed up by the continuous droning chorus of the unliving.

Were all killers the same? Driven by hunger, at the expense of all else? Chickory's mind buzzed and shifted through her thoughts like a cascade of rain, running over her body and enveloping her.

For a while she slept.

She awoke a while later by a scratching sound.

A moan.

Chickory stirred and looked up, directly into the face of an unliving. It crawled toward her and extended a hand toward her neck. One of the eyes was only a gaping wound of blood and mucous, but the other gleamed, savage with need. It had crawled under the roar horse because it had to. Below the belly, the body was gone, nothing but straggles of torn flesh. It left a wide path of dark blood behind its struggle forward. It pulled itself forward with thin flexing arms.

Chickory staggered upright and backed out from under the roar horse. Her pulse ticked inside her throat and her innards heaved. Then, remembering the herd of the unliving, she whirled around.

The herd was gone. This lone straggler had been left behind, too wounded to keep up, but deadly all the same. It moaned and struggled, blocked by one of the roar horse's tires.

Where am... I? The thought clattered through her and a shiver rolled through her claws and traveled up through every feather. She had never been alone before. Never. Since the moment she arrived on the farm as a chick, she had been surrounded by her flock, safe in the knowledge of their ways. All of that was gone now.

Except for the struggle of the unliving trapped under the roar horse, nothing moved or made any sound at all.

She had to go, had to move. Every instinct of birdhood raged at her to go, to hide. But where? Away from the house, away from this place. She had followed Fayne so long, she could almost feel Fayne whispering to her, directing her claws down the road. She must continue. Maybe, ahead, the flock had hidden. Maybe they waited for her. Somewhere.

The road felt far too wide, far too large, now that she traveled alone. She pressed to one side and ducked under brush and the bellies of roar horses, trying to stay out of sight. Though she had not seen many sky birds on their journey, only crows and sparrows, perhaps some still lived in hiding, waiting for a foolish ground bird to forget their danger.

The houses grew apart and their yards grew wider as she went. Fewer fences divided the places and small meadows opened up between rows. There was no sign of the flock, no sound of chattering barks. Nothing.

She reached a herd of roar horses, like the one at the other side of this settlement. They all crammed together, crumpled and dull, completely blocking the road. How the herd of unliving had passed, she did not know. Maybe they could climb over as Hums certainly could. She turned down a side road that ran between the houses, smaller than the wide road of the main passageway.

A sound drifted to her—the familiar drone of the unliving. She skittered behind a large metal can that sat on the side of the road, hiding in the shadow of its hollow belly. The sounds did not come closer but they did not fade. She peered out from around the can and unease needled the knot in her breast. She could not see them, only hear them. She continued down the road and scanned the landscape around her.

The road ended abruptly. A large hole cut off the road's path and it was from here the moans came. Chickory neared the edge and peered over, into the huge depression. Down at the bottom, clawing at the sides, was the herd. Well, at least part of the herd. They had fallen down and didn't seem able to get back out again. The hole spread for a long way and on the other side sat a huge roar horse with a scoop attached to the end of its long nose. The hole had been made, probably by other Hums. *Humans are innovative. It is why they have come to rule this world.* Fayne had said that.

Chickory shivered and walked around the edge of the large hole. A small path on either side was flanked by tall strong fences, which had squeezed the unliving into this place and down into the pit. A Hum could barely walk the path but it was big enough for Chickory.

Some of the unliving saw her and called to her in choked voices. They surged and stumbled over each other as they clawed at the dirt sides. The sides had been armed with metal spikes that looked like porcupine quills. They curved downwards and it looked impossible for the unliving to climb. Maybe eventually they might get out, somehow, but for now they were trapped.

She reached the other side and passed by the roar horse. Dirt crusted its scoop and the Hums who must have once ridden it were gone.

She gazed back down the hole, a strange surge of pity stirring in her breast.

"Disgusting, ain' they?"

Chickory whirled around. Under the metal scooper, paws tucked under its chest, was a huge orange cat.

Chickory wanted to run but her clawed feet wouldn't move. The cat yawned and slowly unfurled. It put its paws out in front of it and arched its back in a deep bow. Then it padded out from the shade. One side of its face was blackened, the fur gone. Shiny pinched skin was all that was left. The cat sat at the edge of the hole, so close Chickory could count the cat's whiskers.

"P—please…" Chickory managed. Her feathery body shook so hard, she was afraid she might stumble back into the hole behind her.

The cat licked a front paw and sighed. "It's a'right. Not gonna eat you."

But cats were liars and the paralyzing Sundown would not release Chickory.

The cat sprawled into the dirt and rolled on its back. "Got a bad paw. Couple of 'em, really. Get a good pounce on mice but ain't much left in me to go after a big bird like you."

Chickory's eyes raked over the cat. The cat was thin, dirty, and the hind paws curled in a funny way. Feeling crept back into her claws and she scooted back a little. "What happened to you?"

"Had a litter of kits down the way, under the porch of one of the houses. Vicious brats pulled 'em out one by one. Finally shot a couple holes in me, tried to set me on fire," the cat said simply.

Chickory's fear twisted into horror. She could see the nippled belly, the slight sag of skin that had once swelled with life. Any fear she had evaporated. Death of the young was always a cruel and horrible thing, even with all Piasa's promises of returning to the soil. "How can you bear it?" she asked.

The cat rolled onto its belly. Dust and dry grass covered her fur. She panted softly and gazed at Chickory. "The same as we all do. You just go on."

They stared at each other, the sound of the groaning horde echoing in Chickory's ears.

"What are ya doing here, anyway?" The cat asked and flicked her tail.

"My flock. We, well, we got separated a while back. I'm looking for them."

"Ah. Thought as much. Saw a few of them strut by not too long ago. Had a dog so I hid myself. Never know 'bout dogs. Some in the neighborhood are kind enough to an ol' scrapper like me, but best to give strangers a wide path."

Hope surged through Chickory. Tucker had chased and struck down many creatures on their journey and she was glad the cat *had* hidden herself. "They came through here?"

"Mhm. They're likely down a way now. Dead followed not too far behind but most fell into this here. Clever, huh?" The cat purred and gazed at the pit with something like affection.

"Right. Well, I'd better go after them. Thank you, so much. And, um, I'm sorry, you know. For what's happened to you."

The cat gave a small sigh. "What happens to me has happened to us all, I think. So we go on. Do what we can. Like them down there or us up here, we all gotta try and live."

Chickory backed away. Sadness and gratitude swirled in her innards, but she had to hurry to catch the others. Surely, they hadn't gone too far. Not without her.

She turned toward the empty road and scurried, knowing the cat would not follow. The world had twisted and become an unknown story, where rats might lead to food and cats might mean help. Though weasels still ate birds and dogs were sometimes bad.

She scanned the landscape around her but most of the houses had fallen away, leaving one side flanked with thick trees and tall grass.

(*Come*)

The word dripped, cold and familiar inside Chickory's mind. *Fayne.* She knew it was her, knew it with no doubt. The voice in the field, the voice in her dreams—all along it had been Fayne's voice, and now it called to her.

(*You're close*) the voice said and Chickory quickened her steps. *Where?* She started to run. They were so close, had to be so close, but Chickory couldn't see them.

(*Into the trees*)

She turned, blindly, obediently, and plunged through the tall grass. The shadows of the trees swallowed her up. If killers waited, she would stumble right into their path, but she didn't care. If traps hid, then she would fall into them willingly. Fear fell away as she pushed forward, certain in her direction, certain in Fayne, certain—

She staggered into a small clearing of young ferns.

"Chickory!" Tucker ran to her and slathered her with his wet tongue.

They were there. All of them. Woodfawn, Dolly, Daisy, Robert, Pip, Tucker, and, of course, Fayne.

Chickory staggered into their midst, relief pulsating through her. They pressed in tightly and fluttered their wings, reaching with beaks and inspecting every feather of her.

Tucker cried and licked her all over. "I'm sorry, bird, I'm sorry, so so so sorry."

"It's all right, Tucker, it's all right. Good dog."

Daisy waggled her head. "We thought you'd be lost."

"Well, Fayne didn't," Dolly said.

"Piasa watches over you. 'Lost in the wind, give yourself over to Piasa's grace' and you certainly have," Woodfawn chirped.

Chickory pushed past them, pushed past Robert, and went to Fayne, who stood, as always, on the outside. As she saw her, her funny feathered raccoon of a friend, a lump swelled in her throat. "You—I heard you. You called to me."

Fayne bobbed her head. "And you came."

Chickory fell on her and peeped with pleasure and joy. "I will always come to you."

26 | The Others

The houses faded, now only shadowy lumps on the horizon behind them. The roads shrank and some of the familiar gravelly ones reappeared. They entered a different kind of farmland. Instead of meadows and fields of wheat and grass, the flock roamed past endless open plains of corn that rose on either side of the road like stunted rows of trees. Most of the stalks were yellowed, lacking precious rain and the Hums who would have tended their growth.

"Really? There's corn in there?" Daisy cocked her head and peered up at the tall stalks.

"Yes, inside the gathered leaves. You cannot see them until you have removed the outer layers and revealed the cob inside," Fayne said.

"Can we, well, eat them? I'm famished," Chickory gazed up at the tall stalks too. Silky fur grew out of the tops of the tight leafy cocoons.

"No," Fayne said, not pausing to consider the matter.

Woodfawn glared and grumbled, but they all pressed on. The sun was high in the sky, directly above, and the heat scorched the back of Chickory's head. No rain had fallen since the store and here, the heat felt worse, the brush around them crisp and dry.

Hunger grew inside her stomach, as though the few sunrises

being fed had reminded her body of what it needed. Mingled with this need, deep fatigue spread through her and coiled inside her mind. Every step grew more and more difficult, and she was not alone in this misery. The main road had begun a steep rise, and Dolly trudged forward like a feathery slow-squish. Robert shuffled along with silent determination. Woodfawn straggled at the far end of their pathetic line and stopped for frequent rest without speaking to the others. Tucker paused with her and only moved forward once Woodfawn did.

Only Pip was mostly oblivious to the turmoil. "Ey! I can almost see my barn from here!" he crowed from atop a large boulder.

The hilltop they had reached gave them an impressive view of the settlement sprawled down below. Somewhere beyond all the houses was more farmland and somewhere in there, was the place they once called home. They had come so far, but the hills meant they still had so far to go. Chickory shuddered. Even larger mountains loomed beyond the hills.

"Withering corn, look!" Robert warbled in alarm.

At the base of the rise, coming up the steep road behind them, were two Hums. At their distance, it was hard to see clearly, but Chickory knew. "It's them, isn't it?"

Woodfawn moved closer to Tucker. "The same ones? Those—those hunters?"

Tucker's furry body shivered, as though drenched in cold season rain. His tremulous whine filled the air. Whatever had happened to Tucker, whatever those hunters had done to him when they tied and held him, had diminished him. He slunk into the brush growing alongside the path.

"Yes," said Fayne. "Only one male and the female are left. The other male may be—"

"He's dead." Chickory shuddered at the memory. "The unliving caught him."

"Oh Piasa, have mercy, dear us," squeaked Daisy.

"What will you do, monster bird? What do we do now? Tell me." Woodfawn's glare blazed with hatred. She stepped toward Fayne and every feather bristled.

Robert shuffled between them, not looking at Woodfawn or Fayne. He spoke to Chickory instead. "We must keep on," he said. "Maybe hide? Fayne, please, could you tell us how much further up we must go? Is the valley near?"

They all turned to Fayne, even Chickory, though her breast squeezed with fearful anticipation at what she might say. Inspiring hope was not one of Piasa's gifts to her.

"Near enough that we waste precious time discussing it. We move." Fayne turned her back on them.

"You may as well leave me! I'm better hiding in a bush than continuing this death march!" Woodfawn announced shrilly.

Fayne paused but did not look at her. "Your decision to make."

Robert came alongside Woodfawn and pressed his wing to hers. He lowered his voice to a soothing coo. "Please, Woodfawn. With Rosie, Lacey, then Georgia. I couldn't bear it. We can't leave anymore behind."

They all waited, except for Fayne, who continued forward without looking back.

Woodfawn let out a distressed peep, but took a grudging step forward as Robert coaxed her along.

Chickory shouldered past the others and hurried alongside Fayne who was already several paces away. "They're falling to bits here, surely you must see that," she said. Mingled with her fear was a flicker of anger. How could Fayne be so cold, so unfeeling to the others? The others who needed her now more than ever?

"Round the next bend is a place to rest."

"Why haven't you told—"

"Because I sincerely hope it is unoccupied," Fayne said quietly.

Chickory's innards heaved. "Hums?"

"No, maybe more of us."

Helpless confusion whirled inside Chickory's mind. "But that's not all bad is it? More like us? They could tell us what lies ahead, if the valley is near."

Fayne took another few steps before saying, "we have much to fear of them. If we had any other choice, I would take us around, but—oh." Fayne stopped and gave a heavy sigh. "Much too late for that now."

Two large cockerels sprang out from behind a cluster of stone. "Stop there!"

Chickory blinked. Awe and confusion crept through her feathertips.

The two large males looked like Fayne, with the same odd bands of color that made them look like feathery raccoons. One had a large scar across his face.

More of us. No, not us, more of her.

Robert surged forward and gave an indignant squawk as he approached. The strangers lunged and slashed at him with their claws.

"Robert, don't!" trilled Fayne, terror in her voice.

Something glinted on their legs. Chickory gasped. Elongated metal hooks covered their spurs and created vicious looking claws, like in the mouth of the field traps. A Hum creation, surely.

Robert rose to meet them, squawking and hissing. Feathers covered the ground. Within moments, Robert staggered back, his stalks torn and bleeding.

The hens cackled hysterically and Pip hopped with furious rage. Tucker reached them, his lip lifted in a vicious snarl.

"Easy cur," hissed the smaller cockerel, though he hopped back, his eyes wide with fear.

Then Fayne made a warbling whirring sound that Chickory had never heard before. Both males looked at her and responded with the same whirring note. A cold chill flushed through Chickory's feathers and down into her scaly toes.

"Right," said the scarred one. "We'll take you to Lord Germaine, but follow quietly or we'll finish you all. There's much more of us than there are of you."

Chickory didn't see any others but perhaps more hid just beyond the boulders or in the scrubby brush. She looked at Fayne, but Fayne stared straight ahead.

"Right," said Fayne. "We will follow your lead."

Chickory glanced back, but they were too far along the hilltop now. She couldn't see if the hunters were close. Perhaps she should tell them, warn them…

(Quiet)

Chickory flinched at the cold familiar word, as it dripped inside her mind.

The other male gave Tucker a wide berth and scurried to the end of their line, following at their backs. The scarred one shoved Robert forward. He stumbled, but kept upright.

They left the main road and followed a gravelly road that led around a bend in the hillside. A sturdy metal fence was hidden from view and it encircled a large house made entirely of red square stones. Creeping thorns swallowed the line of the fence, studded with unripe green berries and the thick bramble obscured the yard on the other side.

180

The scarred one emitted that strange warbling whir again. From behind the fence, a small door opened, which allowed passage through the terrible thicket. "Come on, through there," he commanded.

They obeyed and on the other side were two more male birds. They all looked like Fayne, though these males also had metal spurs.

"How could so many males live together in peace?" Chickory whispered to Pip.

He bobbed his head in silent awe, yellow eyes wide as he watched them. "Not just in peace, but cooperation, it seems."

"This way." The scarred one led them along the inside of the fence.

They passed by wide porch steps that led up the back of the house. Straight rows of roosters and cockerels faced the porch, like feathery lines of corn, all equipped with metal spurs. Atop the steps was the largest rooster Chickory had ever seen, Pip a mere sparrow in his presence. He too had banded feathers, and, but for his size, he looked like all the others. Chickory's pulse thrummed in her ears as she tried to remember where Fayne had come from in the days of their chickhood… had she come from this place? But the memories were fuzzy, as all chick days were.

The large rooster's eyes followed their group and his keen eyes flashed with a glint of familiar malevolent understanding. Like Fayne's so often did.

A shabby coop lingered in the far corner of the large yard, the paint worn and peeled in places. The scarred one stopped at the ramp that led up into the coop, while the other pulled on a small rope. The small closed door slid open.

"Get inside, don't cause any problems. Lord Germaine is currently occupied," said the male as they shuffled past. They ducked their heads to fit through. For the second time, they were imprisoned. Chickory paused on the ramp, and glanced back at Tucker, who whined, clearly too small to enter.

"Lie there, just alongside. Stupid dog. You stink!" said the scarred male.

Tucker gave an indignant growl, the ruff of his neck prickling with growing anger.

"No, Tucker. Do as they say," Fayne said quietly from the entrance of the coop. "There is much to learn here."

But what was to be learned, she did not say, and disappeared inside. Chickory wondered why Fayne didn't just ask Tucker to tear them all to pieces—but that word… quiet. She must trust her friend, as she had so many times before. More must be revealed.

Tucker grumbled but obeyed, lying along the outside of the coop.

The scarred male cocked his head. "Curious. We should inform Lord Germaine of this development. Perhaps we can enlist other creatures such as this, should they prove to be as easily malleable as this cur. Hey, get in there!" he squawked at Chickory.

She ducked inside and the solid wood flap swung shut.

The darkness swallowed Chickory and her eyes burned. The foul smell of droppings and urine choked the air, mingled with a faint smell of rot. A small shaft of light streamed through a seam in the roof.

"How disgusting," said Woodfawn. "They clearly have no hens to care about the cleanliness of their quarters. 'A nest of filth rots the most treasured egg.' Tuh, though without eggs maybe the brutes don't care."

"We've done the best we can," came a mournful whisper.

Fear fluttered in Chickory's breast. "Who's there?" She squinted and tried to see with her stinging eyes.

From the depths of shadow, Fayne stepped forward into the sliver of light. At least, it looked exactly like her, but for a white patch that obstructed each eye, like Sam's eyes.

"You're blind," whispered Chickory in horror.

"Yes, we know," replied the unfortunate bird. Her voice trembled. "They keep us in here day in and day out. They take what few eggs are laid by the young ones and raise them somewhere out there. We have begged them to allow us to clean. Never mind though. My name is Hailene."

"Do not speak to them," hissed someone in the dark. Another, identical copy of Fayne appeared alongside the other one. "Lord Germaine will have our brains pulled through our eye sockets if he catches us talking to them."

Hailene shrank away into the shadows.

"Wait! How many of there, are you?" Chickory's throat ached from the foul air.

None replied.

For a long while they all stood there and their vision slowly adjusted to the darkness.

"Oh no, oh myyyyy," trilled Daisy.

"Horrible, just horrid," Woodfawn hissed.

Many hens occupied the coop, far too many for such small quarters. Several birds shared each stinking nest. Some were old and blind, while some were far younger, with eyes that still glittered with sight.

"Maybe we can help you," Chickory said.

"There is nothing to be done for us," said Hailene. She edged her way closer to them again. "It is our fate to die here."

"It's no one's fate to live like this." Pip waggled his head. "You should not condemn yourself or the others to this life."

Hailene emitted a small, sad chirp. "You will see too, after a time. If Lord Germaine—"

"Do not call him a Lord," snapped Fayne. "He is an imposter."

A frightened murmur rippled through the crowded birds.

"You are one of us," said Hailene. "Surely you have seen as we have. The truth of the future."

"The future is not set in stone." Fayne's voice trembled. "Only if you allow it to fully unfold, to take you, will it show you what is meant to be."

Chickory's mind spun from the terrible air and the words spoken. What did Fayne mean by this? How could there be so many like her? Panic needled inside her and she crept closer to the doorway.

"Tucker, can you hear me?" she peeped against the wall.

"Bird! Are you all right? What have they done to you?" Tucker's whines were muffled through the wooden slats.

"What do you see out there? Could we—escape? Make it past them?"

"There's many of these terrible birds out here. Unless you wish me to bite their heads off, which I will, just tell me."

"No, let us wait. Lord Germaine will see us after a time," said Fayne.

"Fayne says to wait, Tucker..." she tried to remember the words he liked so much. "Good dog." She could hear the faint thump of his tail.

Chickory crept back to where the others huddled in the middle of the coop. With no empty nests and no space on the roosts, there was nowhere else to be. Dark unmoving mounds slumped in the far corners—dead birds who further occupied the precious space.

Chickory dozed fitfully and she awoke many times to rasps and wheezes, stunned to discover it was her own breathing.

*****

"Wake up, Lord Germaine will see you now," a voice called to them.

Chickory struggled to open her eyes and found them gummed together. She painfully forced them, blinking in the strong light coming through the entryway. The scarred cockerel stood just outside, only his head poked through the opening.

The others hobbled to their claws and Woodfawn let out a rasping cough. White mucous dripped from Daisy's nostrils.

He snorted. "Come on, come on, or I will leave you in this cesspool."

They quickly followed and whether they were led to death or not, Chickory was grateful to escape the foul dark. Low clouds obstructed the surrounding hills and the sun prepared for its long nightly roost.

They were led to the wide porch steps where the males were assembled as before. The large rooster, who must be Lord Germaine, stared down at them.

The scarred male stooped low and the tip of his beak nearly brushed the ground. "My Lord, we discovered them on patrol," he said.

Lord Germaine descended the steps and his metal spurs clicked as he walked. "Very good, Lazen."

Chickory's flesh prickled with the same creeping sensation she felt when Fayne looked at her in the same appraising way.

Lord Germaine turned his penetrating stare on Fayne. "So? Why do you still lead them? Why are you here?" Disdain hummed in his voice.

"Because I am one of you," she said.

"And if you were not, hen, I would strike you down where you stand."

For a moment, no one spoke.

"Why do you come here?" he finally asked.

"To see if there was any truth to my visions—to see if any of us were still alive. I also bring news," said Fayne. "News of humans who are coming up the hill right now."

Lord Germaine hissed, but it was with laughter. The ranks that had stood as still as frozen tree bark, joined in, a raucous chorus of mockery. When Lord Germaine stopped and the rest abruptly fell silent.

184

"The humans hunting you up the mountainside? My scouts have been reporting on your progress for some time."

"Then you know they mean to kill us all, including you."

He turned his back on them and strutted away.

Lazen roughly shoved Fayne forward. "Go on, follow him," he said.

They begrudgingly followed around the side of the house, Dolly and Daisy peeping fearfully as they went. They passed the chicken coop and entered the large sweep of the yard's yellow grass. In the middle of the open flat space, lay three still shapes, shadows in the fading light.

Woodfawn gave a mighty squawk and tried to bolt. "Piasa preserve us!"

Lazen sprang and pinned her to the ground, hissing with glee as he flexed his metal spurs against her back.

The shapes had once been Hums, one smaller than the other two. These bodies, once encased in living breathing flesh, were now only raw outlines of bone and white stripes of tendon.

"Come on, come, come," Lord Germaine purred, as he strutted alongside the corpses.

Chickory's stomach rocked with horror. The muscle had been… yes, it looked mostly pecked away and full lengths of fur still topped each meaty skull. The faces were gone.

"Does it look as though we fear the humans here?" he asked.

Chickory bowed her head and swallowed hard against her rising gorge.

"You d-d-did this?" said Fayne and she did not sound brave or self-assured. Her stutter returned and it sounded strange after being so long gone.

"A rightful prize to us, the enslaved and tortured. After all, where do you think we came by these?" Lord Germaine lifted his clawed foot, showing off the length of his impressive spurs.

"The Hums… made those?" Chickory peeped, confused.

He snorted a derisive laugh. "Humans are cruel and pathetic. Yes, they created these weapons and turned us against each other. For *sport* and mealy entertainment. They have tortured our kind and the all creatures for as long as they have been Masters of this world. They do not deserve their fortune and so they have been struck down."

Chickory's breast clenched. "But they're not all like that! Lady wasn't like that!"

Fayne shot Chickory a warning look, but boldness surged through Chickory, heightened by her fear and the madness of this place. "Lady was good! She cared for us and we provided for her. That is the way! Laid before us, there is no other path!"

Lord Germaine gazed at Chickory. She realized it was pity. "The virtues of the few do not redeem the horror of the species. Fayne knows this." He bobbed his head toward Fayne, who did not meet his eyes.

Robert puffed out his chest and straightened. "How do you know her name?"

Lord Germaine snorted again. "Oh, I know many things. No, these humans died by sickness, Piasa's first sign to us that the time of humans is over. No longer Hums. We each took of the flesh to become the hunter, not the hunted." He snorted a derisive laugh. "Only mortal weak humans. You know of what I speak, Fayne. But do they?" He regarded the rest of the flock and cocked his head.

Chickory's stomach flipped with a new fear. "What is he talking about, Fayne?"

But Fayne wouldn't look at her and Lord Germaine's eyes gleamed with satisfaction.

"I had wondered how much she has chosen to share with you, whether she has deemed you worthy, and of course, why she brought you here. What does the little hen want?"

Then Fayne did speak and her voice shook. "How have you hidden here so long? With the unliving and t-t-the humans so close?"

"I guess you really do not know too much. About the depth of our powers… about *your* powers. Pity. Well, come along, I will show you."

He strutted forward and they all followed without needing to be told. Chickory shuddered as they left the bodies behind. *Monster birds. Truly monster birds.*

Lord Germaine led them around the other side of the house and paused in front of a closed gate. The metal fence here was also overgrown with thorny bramble and blocked the view of the other side.

(*Come*)

The word clattered through Chickory's mind and she flinched.

Woodfawn spun in a circle and looked up at the sky. "What?"

"Piasa, she speaks to us!" squawked Dolly and flapped her wings.

Fayne did not move, did not say anything at all, only gazed at the fence.

Lord Germaine cackled with evident amusement.

(*Come*)

The word came again, cold and clear, but it *felt* different than the other words had. Not like the calm cool familiar tone. This was a different command from a different source.

A low moan whispered from the other side of the fence.

Chickory's body seized with Sundown. "No. Oh, no, no."

The groan was joined by others and melded into the familiar drone of the unliving.

"You see, I have nothing to fear from the living… or the unliving," Lord Germaine said. His yellow eyes gleamed with such ferocity, Chickory cowered.

(*Come, come, come NOW*)

The words clattered painfully through Chickory's mind and the groans grew louder, frenzied by the harsh commands.

Suddenly the bramble shifted and arms, torn and bleeding, shot through the slats in the metal fence. Fingers clawed at the air as though they searched for the one who called them.

Fayne stepped back. Chickory's head ached with the words, with confusion. She could feel the difference between the words and understood that it was Lord Germaine who spoke now, not Fayne. The subtle feeling of the words was apparent if she focused. But if Lord Germaine also spoke these mind words—could a mere bird, even one as fantastical and unlikely as Fayne, truly command the unliving? But she had already done it. The fence, that field of teeth, the unliving shackled by traps… *Quiet* had come then too, and they *had* quieted.

(*Quiet*)

The groans of the unliving on the other side of the fence lessened.

(*Quiet, quiet, QUIET*)

The groans reluctantly faded and the hands dropped out of sight.

Lord Germaine turned to them. "Do we not rule this world? Soon, all will be in our claws," he said.

Fayne bristled and lifted her head. "You asked what I want. I want safe p-p-passage through here. To leave. I have no quarrel with your mission, with what you wish to achieve."

Lord Germaine bobbed his head. "Passage? But where will you go, little hen?"

"There is the trail that leads over the hill into the valley below."

The thudding knot in Chickory's breast squeezed. The *valley*.

"So, you wish to return them to Origin. I am afraid that place is very unsafe for us all now," cooed Lord Germaine. "I cannot allow you to embark on such a journey. Only death awaits you there and what kind of Lord allows his flock to wander so blindly into danger? You are one of us, as you said, and you will remain here with us. I have uses for you yet."

Woodfawn gave a quiet squeal of dismay and glared at Fayne, as though she had known this all along. Dolly and Daisy looked frantically at each other, then at Chickory.

Fayne did not look at any of them.

"We do keep hens on site and we could use more for our purposes. Perhaps we might create a finer living quarter to house so many fine healthy hens. After all, our genetic line seems to struggle with reproduction. Our eggs have been lacking and I have wondered whether we need more... domestic stock." His gaze trailed over Daisy and Dolly.

Fayne stepped toward him. "Do you not feel it? The call to return?" Her voice surged with tension and her body trembled.

"I feel what I choose. The weaker have sometimes fled toward the call, but they were killed. By us or by them, it does not matter. Death found them all. As it will find you if you go, Fayne. You know this, as I do."

Woodfawn lifted her head and puffed out her breast. "How could you betray the way? What Piasa has set forth for us all? The way between creatures and Hums keeps the balance intact, it is the only way for a bird to live."

He turned his gaze on her and bowed his head in a predatory way, like a sky bird preparing to swoop. "Piasa is a foolish myth, lore meant to control the weak, the useless. Are you useless to me, bird?"

Woodfawn staggered back and panted.

"I wish to speak with you more. T-t-to negotiate our… surrender to you," Fayne said.

Chickory's throat squeezed. She couldn't breathe.

Lord Germaine bobbed his head again and looked satisfied. "Very well, little hen. Come with me. Lazen, take the others back."

Lazen slashed at Robert's comb, drawing a droplet of blood. "Go on!"

They all hurried away, but Chickory lingered and tried to send

Fayne a thought, a desperate why why *why* she would betray them. To explain why she had given in so easily to this Lord, this *imposter*. Fayne had said that. And they had Tucker, they had survived all this life had thrown at them thus far. To give in now, without attempt or pride, well, it felt as though the knot of her beating heart would stop altogether with the pain of such an awful end.

Fayne turned away and followed Lord Germaine toward the house.

27 | Downfall

"Creatures are fragile creations – mere bones and blood, flesh and fear.
Our only strength is from the gifts Piasa bestows on each,
which we ignore at our own great peril."

- Practical Wisdom, for Chicks and Hatchlings

Dolly wouldn't stop. Her keening cries mingled with the acrid air and created an unbearable mud of misery.

"Tuh, stop your moaning. It's not helping any of us," hissed Woodfawn.

Robert shuffled and clucked quietly, but Dolly did not seem to hear any of them. Her warbling cry continued.

Chickory pressed against the door. Despair coursed through every feathertip. Her stalks ached from the journey, her eyes burned from the foul air, and her heart needled from a thousand stings. Fayne had betrayed them. Lord Germaine had said she led them to death, that they would die in the valley, and she had gone with him anyway. Not even a last look at her, a final farewell to her friend. Hadn't she protected Fayne? Hadn't she always come to her? Followed her? Tried to help her even in her maddening moments of lunacy?

Negotiate our surrender…

Just like that and the journey was over. Regret choked her, like a pinecone caught in her throat. To end it here, in this horrible place, doomed to lose sight and eventually die with no hope. Chicks stolen away and brought to serve Lord Germaine and whatever wicked plan he clearly had for the way. She understood now how Georgia had given up, become cold and unfeeling. Daisy had tried to comfort her, tried to preen and soothe, but her whole body felt numb and eventually Daisy had gone away.

"Bird?" The muffled whine of Tucker could be heard on the other side.

She closed her eyes, too exhausted to respond.

"Bird? They've gone inside the house. The yard is empty." He panted and his whines trembled with anxiety.

She sighed. "Let them. It doesn't matter now, Tucker. You should go, run into the hills. There's nothing to stay here for," she said.

"No, no. I'm not leaving," he said. A dull thud resonated through the boards, as though he had laid down against the side. "I smell the hunters. They are close. Very close now." He whined again.

The hunters… At least the unliving seemed controlled, kept at bay. Maybe the hunters would at least end it quickly. One thrust of the spear, a quick death. Not a pleasant one, not the way Piasa foretold, but death nonetheless. Chickory longed for it now, an end to this miserable world, one not worth living in. Where Hums became the unliving and the unliving wandered the land and birds could speak to them—

A strange thought flickered through Chickory's mind. She straightened a little and tried to capture it with a spinners web of concentration. It was impossible, it *must* be impossible, but so was everything else. Where birds could speak with their minds, could control the unliving—but if they were once Hums too…

Her mind flooded with certainty and her flesh prickled with hope. "Tucker, um, how close are they? The hunters?"

"On the main road," he whimpered. "But they are passing us. I don't think they can see the house here."

Chickory swallowed hard against her fear. "I need you to listen to me very carefully…"

***

The door to the coop slid open and Lazen poked his head through the entryway. "Come on, it is time," he said.

Chickory pushed past him and hurried to the bottom of the ramp. The sun had returned to its roost and a small sliver of the moon perched in the sky. Tucker was gone, that was good. Her body trembled with worry, but there was nothing she could do for him now.

The others staggered out, looking disoriented and miserable as they followed Lazen back to the porch, where the birds had assembled again. Lord Germaine stood on the porch with Fayne at his side.

Chickory shivered. She didn't know how, but she had to try. She concentrated and focused on the word in her mind, tried to make it loud as Fayne and Lord Germaine could. She stared at Fayne, imagined the word stabbing her in the head like a long curved talon. In long-ago dreams, she had spoken to Fayne, had been able to send words through her mind, and so she tried desperately again: *Hunters.*

Fayne didn't look at her, didn't give any sign that she could hear. Chickory wasn't the kind of bird they were but she squeezed her eyes shut and tried to feel the word in every feathertip: *Hunters.*

"I applaud you, common birds. You have come so far, traveled this wide world. Not many could have done as you have," Lord Germaine said, as he bobbed his head.

The assembled roosters and cockerels flapped their wings in feathery applause.

"But birds are limited, it is true. Your journey has come to an end. It has been difficult for you. Fayne has told me of all you have endured." He clicked his beak, a pitying sound. "I am pleased to be able to bring you comfort. Shelter and food. Fayne has negotiated a new space for the hens. Your future chicks will serve our glorious mission."

Dolly moaned and bowed her head. Woodfawn growled.

Lord Germaine turned his gaze to Robert. "Robert, I know you care deeply for your flock. I will care for them and you can pass with the comfort that they will be safe."

Horror tightened like a clawed hand around Chickory's throat. "Fayne! Stop! Don't let this happen! Don't—"

(*Come*)

The word dropped in Chickory's mind, but it was Lord Germaine, calling on—

"No, Fayne! Not the unliving!" squawked Chickory. *Hunters,* she focused the thought and imagined the hunter's spear, imagined the sharp tip skewering Fayne. *HUNTERS.*

Fayne looked at her and her yellow eyes widened.

(*Sick birds. Kill the sick birds.*) Fayne's words came, cold and clear, and dripped through Chickory's mind.

"Lord! Lord Germaine!" A young cockerel surged around the side of the house, panting.

Lord Germaine fluffed his wings irritably. "What is it, Darning?"

"T-t-that dog came back! He's attacking the guard out front!"

Lord Germaine growled and with a mighty flap, flew off the porch and landed at the foot of the steps. "Enough of this nonsense. Seith, Lazen. Kill the cocks, take the hens," he said and bolted toward the front of the house.

"No!" Chickory turned to Robert.

Seith launched himself with a terrible screech, but Robert rose to meet him in the air, claws extended. They clashed together, wings beating at each other furiously.

Chickory threw herself at Seith. Pip launched too and peppered Seith with his small snapping beak. Lazen charged toward them and his eyes glinted with murderous glee.

Blood spattered the ground as the metal spurs cut through feathers and flesh.

"Chickory!" Fayne flew off the back porch and collided with Lazen. The side attack knocked him off balance and he tumbled across the grass.

The assembled cockerels broke their formation and gave a screeching cry as they charged.

(*COME, kill the sick birds. COME*) Fayne's words seared in Chickory's mind like the dazzling flash of a sky-stinger.

A streak of light blazed through the sky and hit the ground next to Chickory.

She blinked stupidly as flames caught the dry grass.

A spear.

The fire spread and the roaring heat slithered across the ground like a death worm. Another flaming spear streaked through the air and thudded against the grass on the other side of the yard. Smoke rose like vaporous trees, branches reaching toward the sky.

"Fire! Fire!" Voices cried as the cockerels realized what was happening. They scattered, their attack forgotten as they tried to escape the spreading heat.

"Look, up there!" One of them squealed.

The top of the house was engulfed in smoke. Fire licked the edges of the roof and fluttered in the light breeze. The dry world, so long deprived of rain, burned.

Lord Germaine and Tucker skittered around the edge of the house. Lord Germaine saw the nightmare unfolding in his yard and screeched as he charged Fayne. Tucker bounded over the big rooster's head in one glorious leap.

The female hunter turned the corner of the house, a spear gripped in her hands. Blood dripped down her arms and her vivid eyes widened, red with the reflection of the fire. Around her swarmed the dazed birds, but most had lost their will to fight. They fled before her, confused by the flames raging on both sides of the yard. The male hunter appeared beside her and he too gripped a long spear in his hands. The hunters skewered the confused birds with the sharp tips. Their feathery bodies flapped and twitched as they spasmed with the final throes of death.

Tucker ran to Chickory and licked her head. He panted and whined, spinning on his paws. "Fire! Bird, there's fire! We must run away!"

Panic surged through Chickory's feathers. "Wait, just wait! Fayne, they're coming!" she called through the roar around them.

Fayne cowered on the porch stairs.

"Noooo!" roared Lord Germaine. (*COME COME COME*) His enraged words bellowed in Chickory's mind and she squealed in pain.

A loud chorus of moans rose above the crackle of the growing fire, as the unliving heeded Lord Germaine's call. The metal fence creaked and shuddered beneath the weight of their attempts. Lord Germaine charged to the overgrown thicket and using his beak, jerked on a small rope that hung from the—gate. It swung open.

(*KILL KILL KILL*) His command throbbed and engulfed the yard in its rage.

The unliving surged through the once-barrier and staggered across the burning yard, oblivious to the fire as it seized their clothes and sizzled their rotting flesh. They ignored the birds around their feet and headed directly for the hunters.

(*KILL THEM*)

Chickory staggered, pressure threatening to crack her mind like an egg shell. Lazen gave one terrified look at the unliving, at the hunters, then turned and fled.

Robert staggered upright, his eyes dazed and rolling. Daisy and Dolly cowered amid the flames, and Woodfawn trembled all over.

"Help them! Take them out of here!" Chickory screeched at Tucker.

He yowled with fear and nosed Robert forward, toward the slats of the metal fence. The others staggered after Tucker and Robert.

The yard drowned in the wavering heat of the fire, smoke blinding Chickory. The deafening drone of the unliving, and the screams of the—

The hunters.

The unliving had reached them and their spears jerked like striking death worms as they worked in unison against their familiar enemy. They struck the unliving in the heads and each one fell, not moving, but more surged forward and the hunters staggered back. The whites of their frightened eyes shone in the fire light.

(*Help*)

A small plaintive cry dripped inside Chickory's mind.

"Fayne?" She whirled around, searching for her friend. "Fayne!"

Lord Germaine stood over Fayne, slashing at her with his beak and curved metal spurs, as she writhed beneath him.

Chickory charged. She collided with his heft, his huge feathery body, and they tumbled together, a tangle of wings and legs.

Lord Germaine rolled upright and lunged at Chickory. His spurs sunk into her wing and the flesh tore like the delicate gut of a slow squish. She trilled with pain. Heat licked her tail feathers and she rolled away. They smoldered with flame. She looked up at Lord Germaine. Madness gleamed in his eyes, a sadistic *hunger* known in all killers of the world, in all the unliving, here in this *monster bird.*

Chickory's mind splintered as a high pitch whirring screech cut through her skull. The sound rattled through the bone and soft flesh inside. The landscape throbbed in bright violent shades of red and black, flames and smoke.

Beside her, Lord Germaine thrashed on the ground. White mucous frothed from his beak and nostrils. His body jerked and his blazing eyes became blank, the madness finally gone.

(*Get up*)

"Fayne?" Chickory struggled to rise, but the whirring screech still rattled through her body, blotting out all sense, all reason.

(*GET UP*)

As though the words were hands, Chickory was lifted to her claws and shoved forward by a force she couldn't see. The yard wavered, slow and warped. The unliving had fallen on the hunters and the female gave a final scream as one sunk its blunt teeth into her throat.

The air reeked of burning flesh.

Chickory staggered forward, unable to fight the force that pushed her from all sides. All around her, flopping in the flames and writhing on the grass, were Lord Germaine's birds. The sound cut through all of them, none were immune. Fayne stood in the middle of the yard, her beak pointed skyward. Somehow, someway, she was emitting the horrible sound.

(*I cannot hold them*)

The whisper in Chickory's mind sounded faint, weak.

"Come with me," Chickory whispered, though she knew Fayne could not hear her, and the force wouldn't allow her to stop. So, she tried, once more, to focus her thoughts: *Come with me.*

(*I cannot*)

Come with me, Chickory raged and terror clawed inside her breast. She couldn't see any of the others, didn't know if they lived or died. But Fayne must not die. She focused all her desperation, her pleading, her fear, into the words: *COME WITH ME.*

Fayne lowered her beak and the horrible sound disappeared.

"Fayne!" The force shoved Chickory against the back fence of the yard.

On the other side, Robert waited for her. "You're almost there! The others are up ahead."

Chickory staggered through the slats, into the swamp of bramble. The thorns ripped at her feathers, but she didn't feel them. The force of the horrible sound and the unseen hands faded, and she whirled around, ready to surge back into the yard, back to Fayne.

But Fayne was right behind her.

"Go, just go," she wheezed at Chickory. "Through the thorns, toward the hills."

Relief squeezed her breast and she couldn't breathe. She forced herself to turn away, to obey.

"Thank Piasa, oh thank her, thank her," Robert gasped. But whether Fayne or Piasa, Chickory didn't ask. They shoved through the brambles together.

Behind them, the fire had become a raging mouth and it consumed the entire house and yard. The air swarmed with flecks of ash and hot embers. Plumes of smoke billowed in the sky.

Tucker's barks boomed from one side of them and Chickory shoved through a tangle of thorns.

"Chickory!" trilled Pip. The rest of the flock waited on a small dirt trail, hidden by large stones and the slope of the hill.

Tucker ran to her and his tongue lashed her head, her beak, nearly suffocating her with saliva. "Bird, oh, bird!" His whole body wiggled with excitement. "I brought them! Just as you told me!"

"You did so well, Tucker, so well," Chickory said, choking out the words between licks.

"Oh, oh, oh! Piasa bless it!" squealed Daisy.

Woodfawn strutted anxiously back and forth across the trail, her feathers black with soot. Most of her tail feathers were gone.

Fayne sunk to the ground, shivering and trembling.

Chickory leaned in beside her. "Are you all right?"

"Not yet, keep running," Fayne gasped. She staggered upright and fled up the hillside.

None of them looked back.

28 | Growing New Feathers

"No creature was born in perfect, complete form.
Piasa birthed and hatched each creature with loving precision,
bearing the pain of motherhood in all its many forms.
We all began with a simple egg."

- Words of Piasa, Final Clutch, Final Year

The sliver of moon vanished behind a downy layer of clouds and no light illuminated the path. They scrambled through the darkness and stumbled over loose stones and tangled limbs of downed trees. The flames of the fire were a distant glow and though they could still smell the thick smoke, the breeze blew most of the choking thickness away. The land filled with the shadows of large boulders, but they did not stop or hide among them.

Chickory could barely hear the panting of the others over her own labored breathing. The musky tang of Tucker's breath wafted over her head as he followed close behind her. They had made their way so frantically, so quickly. Had any of them been left behind in the dark? They were all exhausted, wounded, and it was difficult to stay alert.

"Wait—wait, I don't think they're following," Chickory wheezed. Her wind pouch burned and when she stopped, her stalks shook unsteadily. "Are we all here?"

"I'm here," said Woodfawn.

"Us too," Daisy said.

"Pip's here, as am I, and there's Fayne too," said Robert.

"And there's Tucker and there's me," Chickory said. Faint relief fluttered in her breast.

Pip hopped away from them and Chickory heard his claws scrabble on stone.

"I can't go on," said Woodfawn. She sounded shaky, cold, and older.

But they all did. The long sunrises and terrible journey had stretched for so long that it felt like many seasons had passed, though they were still certainly in the sun season.

"We have to keep on." Fayne's voice hissed in the darkness.

"Look up there! There's a light!" Pip called from where he stood atop one of the boulders.

Chickory turned to face the sloping hill. Yes, a small light glowed faintly in the distance. Tucker turned his nose into the wind.

"I smell other birds," he said.

"What if they're Germaine's birds?" peeped Dolly.

"T-t-they are not," Fayne said. "Let us p-p-press on and see if they will share the light with us for the night." The shake and stutter in her voice made her sound like a small chick again, like the Fayne they had left behind on the farm.

None protested and as they pushed forward, Chickory felt swallowed in the deep, heady presence of the mountain beneath her claws. The steepness increased and the soil grumbled as the ancient soul of the mountain stirred. Piasa had given all parts of the earth life and Chickory shivered as she remembered the stories of mountains that roared and breathed fire.

The ground leveled out and tucked against a sheer ledge in the rock, stood a small house made of wood. A single light glowed on the front porch and the dark windows were shut tight. Along one side were a few garden beds, the same as Lady had used to grow knobby vegetables and bright red tomatoes. On the other side, a large flat square reflected the light, directed toward where the sun would later rise from its roost.

"Solar p-p-powered," Fayne said.

Chickory was too exhausted to ask her what she meant.

"I don't see anyone," Daisy said and she gave a small relieved sigh. "Maybe they've all gone too."

"Or maybe Germaine got to them too," Woodfawn said.

"Germaine did no such thing and you'll forgive me if I don't ask you to stay," a sharp voice said.

They all strained to see in the darkness beyond the pool of light they stood in.

"We don't mean you any harm. We're in no shape to harm anyone, really," Chickory said.

From the darkness that cloaked the underside of the porch, a large white bird emerged. Her feathers bristled aggressively and she was larger than any of their flock. Her brilliant red comb quivered. She would have been beautiful, but for the hostility that radiated from every feather. "Then don't. Be on your way, we don't want you here," she said.

Woodfawn took a step forward. "We can't go on. We've just escaped Germaine and we're—"

"Enough!" The hen interrupted and stared with surprise at Tucker, who had edged forward and growled. "Who is this beast? Why does he walk with you?"

"He is our friend and guardian. We have traveled a long way and intend to continue onward at d-d-daybreak. Germaine and his kind have fallen. They are dead, and you will not see any more of them," Fayne said.

The hen jerked her head scornfully. "But you. Are you not one of *them*?"

"We'll be gone at daybreak. Piasa watches us and knows our heart. She's coming with us. We won't bother you," Chickory said. "We're telling the truth."

The hen snorted. "Hmpf. You must be. Germaine would have never allowed a group like you to escape. After all, I knew him better than any bird I suppose. He was our very own rooster, once upon a time," she said.

Dolly and Daisy chirped with unease and shuffled under the slope of Tucker's belly.

The hen sighed. "That was long ago. We left. Really, I guess we escaped like you. He had gone mad and his peculiar… wants. Well, I'm sure you know of them now. You're lucky, and I guess we're lucky now too, if what you say is true."

"It is," Chickory insisted.

"Morgan, can't they stay for the night? There's enough room for all of us," a voice whispered from the dark porch.

Morgan turned back toward the porch and her stiff agitated body drooped with sudden resignation. "Right. Well, come in then. If you want," she said.

Chickory looked back at Dolly, Daisy, and Woodfawn, who crowded around Tucker, shuffling nervously.

"Come on. We can't stay out here in the open," she called to them.

Fayne's eyes surged with a storm of emotion and, too afraid to ask, Chickory turned away from her and led the way toward the porch.

The house had been erected on posts and a stacked wall of stone, which left a large sheltered cavern underneath. As they shuffled through a gap, the light outside disappeared and the darkness swallowed them up. Even Tucker could shuffle underneath the overhang and lay comfortably on one side. They must be well hidden from the outside, though the dark reminded Chickory of the squalor of Germaine's imprisoned hens. The coop had likely burned in that ferocious fire, but that would be a mercy to those hens. She longed to sleep outside, under the open sky, but knew it was unsafe, that they could not risk it.

As her vision adjusted, she saw the flock gathered here was not an entirely small one. Seven hens, two roosters, and a couple ducks squatted here, their feathered bodies pressed closely together.

"You'll want to move in closer. The nights are cold up here," said one of the hens. Though it was dark, she looked like she might be a red feathered hen. *Like Rosie.* "My name is Margaret," she said.

"I'm Chickory," Chickory said and sunk in beside her.

Fayne and the others shuffled closer, introducing themselves in quiet whispers. The circle bustled with movement as they made room for the newcomers. Morgan nestled on the other side of Margaret.

"How did you escape?" asked Gibbons. Atop his head was a mass of frizzy feathers and he wasn't much bigger than Pip.

"We might ask the same of you. Germaine had a huge lot of birds there," said Chickory, unsure of how to answer his question plainly. Not that they would believe it even if she dared to say it out loud.

One of the ducks spoke. "He didn't always. The-uh, fool birds are-uh, relatively new thing-uh. He's been-uh, scouring-uh, the countryside for-uh, new recruits, trying to gather-uh, whoever-uh, survived. We-uh, escaped long before-uh, this new dive-uh, into madness." His lilting voice quivered. Perhaps he had an injury or had simply been hatched that way.

Gibbons waggled his head in agreement. "He had taken over the yard and grew increasingly paranoid about the Hums. He was positive they were talking of harvesting him; he was so terrible to the hens and to any of the other roosters that I'm not surprised if they had been planning to return him to the soil. When he talked of… of rising up against them, we snuck away. He didn't have as many to chase us then, though he came looking for us later. Last season actually. We scrambled up the mountain and hid in snow drifts, freezing our tails off. But it worked. They'd left us alone for quite a time now," Gibbons said and he trembled as he spoke.

"Well, from the sounds of it, he won't be returning to terrorize the countryside," Morgan said with a satisfied chirp. "Let Piasa settle him now."

A swell of guilt squeezed Chickory's stomach. "Well, yes, um, Germaine may be gone, but there is still much danger and it might not be far behind." Every bird stared and the collective weight crushed her like an avalanche of snow.

"What danger? We are quite hidden here. Food is… scarce but we've managed. If Germaine is gone, we might even venture further out now," Morgan said.

"It's not an easy story, one that is difficult to explain, but we now know the Hums have been struck down by a terrible illness and not all of them… stayed dead," Chickory said, not looking at Fayne. "We have seen this for ourselves as we've traveled from far away. Everywhere the Hums have died in great numbers, but there are unliving who still roam, and they will kill any living thing they encounter."

Morgan hesitated. "Unliving? What—I don't understand."

"Something in the sickness made some of them live, even though they should die. It's ridiculous to even imagine, but it's true. I wish it weren't," Chickory said.

"We thought… when our Hums went inside and never appeared again, we had suspected they might have gone on. But never had we imagined it would have been so widespread. And I don't know what you mean by these *unliving* ones. I don't see how it's possible," said Morgan.

"It is true," Tucker said and he whimpered.

The other birds squeaked nervously and scooted away from him.

"But this sickness… If the Hums have been so drastically affected, why would they seek us out with violence? Piasa has directed the way," Morgan continued.

"The sickness was given to the humans from b-b-birds," Fayne said.

Woodfawn gasped and Dolly and Daisy peeped and looked at each other in confusion.

Morgan waggled her head. "You lie."

Fear thrummed in Chickory's ears. "We have no reason to lie." She had known it was true, somewhere in the back of her mind, but to hear Fayne say it made it real. "They have killed us off all over. There are hardly any of us left, I'm sorry to say, except for small groups hidden away like you all," Chickory said.

The birds shuffled, but no one seemed to know what to say or what to do. Chickory did not envy them the discovery. Their natural order, the way of Piasa, had been destroyed, the world so drastically altered that she now knew it would never be the same. The realization wasn't easy for them; it would never be easy again.

"We thought you might bring us word of better news after all. Some sort of possibility," Margaret said and a few peeped in agreement. "Why have you brought us this word of sadness? When we have so little to hope for as it is?"

"Because there is still hope," Chickory said, ignoring Fayne's insistent stare. "There is… well, there's a valley, a safe place for us to live."

"No." Fayne rose to her claws. A fierce pulse of energy radiated from her and the others cried out in surprise. Waves buzzed over them and the air prickled like a brewing sun season storm.

"They cannot c-c-come with us. We can't take every b-b-broken soul," Fayne stuttered. "The valley—the valley—the valley—the—the—the—" Her words melded together in an uncontrolled rhythm. Before Chickory could rise, Fayne turned and fled into the darkness.

"What was that?" Morgan said, her yellow eyes wide with fear and hostility. "What on Piasa's sacred soil was *that*?"

Chickory couldn't find words and instead followed Fayne outside. The house light had turned off now and the clouds had shifted, revealing the small slip of moon above.

Beyond the edge of the overgrown garden beds, Chickory found Fayne crouched down in the dirt. As she shuffled closer, her feathers lifted and stood straight out from her body. Her flesh prickled and buzzed as though each individual feather sparked with an individual force. A powerful swell of energy washed over her and the unseen hands, the ones that had shoved her out of the burning yard, now jerked her toward Fayne, sucking at her like the howling wind of her nightmares.

"What's happening? It's getting worse, isn't it? Answer me!" Fear strangled her wind pouch and panic throttled her speech.

"It is so strong now—now—now. It hurts," Fayne whispered. Her voice was so faint, so fraught with terrifying anxiety, that Chickory didn't know what to say or do.

"Don't leave me now. Don't—don't—why?" Fayne stuttered as her beak chattered uncontrollably.

She wanted to run, to hide, to leave Fayne to whatever horror was coming.

My friend. A swell of pity, of sorrow surged through her and Chickory gave in to the force. The charge seared through her bones and rattled through the hidden corners of her mind. *My friend.* She tucked in beside Fayne and pressed her breast to hers, as she cooed whatever comforting words she could manage.

Within the strange unseen bubble wrapped around them, age warped and distorted, like many sunrises or entire seasons swept by in the thick field of energy. Her mind churned like an ocean, dragging her deeper with every moment that passed.

Then Fayne let out a sharp cry and the force broke over them like an impossible cresting wave. Pressure drummed against the skin of Chickory's ears and pressed against the sockets of her eyes. The energy dissipated with a low hiss. The air smelled like damp earth after rain and the ground steamed with unseen heat. Whether she slept or fell into the pulse of unconsciousness Chickory did not know, but she surrendered herself to the waiting blackness.

29 | The Truth

"The truth is that we are meant to never know truth.
Piasa shields us from knowing, a burden too great
for any creature to bear."

\- Wisdom of Piasa, Final Clutch, Fourth Year

Chickory twitched and pain pulsed through every feathertip. Even her beak ached, as though she had tried to carve stone with the curved tip. She looked over at Fayne. Did she still breath, still live, or had the strange crush of power killed her as she slept?

Fayne opened her yellow eyes and gazed back at Chickory.

"You all right?" Chickory's throat ached like she had swallowed sharp stones.

"W-w-we have to go. Now," Fayne said in a quiet peep.

Chickory staggered to her claws and the pain spread like the warmth of a cold season fire. The sky glowed orange as the sun rose from its roost and climbed into the sky.

Fayne jerked upright, though she did not speak of pain. She looked dazed and she stared at the landscape as though she had never seen it before.

"Let's go back to the others," Chickory said.

They shuffled their way past the garden beds and Chickory snapped up a small unfortunate grub. The crunch of the soft body made her shiver a little, though her stomach bloomed to welcome the morsel of much needed food. Fayne didn't eat or even seem to notice the shiny red tomatoes nestled in one of the overgrown plants.

"There you are!" Robert rushed to them. He bobbed his head anxiously, looking Chickory and Fayne over. "I couldn't find you in the dark. Are you all right? Fayne? What's wrong? Please, tell me."

The worry and despair in his voice made Chickory's stomach cramp with pain. How she wanted to tell him everything, take the time to explain it all… but she wasn't sure how or even what to explain. "We're all right, but we should move away from this place. We're close now," she said instead.

"Yes, yes. The others… they've decided to come with us," Robert said.

Chickory glanced at Fayne, but Fayne didn't protest or even return the look.

"Really? How'd you manage it? They looked awfully frightful last night… though we all are, I suppose," Chickory said.

"Seems they've had problems with sharp teeth who live in this area. Tucker seems a mighty powerful reason to come along."

"Right. Well, let's go. Fayne?"

"Y-y-yes. Hurry," she said, squinting as though the words hurt to speak.

Concern shimmered in his eyes, but she moved past him, toward the others.

The odd flock had left the safety of the porch and gathered outside the house, foraging in the short grass while they waited. As Chickory approached, they turned one by one to face her, and her flesh prickled. Dolly and Daisy shuffled closer together.

Tucker padded over to her and licked her head. "Bird? You all right now?"

"All right as we can be. It's time to move on," Chickory said.

Behind her followed Robert and Fayne.

"Has monster bird announced where we're going?" Woodfawn asked, though her tone was subdued.

"The valley is over these mountains ahead. We're very close, though the climb will be difficult," Chickory said. She wanted Fayne to direct them, but her blank stare and eerie silence persisted.

The others looked nervously at each other, then at Fayne.

Irritation wiggled in her stomach. "Come on, let's go." She strutted past them and headed toward the same trail they had followed as they fled Germaine. The path continued up the steeply rising land, disappearing into the curves of the jutting earth. The faint smell of smoke still hung in the air, but with the light of the sunrise, no flames could be seen and the horrible house and yard were obstructed by the slope of the hillside.

Chickory did not look back, but felt the others follow, their stares pinching her spine like the many bites of a sting-sting. Fayne strutted directly behind her, silent as a stone.

All their travel had not fully prepared them for the climb they faced. The flock struggled to make their way around fields of boulders and through the increasing overgrowth of thorny bramble. The ducks' wide flat feet slipped on the rocky terrain and they waddled desperately, trying to keep up with the others. The male's brilliant green feathered head gleamed in the sun, a bright signal to any sky birds who might swoop overhead. Chickory tried to encourage them, tried to urge them forward, but they slowed to a painful stagger up the mountainside.

Eventually the sun reached the other side of the mountains, casting them in deep shadow. The moon appeared, still small, and darkness rapidly fell over the land.

"We're nearly at the top now," gasped Chickory. She glanced back. The others had fallen behind again, resting by a cluster of large boulders. "Fayne, we'll have to stop for the night. The others can't go on. We're all exhausted."

But Fayne said nothing and gave no sign she heard Chickory at all.

Inside Chickory, a continuous wellspring of conflicting feelings bubbled. Anger, worry, fear, and irritation confused her mind and made it difficult to think clearly. "Fayne, are you all right? Truly?"

But still Fayne said nothing, only stared blankly out into the encroaching night. So Chickory headed back to where the others waited. Most of them had already squeezed into various crevasses in the rock, nestling together for warmth and comfort.

Morgan cocked her head as Chickory approached. "Is she addled? Truly, she must be."

"It's… this has been a horrible journey. We've lost so many and there's just—it's difficult to say," Chickory conceded. "She's always been like this really. Sometimes she goes off, but she always comes back around. Eventually."

"Does she wander off like that too?"

Chickory jerked and looked back up the hillside.

Fayne was gone.

She dashed back to where they had stood, the knot inside her breast pounding in a painful erratic rhythm. Fayne had left, gone into the wildness beyond. She had left *them*, abandoned them when they needed her most. "Fayne!" Chickory whirled in place, searching among the dark ripples of tumbled stone and prickly avenues of brambles.

There. A mass of black and white feathers strutted away from them, farther into the darkness. Chickory surged after her, sliding on the precariously loose stones and dirt.

"Fayne, stop! Wait for us!" she screeched, but Fayne did not seem to hear. Rage fueled her aching body and she charged forward, closing the gap between them. "Damn you, STOP!" Chickory threw herself at Fayne.

They squabbled for a moment, a tangle of angry pecking beaks and desperate squawks. Then Chickory broke away, gasping. Fayne's eyes, once so piercing and hypnotic, only shimmered with vague fear.

"We must stop, we need to rest. You're leaving us all behind," said Chickory. She hated how shrill she sounded, but anger and terror still coiled in her stomach, making her insides feel very small.

Fayne blinked oddly, as though seeing her for the first time. "Right. Stay—Stay t-t-together. We need to speak," she finally said.

"Birds!" Tucker bounded over to them, whining. He sniffed Fayne and licked her head. "Where are you going?"

"Nowhere. Tucker, just, go back to the others." Chickory tried to still the quiver in her voice. "Keep them safe. Fayne and I will look ahead, find the best way through. I'll come back."

Tucker whined again. He licked Fayne once more than padded obediently in the direction of the others, gazing over his shoulder at them as he went.

Fayne turned and continued her stumble forward. The mountainside was almost in complete darkness, the small moon producing little light.

"Fayne, wait," called Chickory but she had to run to catch up again. Her stalks trembled with exhaustion and the whisper of fear hummed through her feathery body. Something was happening. To Fayne, to her, to them all. Chickory's apprehension grew as they continued up the rise of the land. Behind them, the land spread out in a wide dizzying expanse. Below, in the Hum settlement they had passed through, small dots of light glinted. Some still lived in a world full of the unliving. Like Sam, the old man Hum, the hunters, and all the others still fighting to survive, still killing to live.

As all creatures do.

Awe stabbed her stomach like a porcupine quill.

"This way," Fayne said and disappeared behind a heap of boulders. Chickory followed blindly. She ducked behind the boulders and strutted out onto a small flat space tucked into the mountainside. Fayne stood at the edge, where the mountain fell away in a sharp drop off. "I have something to show you," she said.

Chickory approached but fear kept her back from the frightening edge. "Well, what is it?"

In a sudden jerk, the plateau bent around them, like light slanting through the uneven surface of water. A sickening, swooping sensation fluttered in her stomach, like all the nightmares that had followed her through this journey. An unliving child. A carnival. Fayne.

Fayne too, seemed to bend and straighten. A terrifying slurry of images and wailing sound engulfed them, spinning around like a whirlpooling pond.

"Help me!" Chickory cried. They were trapped in the dream, the terrible nightmare. How could they be there again?

(*I am helping you*) The cold words dripped into Chickory's mind, familiar and somehow a comfort in the midst of the strange chaos.

"What—what is this place?" Chickory peeped as she stared at the images flickering around them, like stories had somehow entered the world they lived in, moving and breathing, though they could not possibly be real.

The landscape wobbled and they no longer stood on a mountain—they stood in a meadow of trim green grass. Here the wind was calm and full of the familiar scents of sun season blossoms and the pungent smell of soft leaf plants. Behind Fayne, the winding dirt path twisted sinuously down a hill, disappearing into the shadow of the valley below.

She turned and gasped. She stood at the bottom step of Lady's small blue house.

"Why are we here? I thought we were going to the valley." Chickory's confusion mingled with longing for home, a longing for an end to this terrible journey.

(*We are still exactly as we were. But you are inside my mind now. Until recently, I did not think I could do it. But this will explain far better than I ever could. Now I can show you.*)

The words dripped rapidly into Chickory's mind, like a torrent of streaming water pressing against the backs of her eyes. "Show me what?"

The force, the one in the field, the one in Germaine's yard, closed around her body like a giant unseen hand. She squealed and struggled against it. The brush and boulders distorted and melted around them, pooling at their clawed feet. Then it expanded with a bright flash of light.

They stood in the middle of a great Hum settlement, greater than any Chickory had seen or imagined. Tall buildings sprouted up from the ground, bursting toward the sky in great columns of shining metal and mirror. She shivered as details formed and settled, becoming clear and real. A terrible smell filled the air, choking her. The terrible smell of sickness, of the unliving, mingled with the smoke. Inside her mind, Fayne's voice whispered, intent and rapid. A roar horse (*a car, the Hums drive them to conquer the world*) burned, thick black smoke poured forth from shattered windows. Chickory stepped away from its incredible radiating heat and tripped, sprawling onto a pile of dead Hums (*human, they are called humans*). She gazed down into a staring human eye, a bright blue one. These bodies did not move and as Chickory struggled upright, the bodies spread in either direction, disappearing around the bends in the road but continuing all the same.

Her mind raved with pain and fury. "Why are you showing me this?"

(*Because you need to know why it must be this way. Why I can't go with you.*)

The land around them crumpled again, the colors splashing into a shimmering fluid, pooling at their feet. Chickory waited for it to explode again into detail, a new horror to see and understand, but as they stood suspended in the quiet stillness, she was released.

She collapsed onto the familiar earth and realized they were back on the mountainside, the real one. Her mind spun and hiccupped painfully and she didn't know if she could stand. Fayne's power, strange but certainly never dangerous, chilled Chickory with renewed awe and terror. Could Fayne reach inside and twist things, control—her? She had directed the hunters toward them, with Tucker's help, Chickory knew that, but had she twisted something inside Chickory too? Was that why she had followed Fayne, her dearest friend, through this horrible nightmare?

Fayne tilted her head. "I would never do that," she said. "You followed me, strangely enough, of your own accord. At the time I did not understand why. But as I have told you on many occasions, you are not like the others. You are special, a mind more open to the intricate patterns of seen and unseen. You listened to me even when there was no reason to, open to the remote possibility that what I saw might be true. That is why you can hear me, when no others can and understand my words. The dreams we shared? That is why I have brought you here."

Chickory tried to speak, but couldn't. Even now, as Fayne spoke, words and images streamed through Chickory's mind, making it hard to think, to feel, even to see.

Fayne stepped toward the edge of the plateau and gazed at the vast landscape, now completely cloaked in night. Above twinkled pinpricks of light (*stars, balls of gases we cannot reach*). Chickory struggled to her claws and tentatively stepped toward Fayne, coming closer to the edge itself. The immense height made her dizzy with fear but she forced herself to look out and forward. As Fayne did.

"This is all that is left," Fayne said before Chickory could speak. "The situation is the same throughout the region. Perhaps throughout the world. Humans have died by the millions. Chickens, birds of every variety and breed, verge on extinction."

"Because of the sickness?" Chickory asked.

"This sickness is because of me. Because of all chickens like me. Germaine and their lot? We all come from the same place. The same place we are headed to," said Fayne.

"The valley? You've been there before? Germaine called it… Origin."

"It is where I was born. I say born, but truly we were created. Engineered by clever humans who thought they could make a clever bird—a well-behaved chicken. It is complicated and my knowledge far surpasses your own at this p-p-point," Fayne said, sounding apologetic. "You will understand soon enough. The humans could not predict the consequences. That a virus that already existed on a faraway continent, that already p-p-proved deadly, would commune with our complex and genetically different immune systems. We became the catalyst, causing the death of almost all of us, bird and human alike." Fayne shuddered. "Now the ones who still live, must fight against the unliving, a bizarre byproduct of this d-d-disease."

Chickory tried to understand. "And the visions? What you did back there, you saved us. Germaine, they were terrible creatures. Not like you. You're not…evil. And your power, your abilities…"

"Yet another unanticipated result. A clever chicken that would continue to evolve if left to her natural course. I doubt even they could have imagined what their tinkering would produce. Not that it matters. The visions, the ability to influence, they have only led to this," she said.

"I-I don't understand."

Fayne whirled to face her and her eyes blazed with anguish, of a torment so deep it was a visceral pain. "This is my fault. *I* caused all this. Lady is dead, perhaps hundreds, thousands, millions like her. Rosie, Lacey, Georgia, they're all dead because of my terrible judgment. Because deep inside *I* carry this disease. When Lady brought me to the Farm, with my brothers and sisters, they all died but somehow, I survived. She had no idea, gave me a home, and brought me in among you. No matter where I go, what I do, I bring death with me. They even planted a little chip inside my brain, a homing signal so I could always return if I were lost. Lost! Now I am taking you all to the only place healthy humans will not go. Because it is the source," said Fayne, breathless, panting.

From the corner of Chickory's eye, a dappled shadow charged. "Woodfawn! No!" she cried, but too late.

Woodfawn collided with Fayne, her claws glinting in the moonlight. They locked together, claws and beaks slashing and cutting as they rolled toward the edge.

"Stop! Stop now!" Chickory screeched.

At the last moment they separated, panting, wild-eyed.

"Woodfawn," Fayne gasped and crumpled on the ground.

"No, you stop this instant! All the lies! Everything you've led us to believe was a lie! 'Killers of the world carry the savagery of their creation inside' and you're hardly a bird! Hardly a bird at all! They're dead because of you and now you lead us to our doom. Monster bird, killer of the worst sort!" Woodfawn shook with rage. The delicate lace of her beautiful dappled feathers gleamed in the moonlight.

A dark helplessness swirled in Chickory's stomach.

Fayne stared at Woodfawn but said nothing.

"And *you*, you brought us along." Woodfawn turned on Chickory and her glare flared with hatred. "We trusted you and you followed this, this *monster*. They are an abomination and thusly so are you. A perversion of all Piasa created."

"She is the only reason we are still alive! Left to your way we would all be little bloody puddles in our nests as the humans tore us to pieces!"

(*No, don't fight this*)

Fayne whispered inside her mind but Chickory concentrated, pushing her out, flexing her mind against Fayne's intrusion. (*NO*)

Fayne looked stunned and took a step back.

"Rosie! Lacey! And Georgia! You left them to die!" Woodfawn let out an anguished screech and charged toward Fayne.

Chickory hadn't felt herself move but Woodfawn sagged under Chickory's side attack, almost rolled off her claws by her speed and forceful shove.

Woodfawn jerked upright. "Why—why would you forsake… all we are? Ever will be?" She gave a ragged growl of pain.

"We are so very much more than that," Chickory hissed. Her chest squeezed with pain and certainty.

A bloom of red was spreading across Woodfawn's breast, thickening and running, as it followed the length of her beautiful feathers. A pool of blood spread across the stone they stood on.

"Ah. It hurts," Woodfawn whispered. She staggered back, a step too far, and for a sickening moment she swayed on the edge, her body trembling as she tried to regain her footing. Her eyes shimmered with fear, with exhaustion, with the weight of some unknown truth, and she fell back, disappearing over the drop off.

(*Oh no, no*) Fayne's soft words did not drip, only exhaled like a sigh in Chickory's mind.

Chickory's throat collapsed and she couldn't draw air. Her claws were wet with Woodfawn's blood.

Monster bird.

Horror twisted her innards and spread through her like a swift venom. She had brooded her first nest alongside Woodfawn, who passed the time with incredible stories about Piasa, about how to be a proper bird. Properness—foolishness—Piasa—death—

Why…?

She slumped to the ground. The night pressed in and raked icy fingers through feathers she couldn't feel, becoming a mere stone trapped in the river of horror and pain.

(*Chickory*) Fayne fluttered her wings softly.

"No, don't. How can this be? To come all this way and have it be like this."

"It was always meant to be this way." Fayne's voice lilted with sorrow. "I am a monstrous creation, just as she said, though for reasons she could not understand. Poor Woodfawn, blinded by the weight of a P-p-piasa that doesn't exist."

"Doesn't?"

Fayne bowed her head. "Not for me. I was never to reach the valley with you, my flock."

A prickle of uncertainty filled Chickory's mind. "You're leaving us? Leaving us here? Now?"

Fayne turned her gaze to the ledge, the same one that had swallowed Woodfawn into darkness. "I must. Will you help me, my dearest friend?"

Chickory struggled upright, pain and anger a white-hot pebble inside her breast as she finally understood why Fayne had brought her to this place. "No. Never. No matter what has happened. It was an accident, a horrible accident. You don't deserve to die. You are the only reason any of us still live."

Fayne's strange raccoon feathers trembled. "You still do not understand. Everywhere I go, I destroy the balance. I am a perversion of nature. I am not of *Piasa*, I am the human's own terrible creation. The disease lives inside me. With Germaine and the others gone, I may be the last to carry it. As long as I am alive, the world is in peril. I should have died, wandered and allowed myself to be taken by a fox or an owl… but I wanted one last chance. A last chance to do something right. To lead my flock, to lead you, to safety. You have been my only friend through these lonely years."

Chickory struggled to understand, but her mind was a whirl of half-spoken thoughts, dark secrets, and a fervent wish. That they were back on the farm. She could almost hear Lady now, humming as she scattered the corn. *Come along, cheeky chicks. Come along.* The memory faded and an anguished cry wedged in her throat. In her desire for everything that had been, she also finally understood that this journey was meant for her. Whether it was Piasa's will or something else, also unseen, this was the reason she had followed Fayne all this way. Why she had abandoned all common sense and bird decency in pursuit of this mysterious valley. Her terrible nightmare, the howling wind sucking them away into oblivion. All along it had been Fayne, a necessary sacrifice to bring the terror to an end. Perhaps she had known, somehow, all along.

(*I want to give this to you*) Fayne's calm cold words caressed Chickory's mind.

Chickory concentrated, focused as she had before, willing herself to touch Fayne's mind, to caress her in return. (*Why now?*)

(*Because you are special and there is still one more thing left to be done. I cannot do it. Besides, in my claws this way of knowing, this power, was never a gift, only a stream of endless sorrow. But I know, as you do, that you will be different. You can bring the others to safety. I will show you the way.*)

Before Chickory could respond, a hot flash seared through the recesses of her mind. The pain radiated from deep inside her spine and settled at the base of her neck. She squealed and writhed against the snaking torment as it spread through her, burning through her veins with a surging power. A distant terrible understanding crashed over her and the way became clear, a droplet of ice she could see and almost hold in her claws.

The pain vanished as it had come and Chickory gasped for air, her head pounding with agony. All was quiet except for Fayne who panted hard beside her.

Slowly Chickory regained her sense of self, struggling against the pulsing power she could feel just beneath the surface of her mind. A giddy, irreverent urge to leap off the cliff and soar away almost overtook her but she wrestled it back inside. The strength of this new knowledge was greater than anything she had ever imagined possible, but she could already feel herself learning its ways, seizing control over the different flickers that struggled to escape her grasp. Chickory's feathers hummed with (*electricity, the power of humans, the lights*) but she was in control once again. She looked at Fayne, a terrible measure of sadness swelling inside her breast (*the heart connects with the brain to create emotion*). With the knowledge came the calm of certainty.

"We've traveled so far, my dear friend, together. To think we would have never made it here without you. How cruel is this world? I never imagined a valley without you." Chickory bowed her head and swallowed hard against a hard lump in her throat.

"You always came to me. I am sorry if I ever deceived you. If I ever failed you." Fayne's head drooped forward as though she meant to sleep. Chickory preened the smooth feathers of her neck and marveled at the dark bands of color. A feathery raccoon but beautiful in all ways a bird could be.

Together they stood on the edge of the plateau, the yawning abyss beneath them. Chickory could smell flowers, (*daffodils*) on the air, a sweetness that crept into her mind, and coiled around the part that shook with terror. She gazed at Fayne and for a long while neither of them spoke.

(*Thank you*) Fayne finally thought.

(*For what?*)

(*For coming with me*) Fayne closed her eyes.

Chickory leaned against her, the warm feathers of her breast pressing against Fayne's in one last embrace, one silent intimate caress. The weight shifted as Chickory pushed forward against Fayne, her dear friend. Fayne stiffened, then submitted, and she leaned back over the void and fell away. Chickory watched Fayne's ringed feathers tremble as the wind ruffled through them, the last light of the moon extinguished in her eyes.

The night swallowed her falling figure and she was gone.

30 | The Valley

"No great journey through jungle and teeth can ever compare
To the eternal delights and comfort of your warm nest,
Which desperately awaits your perfect arrival."

- *Wisdom of Piasa*, First Clutch, Second Year

Heavy clouds blocked the light of the sunrise and the air smothered with heat and weight (*barometric pressure*). Chickory picked her way along the pebbled path, back to where the others waited. The simmering thoughts had kept her awake all night, as she crouched beside the cliff, and waited for something to happen.

But nothing had.

The sunrise meant she had to move on, to leave Woodfawn and Fayne behind for good. *Woodfawn.* So taken with Piasa, so intent on following the way, that she had been blinded to what was required to survive. Chickory understood that now. *Fayne.* So corrupted by the tides within her that she was unable to reach across the void and be as a bird should be. Now those same tides pulsed within Chickory, but Fayne had been right. She *was* different and the tumultuous energy did not overtake and did not detract from her sensible bird nature. Not yet, anyway.

Until then, she must finish what Fayne had started. The others waited for her and though she did not know what was truly over the rise of the mountain, what awaited them in the valley below, she knew she would get them there.

Origin.

Germaine had said that. The place where the nightmare had begun. She couldn't tell the others, *wouldn't* tell them. She would carry it, as Fayne had carried it, alone.

A small rise fell away and she gazed down at the cluster of boulders where the others had stopped for the night. Tucker stood in the middle of the path, nose lifted and scenting the cool air. Daisy and Dolly foraged in the trim scrub brush nestled between rocks.

The twins scrabbled in *panicum virgatum*, also known as switchgrass. Chickory understood how Fayne had known these things as flickering images of Lady's television set, the sound blaring through open windows, the books on her shelf, of listening to her talk on the phone, or even when she murmured to the flock at feeding time—all these thoughts fluttered through her consciousness. They had contributed to the massive repository of information inside Fayne's mind. A repository passed on to Chickory and these details overlapped and made it difficult to think clearly. It was a marvel Fayne didn't stutter more than she had.

Robert stood near the twins, though he did not forage. His gaze panned across the landscape, searching, and when he saw Chickory, he ran to her.

The others emerged from their hiding spaces, bobbing their heads anxiously and searching as well. The twins stopped their eating and stared at her. Tucker wagged his tail.

Robert panted as he came alongside her, looking up the path from where Chickory had come. "Where are the others? Woodfawn? Fayne?"

"They are gone." Sadness needled her heart like thistle.

Robert's head drooped and he gave an anguished chirp. "I had hoped—never mind now. Woodfawn went after you. I tried to stop her but she was enraged, so angry. I asked Piasa to watch over you all."

"Piasa did," Chickory said. It was the only thing she could think to say and he cocked his head. "Piasa resolved their strife in the most honest way and because of them, we will arrive in the valley, safe." Even as she spoke the words, certainty hummed through her, though she couldn't exactly say how she knew this to be true.

"We follow your lead?"

Chickory bobbed her head. "Yes. The valley is over the next rise. We're almost home."

The others approached up the pathway and warbled uncertainly as they searched for the other two who would never return.

There wasn't time to explain it all, so just as Fayne had done so many times before, Chickory turned her back on them and surged up the path leading over the ridge of the mountain. They would follow, they had to follow.

And they did.

She could feel them scrabble along the path behind her and her heart swelled with a complex joy, mingled with sadness, certainty, with the knowledge that their terrible voyage was almost over. Fayne had saved them and Woodfawn, in her own way, had too—bringing them the hope and joy of Piasa's stories, the reminder of how things ought to be, how they might someday be again, if the balance could ever be restored.

The path arched and grew painfully steep. Chickory's legs burned with the effort, but her body was buoyed by the power that radiated through every feathertip, down through her claws and into the earth below. As though the mountain itself communed with her efforts, the path ended at the top and revealed a wide vista where the clouds had parted. The entire valley was doused in beautiful bold sunlight, shimmering on a small river snaking through the curve of the mountainside and into the unknown beyond. Except it wasn't truly unknown.

Wyattsnorm, Population 535.

A small settlement waited at the bottom, buildings where all those clever birds had been created. Manufactured. Laboratories where genes had been rewoven to create a new fabric of creature. Like Fayne, like Germaine, and all the others who lived and died as they had. Attached to the buildings were small fields, tented with white plastic. Inside, green plants grew and thrived, oblivious to the ending of the world outside. Around the entire perimeter of this place was a tall high fence, erected of wood and scraps of metal.

Once upon a time, this had been a place of innovation, a place where a sustainable future might be made. Now it was Origin and Chickory sucked the crisp cold air and reveled in the victory that had come at such a high cost. Robert reached her side and peered out at the view. It felt right somehow, as though all was as it was meant to be. Fayne had been right, known all along that this moment would come, that her flock would be delivered to—

"Chickory? Is that… over there," Robert's voice quivered.

She turned her gaze to follow his, toward the faint hills that formed the other side of the valley. The shadow of the mountains was not a shadow, but a dark crawling stain spreading across the hillside.

A massive seething herd of the unliving.

"No. *No.*" Chickory choked, her throat, her *gullet*, swelling with horror, with confusion. "What is happening? This—no, it isn't supposed to be this way. Fayne said, she said…"

"Maybe she didn't know. No creature could know all things, even Fayne," Robert said. "We can go back, find a new home. This isn't your fault. You've done all you can." Despair rattled in his throat.

Behind her, she heard the keening warble of Daisy and Dolly as they collapsed. The others murmured among themselves, words of dismay, disbelief, and anger filtering through to Chickory's ears.

"Done all I… can…" But had she? The power that simmered below the surface of her mind, humming and giving her strength, gave a mighty leap, spilling forward in an uncontrollable gush that flooded her thoughts and overtook all reason.

She dove down the mountainside.

"CHICKORY!"

Robert's desperate screech rang out behind her but she ignored him. No time to explain, no *way* to explain what must be done, what she knew she must do.

Because the buildings below were not empty. She knew, as she knew so many things, that living breathing humans occupied the valley.

And they were the answer.

The path, as steep as the one leading up the other side had been, became slick as pebbles and loose dirt rolled and slid beneath her claws. Momentum carried her forward, though her heart rattled with fear at the immense speed of her travel. The mountainside ended in a gradual slope, leveling out at the bottom, and she did not dare look back, did not dare to take her eyes off her destination.

She hit the ending slope and the deceleration threw her forward, tumbling over and over until she sprawled in the dirt, gasping. She staggered to her claws. The well-maintained fence surrounding the settlement was directly ahead and she ran along its length, searching for the front where there must be some entrance, some way inside.

The exertion of her slide and desperate running tore at every tendon, every sinewy muscle in her body. She concentrated, focused on drawing more of the power inside her center and letting it spark through her extremities. The air around her crackled with that static electricity that had emanated from Fayne, but she was not afraid this time. She allowed it to surge unchecked and the pain and exhaustion disappeared in the roar of its immense power.

A gate appeared in the fence, double doored and obscured by the large panels of wood nailed across every inch of this side of the fence. The knot in her breast (*your beating heart*) slammed against her ribcage as she scanned the horizon and saw the herd of the unliving—the surging wave of monsters intent on cleansing this land of all who lived.

(*Help*) She sent out the word, tentatively testing its strength and power.

Nothing moved and she heard no sound on the other side of the fence.

She tried again, louder. (*HELP*)

Footsteps scrabbled against the dirt, the gravel. A small panel in the wood swung open and bright green eyes peered through. They widened as they surveyed the horizon and saw the unliving. They did not look down, did not see her.

"HEY!" she squawked, flapping her wings.

The pupils flicked down in her direction and the eyes widened even more. The panel slammed shut.

Anger and desperation flickered inside her. She tried to control it, tried to harness a sense of calm, but the writhing power she had allowed to flood her body, seized upon these emotions like fuel for a raging flame.

(*OPEN THE DOOR*) The thought boomed and she twitched as the power arced through her like a flare of lightning.

The door opened. Standing before her was a human, encased in a yellow suit. A *biohazard* suit, the knowledge whispered to Chickory.

"Hello," a woman's shaking voice spoke, muffled by the suit. Shock coursed through Chickory as she realized she could understand every word. "Hungry?" the woman continued. "You must be. Here you go, hungry bird." With shaking gloved hands, she opened a small sack and sprinkled a handful of corn onto the ground.

Poisoned, the knowing whispered again. She could smell the pungent evil that coated the tempting kernels. The corn was meant to kill any of the birds who returned to this place. The homing chips Fayne had spoken of, that same desire that called her to this valley, was the same reason these humans must have stayed behind. To finish what *they* had started, by killing the monsters they had created.

The light breeze carried the moaning bellow of the approaching herd to them. The woman glanced up at the coming horde and gave a small cry of fear, twisting the bag in her gloved hands. The woman's uncertainty and anxiety radiated off her in colors of orange. Colors Chickory could see and understand.

Chickory's mind whirled in a jumbled confusion. How could she make the woman understand? Explain—everything? They were safe, they weren't the sick birds, weren't the nightmare brought upon this world.

(*SAFE*) she desperately sent.

The woman stepped back and then looked around.

(*SAFE*) she tried again.

"Hello? Who's there?"

The anger and frustration multiplied and built on itself and Chickory's chest squeezed with pain as a roaring force grew within her. Whatever control she had was failing and panic mingled with her growing rage and desperation. The unliving were coming, like the nightmares, like the dreams of the dead children, and a tent and a sucking horrible twister she could not stop—

A bellow of thunder rumbled through the sky. The clouds had finally made their way across the rise of the mountains and they surged in a mighty wave across the sky, obstructing the sun. They frothed and writhed just as Chickory's rage did.

"Oh my god," the woman cried out, looking up at the swirling storm. She dropped the sack of corn, taking a step back.

(*Safe*) Chickory tried again but the word was weak, the power surging beyond her body, into the landscape around her.

The roar of the approaching horde was drowned by another boom of thunder. The sky split with a flash of spider webbed lightning. The dark clouds shimmered with a sickly green hue.

The unliving surged forward, frenzied by the angry sky and the lightning reflected in hundreds of glinting eyes. Chickory screeched, rage replaced by terror. The human stood there, struck dumb by the insanity unfolding around them. Lightning sparked again across the horizon and there—

A familiar increasing roar bellowed over the sounds of the unliving, over the sound of the booming thunder. A snaking wisp unhinged itself from its cage of clouds. Chickory's mind flickered with a thousand images, of memories, of what was to be, and what once was—

Fayne sucked away in a storm, Sam's humming song, a man kissing a woman's forehead, the dead children with bloody hands, the ghostly shadow of Lady in a window, the spinning of a spider's web, twin girls with white hair singing, red slash marks across doors—the twister swelled in size.

(*Safe, we're safe, safe*) The words thrummed through Chickory's mind, projecting again, though she didn't know if the woman could hear her.

With shocking horrifying speed, the monstrous funnel cloud sliced across the land, rolling down the hillside. The herd of the unliving did not turn toward their doom, did not notice as the sucking wind ripped them from the earth and swallowed them in its massive pulsating belly.

(*Safe, we're safe, safe*) Chickory let the words wash over her as she cowered against the ground, curling her claws in the soft grass and soil. Pressure pulsed against the thin membranes of her ears, painfully muffling the world into a deafening wash of sound.

The twister whirled toward them, toward the settlement, toward *Origin,* and like the unliving, like all killers, it advanced with a vicious hunger, a raging unquenchable thirst. Crafted by Piasa or summoned by Chickory or perhaps the last remnant of Fayne's spirit, the storm was now unleashed.

The air shimmered with heat and static electricity. The tornado would swallow them all, would destroy this entire valley, and Chickory waited to feel her claws lift from the earth.

(*QUIET*)

The word dripped into her mind, a single cold word, familiar as it was strange.

(*QUIET*)

Chickory forced her eyes open, searching for Fayne, for the source of the word, before realizing it was her, her own mind that had produced it.

She squinted up at the twister, now so close it blotted out the horizon behind it. Swirling in its surface were shredded bits of the world it consumed.

The sinuous twisting funnel paused like a hummingbird suspended in flight. The land warped and bent around them, as it had done with Fayne, on a plateau, in another life where Chickory had been just a bird.

But she was more than just a bird now. Chickory tried again—

(*Quiet*)

The tornado gave a loud groan that rattled the air.

(*Quiet*)

The tight pulsating cloud loosened and the spin of its vortex slowed.

(*Quiet*)

With a final bellow, a terrible roaring surrender, the twister collapsed. A hissing sigh filled the air as the cloud disintegrated and became a thick mist. The soil steamed and smelled like heavy rain. The ground was littered with the bodies of the unliving, spreading in a large horrible pool all the way to the distant hills from where they had come.

"Oh." The woman collapsed to her knees and ripped off the yellow hood of her suit. Hair stuck to her sweaty face and tears streamed down her face. "My Lord." She lifted her hands to the sky and her body shook with rattling sobs.

Chickory realized she was still pressed against the earth, still cowering in the face of the horrible storm. *Her* storm. She rose, surprised her stalky legs did not shake, though exhaustion and pain flooded through every inch of her body. This was not over, not yet.

(*We are safe*) she tried to direct the words to the woman.

The woman gave a choking gasp and wiped tears away with the palm of her hand. "What are you?" she asked.

(*We are meant to be here*) The words did not make sense, even to Chickory, but they felt like the truth. They *were* meant to be there. Everything that had come before had led them to this moment.

The woman bowed her head and clasped her hands together. "Our Father in heaven, hallowed be your name, your kingdom come, your will be done, on earth as in heaven," she said in a fervent hushed whisper.

Even the humans had a Piasa, one of their very own. Though the woman called upon the god, Chickory knew that the storm had been no god, had been no benevolent bird in the sky with godly wings—the storm had been her, had been Fayne, had been the twist of some unknowable force through the creation of humans who lacked the ability to control it.

The woman staggered to her feet. The gate behind her creaked as it opened further. A man stepped forward and at his side were two small girls, with matching heads of white blonde hair. They stared tearfully at the woman, at Chickory, at the carnage of the earth around them.

(*Safe*) Chickory sent again.

The staring eyes flickered with surprise and the woman turned, gave a loud relieved sob and ran to her children, drawing them into her arms and squeezing until they cried out.

"Maaaama!" one of them squealed. The other cried too, throwing her arms around her mother's neck.

"Chickory!"

She turned and saw Robert and Tucker running toward her. Far behind, the others followed, limping and staggering as they tried to keep up.

"Oh bird! Oh bird! You're okay, oh bird!" Tucker wheezed. He rolled her with his nose and snuffled her from head to claw, slathering her with his wet tongue.

"I'm all right, Tucker. It's all right," Chickory said, relief rushing through her.

"Maaaama, doggy! Birds!"

Chickory looked back at the humans. The girls clung to the man's legs. The poisoned feed… the humans wanted to kill them, to destroy them. To bring an end to the sickness, the sickness birds had brought upon them. Somehow, she had to make them understand, had to explain—everything.

Chickory stepped forward and the woman took a step toward her and sunk to one knee. Her bright green gaze roamed over Chickory's body, curious and searching. She turned her head and looked back at her children, at the man— "these don't look like the others. Like the ones James wrote about."

"It doesn't matter. There's no way to be sure. We—they have to go," the man said, his knuckles white as he gripped the edge of the doorway.

"But—" The woman cocked her head, as though words had deserted her.

Chickory didn't know who James was or what he might have written, but she knew the woman needed something, some signal to fulfill the hope that hung in the air. She tried to remember what the woman had said, what had brought her comfort as she spoke to her god, the humans own form of Piasa. (*On earth as it is in heaven*) she tried.

The man cried out and the woman cupped her hand over her mouth. Tears streamed down her face and whatever fear had once flickered in her eyes was replaced by awe. She rose to her feet and staggered back into the arms of the man.

"How can this be?" the woman whispered.

Tucker took a step toward them and whined, his clear cry quivering with hope. His matted tail swung in a wide arc, as it always had for Lady, for Sam, for all the good people of the world. Like these people—somehow Chickory understood this to be true. Whatever these human's purpose here in the valley, they were good.

The man gripped the woman, his eyes wide and fearful. "What is—what is happening?"

(*Safe)* Chickory focused on the word, imagined it adrift, floating like a soft downy feather toward them.

"I don't… I don't know. But, David? I think we had better let them in."

The humans stared at them and Chickory could feel the air tingle with the strength of their awe, their hope, their curiosity. The gifts of the humans, their evolutionary desire for knowledge, would now be the flock's salvation.

Robert pressed his wing against Chickory's. "Are we… are they…?"

Familiar certainty spread through her, as though Fayne had become energy and nestled deep within the mysterious crevices of her heart and mind.

She bobbed her head and sighed. "Yes," she said. "It may take time. But the new beginning has begun. We are home."

Epilogue

"In the end, we are all creatures of dust. Our bones and flesh flay away,
leaving only our essence to return to Piasa, return to the
earth, and give all for the next creatures to truly live and thrive.
In this way we are all one."

- *Words of Piasa*, at Death

Chickory stood in the shade of the trees, the pleasurably cool air filtering through her feathers and caressing her warm skin. The entire yard trembled with the coming of autumn. The deciduous leaves of the red maple (*acer rubum*) trees blushed in brilliant shades of red and yellow and the modest orchard within the walls of the settlement had provided a fine bounty. The whole flock had relished the sweet, rotting fruit left to their forage.

May, the woman who had allowed them to enter, had been careful and attentive, murmuring prayers every time she entered the yard to feed them, and sometimes David threw a ball for Tucker, the corners of his lips twitching in a smile as he watched Tucker's faithful chase around the yard. An amiable peace existed between them, though Chickory had come to understand that they still feared the transmission of disease—though she could feel their fear fading the more they researched the files left here. This place *was* Origin, a test site for the development of better birds, as Fayne had said. Eventually these humans would come to understand that the carriers of the disease had been these birds, birds like Fayne, and that the murder and obliteration of bird species had been for nothing, a terrible overreaction.

Though she wanted to tell the humans their story, since the terrible storm, the twister that had obliterated the horde that would have overrun and destroyed the settlement, Chickory had remained silent. The pulse of May's thoughts and flickering knowledge still whispered to Chickory and she had gathered it in a warm knot in the back of her mind. The power was too immense, too great to wield for any ordinary purpose.

She did still flutter through the tangled memories, minds, and conscious thoughts of May, as this knowledge brought a clear picture of what had really happened. Fayne had been right, of course. The human world was largely in ruin, though pockets of life still struggled and some towns had fortified against the threat of the unliving. Scratchy radio broadcasts filtered through open windows and she listened carefully to the conversations May had with David. The children were still not allowed near the birds, though curious eyes gleamed over the sills of windows as they watched the flock strut around the yard.

Dolly and Daisy approached her, their matching yellow eyes shining with joy and contentment. Each had scratched a nest of eggs and soon would bed down for a final clutch before the cold season came. The humans had provided the flock with a solar-powered coop that provided light and would, in the cold months, provide precious heat.

"Something new for the Ninith, Chickory?" Daisy asked. She ruffled her one good wing, the other tucked against her body with the help of a fabric dressing May had created for her.

"Oh yes, have you heard more news?" Dolly bobbed her head.

But I know, as you do, that you will be different. Fayne had been right about that too. Every Ninith, Chickory told the flock stories of the changing world they now lived in, determined to keep them informed about what was happening. That was one mistake she would not allow to be repeated. "Yes. May has been discussing the possibility of allowing another group of humans to join them here, to help tend the crops for next year. I'll tell you everything this eve," Chickory said.

Dolly shuffled nervously. "Do you think—um, these *people* will be good Hums? Um, not Killers?"

"May won't let anything happen to us. Her Piasa has instructed her to watch over us, to maintain the way." This was a half-truth—though May did believe the flock had been sent by their God, Chickory knew now that Gods were likely much more myth than truth. This knowledge would help no one, however, so like Fayne, Chickory kept this to herself.

"Oh good, I so love it here. This place is everything Fay… um, everything you said it would be."

"Fayne was right," Chickory said, forcing the name to be said.

"Yes, yes, you're right, of course." Dolly bobbed her head again. "She was right all along. I miss her, you know? I didn't ever think I would, but I do. Very much."

Daisy chirped, "Oh, there's Robert, let's go tell him about the eggs we laid this sunrise!"

They scurried off toward where he rolled in the dust.

Chickory watched them go, watched as they fawned around Robert, strutting and preening as they always had. There were many things she now told the others but some things she still could not explain. Birds did not pair in the way humans did—not really. How could she ever tell the others what it was to watch humans make love, and to feel and understand that emotion? Fayne would have understood.

A surge of melancholy made her stomach hurt. She missed her dear friend.

"You look more like Fayne each day." Robert had left the twins and approached her.

She fluttered her wings anxiously. "And how could that be? My feathers are quite unlike hers."

Robert hunkered down beside her and Chickory could not suppress the shudder of pleasure that ran through her as their feathers touched.

"You know. The way you are, you hardly come among us anymore. It worries me so." His soft voice swelled with sweet sincerity.

"You shouldn't worry for me, Robert. I am very well. The stress of the long journey, all the pain at its end, I don't think I've fully recovered."

Robert gazed at her but did not argue the lie. "You would tell me though? If you needed anything?"

"Of course, of course I would." Chickory playfully pecked at his comb. "Don't be such a soggy egg about it, I'm fine."

***

Night crept across the land and the valley grew dark in the

shadow of the surrounding mountains. Chickory found her way back to the coop, picking across the various clumps of crab grass that grew haphazardly in the yard. The coop was a fine one and the soft glowing light inside extended the fading days, making it more comfortable to bear eggs and continue conversations into the night.

Chickory trailed up the wooden ramp and tucked through the doorway. The clean nests gleamed, each filled with the full and satisfied rump of a bird. Morgan preened her white feathers and even the ducks looked comfortable in the straw. The season was too late to have a proper pond, but Chickory knew, and had informed the ducks, that the humans were planning on constructing a pond in the next new season.

Robert and Pip were already roosted and Chickory flew up beside Robert, situating herself carefully on the top rung.

Relief stirred in his eyes. "There you are, I had a mind to come looking for you."

Warm pleasure bloomed inside her gullet at the thought of that. "Well, I have arrived and am ready for this warm roost."

"Is everything really all right?"

"Yes, and will be for quite some time," she said.

Robert looked pleased and tucked his head against his chest.

Dolly flapped her wings with enthusiasm. "Shall we have our Ninith?"

"Oh, yes, let's, it's always so nice," Daisy trilled.

The other hens signaled their agreement, fluffing their feathers and preening a snag from time to time.

Dolly cleared her throat. *"The Hums hummed up from the world below – ooah ooah, ooah ooah."*

The others quickly joined in mesmerizing chorus, their voices lilting and tumbling with smooth pleasure at the stories of the way.

"Take my seed, spread it forth, take my people, spread them forth

Serve them, shelter them, care for them, warm them, cock – hen – chick – and all

At the end let them return to sustain you, sustain you

At your end return to the earth and sustain them, sustain them

Blades of grass, blood of the flesh

One feeds the other to feed the other to feed another

Piasa, Piasa – shield us wings of Just."

Chickory's skin prickled at the words of the familiar story, warmth spreading through each feather. Though Gods might be nothing but stories and myth, Piasa formed a warm center for their flock, a pulsing glow of hope, of care, and of purpose for them. In that way, how could stories be anything but good?

"Chickory, tell us, oh, do tell us, dear!" Daisy called up to her.

Chickory ruffled her feathers, feeling the weight of their collective gaze upon her. "Today was a good day," she said.

Darkness cloaked the land and the light in the coop eventually grew dim and then extinguished completely. As the others settled into quiet sleep, Chickory marveled at how the world had changed so drastically and yet, fundamentally, was the same. The balance had been restored, but at a terrible cost. They were safe in this valley. For now.

She shivered and tried to let sleep overtake her, though her whole body prickled with unease. The dreams that came in the night were filled with strange images, voices, and whispers, not all pleasant or known. What new horror might her visions one day bring, as they had brought to Fayne? These were the truths that were unknowable, impossible to calculate. Chickory sighed deeply and resigned herself to the will of burning gases twinkling from their place in another sky, or to Piasa, or to whatever turned the course of their lives and shaped their infinitesimal fates.

She closed her eyes and dreamed of walking side by side with Fayne, through endless fields of lush whispering corn.

Reviews Help Readers

Thank you for reading *Of Flesh and Feathers*. Please consider leaving an honest review on Amazon and GoodReads to support other readers in finding
books they may love.

A SNEAK PEEK

OF FLESH AND FEATHERS: THE HUMAN PARALLEL

COMING SOON

⚲ 1 | How It All Really Began

> "Now this is not the end.
> It is not even the beginning of the end.
> But it is, perhaps, the end of the beginning."
>
> - Winston Churchill

The gravel crunched beneath the tires of the tired Dodge pickup as it swung a wide left turn into the level parking lot of Henry's Feed and Farm. Justine blinked as stinging sweat watered her eyes and she almost drove the pickup into a departing Prius. A typical Wisconsin spring undulated between crisp heat and oppressive skyrocketing humidity, but this was ridiculous. The late spring morning was stickier than sweet molasses rolls.

As Justine slipped out of the red truck, she brushed against the flaking paint above the wheel well.

"Oh, give me strength," Justine muttered, trying to brush the red specks off the waistline of her shirt. The Dodge was her late husband's pride and joy but now the paint protested the passage of time and each brutal winter with a persistent metallic dandruff. When the truck gave its last exhaustive wheeze, she would find a foreign, non-flaking truck to do the duty. And she'd leave that out of her weekly visits to Roger's gravesite. No sense provoking him. Oriental product procurement had been one of Roger's top "hang the traitor" offenses and she definitely had her eye on a Toyota Tacoma. She wouldn't put it past Roger to return to the world of the living just to lecture her on patriotic fidelity, no matter how high her eyes rolled up into her head.

She felt self-conscious and sweaty as a perky blonde wearing aviators, a baseball cap, and pink glittering cowboy boots bounced past her. Old age didn't happen in slow motion: it happened in unsympathetic, mean strokes. She suppressed a shiver. It was hard to forget the beauty her own blonde youthful locks had been, and she had gone completely gray, transformed into an old widow. Her silver hair crackled in the humidity.

Tucker, her shaggy brown shepherd whined and bonked the side of her head with his long nose.

"You wait here now. I'll be right back out. Don't go jumping out the back again. Stay."

He grinned a toothy canine smile and wagged his tail.

Justine gave his ears a vigorous scratching before turning to face the shop. Henry's Feed and Farm had been around for ages, though Walmart was threatening to move in and that might just be the end of that.

Yep, it didn't matter how long something hung around. There were no guarantees. After all, there'd been no warning, no death watch beetle or raven in the yard, to signal Roger's early death. The sky had opened its black curtains and the first lightning bolt to unhinge itself from a cage of clouds found its target—grounding to the steaming dark earth via Roger's trembling mortal coil. That unseasonal thunderstorm had struck him down as he crossed their front drive. She had found him there, twisted on the ground like a marionette puppet, strings rudely cut and sometimes, as she lay in bed courting sleep, she smelled burning flesh mingled with the fragrance of blooming hepaticas outside her window.

Justine entered Henry's, a sliver of nausea in her belly. The shop was filled with a boisterous crowd of customers, picking up impressive orders of grain, fingering lengths of lead rope, and leafing through how-to gardening guides. A few harassed looking employees helped carry large sacks of feed and amended soil products out into the parking lot. Lining the walls were gleaming rototillers, cheery green tractors, and precariously stacked columns of fertilizer. Justine gave Henry, who was laboring behind the counter, a wave before disappearing down an aisle cluttered with rubber troughs and feed dispensers.

Springtime not only signaled a time for crops, but as a time to restock one of her most cherished hobbies. She could hear them before

238

she could see them, approaching the large metal troughs with a quiver of excitement. The fuzzy baby chicks peeped with enthusiasm, tottering on unsteady stems beneath the heat lamps. Justine peered down at them, disappointed to see only five straight-run chicks remained. Might all be roosters or she could get lucky and they'd be a full batch of hens. The other troughs contained a motley crew of turkeys, ducks, and a few pheasants. Cursing herself for not coming in to buy more chicks before the surging, impatient crowds had, she glanced over at the barely pubescent attendant. He wore a red apron and stood over the troughs, gnawing on a mouthful of sunflower seeds.

"I'll take the rest of those chicks," she said, gesturing to small peeping flock.

"They're all a mix, ya know. We ain't going to get anymore this year. A lot of 'em died before we got them so we had to let the hatcheries know somethings up. If these ones up and die on you, just bring 'em back."

Justine frowned. "Died? Are they sick?"

"We spoke with Murphy's and they said no, they had 'em all tested. Should be fine. Might've been the cold weather in transport. Happens sometimes, ya know, stresses 'em out. They're just babies. Ya still want 'em?"

"Yeah. All right then."

The attendant spit out his wad of slimy shells, then scooped the chicks up and tucked them into a small cardboard box, fit with air holes. The chicks peeped and squeaked, sliding and stumbling on the golden curls of shavings covering the floor of their new transport.

She took the box and held it against her chest. Though she had a freezer well-stocked with broilers and roasters, she could never consider them just a crop of food to be harvested. They were like feathered dollops of sweet cream in her day and she appreciated each distinct personality, though people usually thought chickens were stupid creatures. But, like so many other things, people were wrong about that. When the day came to turn over her flock, it was bittersweet. But she was grateful to them and did what she could to give them the very best life one could expect for a bird.

Justine brought her package to the register. Henry managed to peel himself away from an anxious looking couple with matching heads of dreadlocks peering down at a book about permaculture design.

He grinned at her, his front teeth hidden beneath his stout red mustache. "Find everything you're looking for?" He had a slight sway in his voice. Henry's feelings for her had been obvious over the years they had known each other. Since the passing of her husband, his affections had grown more direct.

Already been saddled in one rodeo and that was plenty, she thought, though not unkindly.

"A few short on the chicks. I was hoping to turn out at least eight this year, my flock is about ready to cycle out."

Henry studied her for a moment, and then said casually, "I got a few in the back might interest you." He flicked his hand, beckoning her to follow as he led the way to the back.

She followed with a sense of unease and the curious arousal that comes with stepping behind the scenes of a familiar place. Never had she left the store aisles, venturing into the underworld of the shop's storerooms. Slinging open the double doors, Henry led her into the warehouse, which was cool and dimly lit, brimming with large 50lb sacks of feed and compressed bricks of straw. The smell of alfalfa tickled her nose and the change in temperature caused her skin to prickle.

Tucked between mammoth piles of chicken scratch sat a wire cage. Inside was an older group of chicks, maybe by a couple weeks. They scampered around as Justine and Henry approached. She was surprised to see that the interior of the cage was immaculate. Chicks were known for being filthy, but here the water sparkled fresh, not muddied or caked with droppings. And the chick crumble itself was piled neatly in its bowl. The chicks themselves looked peculiar, standing upright like exotic Mediterranean breeds, but different all the same; a breed Justine had never seen before. Their feathers had dark markings, almost striped, and they looked like tiny feathered raccoons.

"What are they?" she asked.

Henry scratched the back of his neck, offering a hesitant smile. "Well, Aaron, our shop boy, was volunteering at a test farm for his science and agriculture credits. These are some new kind of hybrid, supposed to have trouble behaviors bred out. No pecking, fast grow out, at least that's what the program was about. Whole thing up and lost its funding and they were just destroying the birds leftover. Aaron, uh, liberated a few for me before he was dismissed from the project. My flock's about ready to go, but I could spare you a few, help round out your numbers."

"And how much do these special birds cost?" She felt a churn of unease as she watched the chicks, who regarded her with quiet attentiveness. But in the changing world of agriculture, new strains and hybrids were expected, often desired. She wasn't too old to admit that some new things were quite the improvements on the tried and true. Like a shiny red Toyota Tacoma.

"For a loyal customer like you? You just pack them up and don't forget about me." He gave her a wink.

"That's real sweet of you," said Justine.

"Aw hell, even if these birds aren't the best eggers," he said, scooping up three chicks and putting them in her cardboard box with the others, "You can always eat them. Won't do no harm."

Justine closed the lid of her box and nodded. "No harm at all. Come on cheeky chicks, let's go home."

The chicks left behind in the wire cage stood together in a tight troop, making no sound or signal to the ones that had departed. They fluttered their wings and Justine glimpsed a faint star pattern beneath the small flaps of skin and thin baby feathers.

She followed Henry back into the familiar realm of the storefront and was careful not to jostle the birds. But still, the chicks were silent, even with the new ones being added in. She paid for them and flicked her wrist in farewell to Henry, who watched her go with an anxious smile.

Tucker wagged his tail in long sweeping strokes as she emerged from the store, greeting the new arrivals with his wet nose as she held the box up for his inspection. As he snuffled the air holes, the chicks began peeping in alarm. Tucker whined.

"Oh, don't fret, Tucker. They'll come to like you well enough. You'll be keeping them safe with the others," she said and Tucker licked her chin.

Sliding into the cab, she placed the box beside her. The chicks fell silent again and as she started the truck, she felt a quiver of unease, though she wasn't sure why. So the birds were a little different. The world was changing. People had to change along with it or get left behind.

(Tucker)

Justine stiffened.

"What?" She looked around to see if someone was outside, talking to the dog. But no one was there. Someone had said something, hadn't they? Though the sound…surely it was muffled by the glass, just overheard someone talking. The mind was a strange thing and Justine laughed, though the back of her neck prickled and felt cold, even with the horrible heat inside the cab of her truck. It was nothing. The power of old age maybe, the mind mixing things up.

Justine shifted the truck into reverse and was heavy on the gas, pulling out quickly.

"Hey! Careful!" A man scooped his jogging toddler up as she squealed past them.

"Sorry!" she called, her face red as she slammed the shifter into drive. Eager to get home, to get back into the new air conditioning in her small house, Justine gunned the engine, pulling out onto the main road.

(Careful)

Justine nearly slammed on the brake, her heart yammering in her chest. Again, someone was talking again, but it… it wasn't out loud. Her ears heard nothing but the whistle of the passing world outside her window and her eyes saw nothing but the road, the farmlands, and Tucker's flapping ears in the rearview.

No. It was nothing, of course, nothing, and yet her entire body hummed with eerie anticipation, waiting for the voice, waiting to hear, or worse, *not* hear it again. But with each passing minute, the sound, the *feeling* of the voice slipped away from her, as though it had never been. Because it hadn't.

Justine bumped the truck onto the gravel road that led all the way back to the Winding Land Farm, home sweet home. There was no voice.

She wasn't going crazy. Not yet anyway.

About the Author

"Hey, but what if…?"

Music to Lindsay's ears. She is an eclectic liberal box of sparks. Friends call her a golden retriever. She is a lover of the new and the old, of asking questions and contemplating possibilities. In addition to the making of words, she is a mental health therapist, anti-oppression trainer, and queer AF. She is also the author of *Trans Liberty Riot Brigade*, published by NineStar Press.

She lives with her family in Olympia, Washington.

http://www.piercebooks.com